CROOK HAVEN

THE SCHOOL FOR THIEVES

J. J. ARCANJO

ILLUSTRATED BY
EUAN COOK

HODDER CHILDREN'S BOOKS

First published in Great Britain in 2023 by Hodder & Stoughton

1 3 5 7 9 10 8 6 4 2

A CIP catalogue record for this book is available from the British Library.

ISBN 978 1 444 96573 5

Typeset in Sabon by Avon DataSet Ltd, Alcester, Warwickshire

Printed and bound in Great Britain by Clays Ltd, Elcograf S.p.A.

The paper and board used in this book
are made from wood from responsible sources.

Hodder Children's Books
An imprint of
Hachette Children's Group
Part of Hodder & Stoughton Limited
Carmelite House
50 Victoria Embankment
London EC4Y 0DZ

An Hachette UK Company
www.hachette.co.uk

www.hachettechildrens.co.uk

For my grandpa, who has read every word
of every story I have ever written

CROOKHAVEN

legacy bridge

Villa

the lawn

Crooked Oak statue

crooked pier

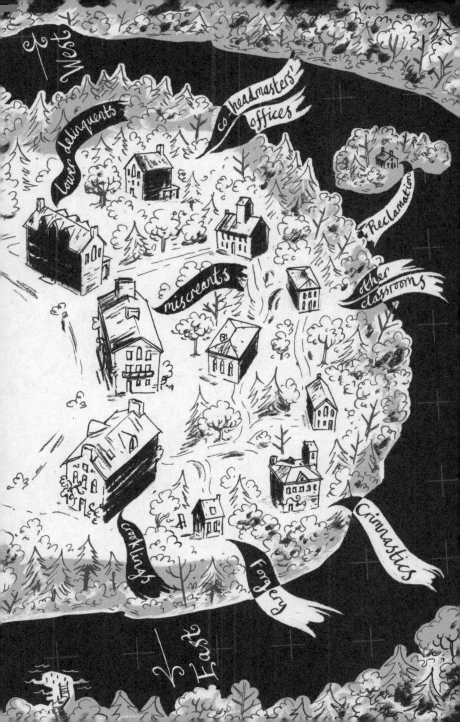

CHAPTER ONE

Gabriel Avery hadn't picked a pocket in weeks and the tips of his fingers were starting to itch.

Summer was fast coming to an end and each week fewer tourists were passing through Torbridge, which meant fewer pockets for Gabriel to pick. Even the tourists who did come never stayed in the village long. After all, there were only so many photos someone could take of the town's main attraction – a hideous granite boulder-bridge – before getting bored and leaving. Thankfully for Gabriel, a steady trickle of commuters still passed through daily. No doubt on the way to faraway places where wonderfully exciting things happened.

Gabriel had only lived in Torbridge for a year and already he felt that pretty much *anywhere* else would be more exciting.

It was early on a Monday morning and Gabriel was leaning against the wall of the train station waiting for the next train to pull in. Soon the platform would be alive with people changing to head north to Exeter or south to Cornwall. But at the moment, only two men in dark suits waited, and they were backlit by the rising sun so Gabriel couldn't get a good look at them.

Probably locals, he thought, yawning. He never picked a local's pocket. They'd only recognise him and tell Grandma. And after his most recent incident he was already in her bad books.

Come to think of it, Gabriel wasn't sure he'd *ever* been in Grandma's good books since they'd moved to Torbridge.

It was before eight and everyone getting off the trains would be grumpy, tired and, best of all, completely uninterested in Gabriel. Which meant he could move between them like a twinkle-fingered ghost. Excitement raced through him at the thought. For the last few weeks he'd been so busy helping Grandma at the mansion that he hadn't been back here, and *man* did he miss it.

He shivered in the crisp morning wind and pulled the sleeves of his blue jumper over his hands. Cold fingers were stiff and clumsy and no good to him at all. He needed them warm and nimble and steady.

To his left, Benson's Café was selling warm drinks from an open window. The sweet scent of hot chocolate and the bitter tang of coffee wafted over on thin tendrils of steam. Inside, the sound of bacon sizzling joined the hiss and glug of the coffee being made.

His stomach growled.

First thing I'm getting with my takings is a bacon sandwich, he thought, *and a sausage one for Grandma*.

A to-go cup of coffee sat on one of the high tables beside the open window, still faintly steaming. Gabriel waited until the barista disappeared inside before edging over and nicking it. He hated the taste of coffee, but the warm cup was perfect for loosening his stiff fingers.

A few minutes later, he heard the gentle rumble of an approaching train and pushed off the wall to get a better view. He placed the cup on a nearby bench and watched as the passengers piled off the train.

Gabriel frowned. Autumn closing in meant he'd have to start contending with coats and jackets, each with several pockets. He never had time to check every pocket so would often have to guess. But after a few years at this he'd gotten pretty good at guessing. And luckily, not all who disembarked had planned for the unseasonal chill in the air that morning.

Most of the passengers stayed on the platform to wait for their connecting train, but a few headed right, towards the café.

Gabriel grinned and took out a 2p coin. He'd had it for as long as he could remember. What was unique about it was that one side – heads – gleamed the normal copper, while the other – tails – was black. Almost as if it had been burned. Why, he didn't know. But it looked pretty cool, and it had become a key part of his gambit.

Gabriel flicked the coin into the air with his thumb, caught it in his palm, then flicked it high again. He was just about to put his plan into action when he heard a familiar voice.

'Gabriel Avery, is that you, boy?'

Gabriel caught the coin, quickly slipped it into his pocket and looked up. Theodora Evans looked back at him. Her face was all deep creases and sickly, greyish skin, brought on, he thought, by a combination of non-stop frowning and fifty years of smoking.

'Morning Mrs Evans,' Gabriel said sweetly.

If possible, her face soured further. 'What are you doing at the train station at this hour?' She pursed her wrinkled lips. 'Up to no good, I'll bet.'

Gabriel pretended to look hurt by the accusation. 'Not at all, Mrs Evans. I came to get Grandma a sausage sandwich from Benson's. They're her favourite.' He shrugged. 'I thought I'd surprise her.'

Mrs Evans' face softened for a moment. Then hardened again. 'A likely story.' She leant closer. 'I know it was you who pilfered the steak and kidney pie from my windowsill last week, Gabriel Avery. I just *know* it.'

Gabriel furrowed his brow. 'What does *pilfered* mean, Mrs Evans?' Of course, Gabriel knew exactly what pilfered – and every other word related to thievery – meant.

Mrs Evans' watery grey eyes were so close now. 'Means you *stole* it.'

Gabriel took a step back and raised his jumper and

T-shirt, revealing a scrawny, olive-skinned torso. 'Does this look like the tummy of a pie thief, Mrs Evans?'

She straightened, thrown by this. 'You've got a smart tongue, Gabriel Avery. A little too smart, if you ask me. No good, honest, *godly* boy allows such lies to slither off his tongue so easily.'

Gabriel let his shirt and jumper fall. 'I wish I *had* been there, Mrs Evans – then I might've caught whoever did steal it. But I wasn't.' Gabriel had been there, of course. And while the pie's crust had been pure buttery deliciousness, the filling hadn't been nearly as tasty as normal. It was, in Gabriel's humble opinion, Mrs Evans' weakest attempt yet.

Unconvinced, Mrs Evans grunted once, loudly, and turned out of the train station muttering under her breath.

Gabriel dug his coin out of his pocket again and turned back towards the platform. A few people had already formed a queue at the café's window. He frowned. Queues were difficult. If something happened to one person in the queue – be they bumped or tripped – the rest often looked over. And more eyes meant more of a chance one of them would notice a wayward hand. Gabriel turned to see if anyone was approaching the café.

Two people were. But they were too close together to try anything.

There was, however, a silver-haired man walking just behind them.

What about him? Gabriel thought, eyeing the figure.

No coat. Loose-fitting trousers. A wallet-sized lump in his left pocket. Distracted by his phone. Looks perfect to me.

Gabriel started to flick his coin in the air again. He waited for the other two to pass, then hurried directly towards the man. They collided, shoulder to hip, and Gabriel's coin clattered to the concrete floor.

'Sorry lad, that's my fault,' the man said, slipping his phone into his right pocket and giving Gabriel an apologetic smile. 'Here, let me get that for you.'

'It's OK,' Gabriel said, pretending to look flustered. 'It's just an old coin.' But the man was already leaning down, exposing the thin, black leather wallet in his left pocket.

One minute it was there, the next it wasn't.

The man straightened and held out Gabriel's coin, heads up. 'Where'd you get this, then? I've never seen a coin in such bad shape.'

'It was a present,' Gabriel said with a shrug. 'From my parents.' That, at least, was true. The only other things those two had ever given him were his honey-brown hair and burnt-amber eyes, and he didn't much care for those features anyway.

The man dropped the coin into Gabriel's hand and Gabriel pocketed it. 'Better than a screen, I suppose.' The man pulled his phone out of his pocket. 'These things are evil, lad. Stick to playing with coins for as long as you can.'

Gabriel nodded politely. 'Sorry again for bumping you.'

The man tapped him on the shoulder as he passed, eyes already glued to his phone. 'Not at all, lad. Not at all.'

Gabriel turned the corner and, after snatching a glance over his shoulder, carefully pulled the black leather wallet out of his pocket. He grinned. *As easy as taking a steak and kidney pie off Mrs Evans' windowsill.*

He opened it and . . .

That's strange. It was almost completely empty. Inside there was just one ten-pound note and something white – a card, it looked like – poking out from one of the sleeves. Gabriel slid it out and read.

> YOU'RE GOOD.
> I'M BETTER.

Gabriel swivelled and sprinted back towards the café. The queue was down to two now.

The man wasn't either of them.

Gabriel turned, eyes frantically scanning the platform for the silver-haired figure. The train was just starting to crawl away and—

Oh no . . .

The man was sitting in a window seat on the train, smiling. Gabriel locked eyes with him. Slowly, the man held something up against the glass. It was small and circular and looked burnt on one side.

Gabriel, heart thumping, dug into his pocket and pulled out a 2p. But it was not his coin.

CHAPTER TWO

The train sputtered into the rising sun, taking the silver-haired man and Gabriel's coin with it.

Gabriel slumped against a nearby wall, mind racing.

To anyone else it was just a 2p coin, but it was important to Gabriel. It was the only thing his parents had left behind when they abandoned him. The one item that might help him track them down one day. He never went anywhere without it, used it in almost every con, and now some thieving stranger had nicked it.

But *why*?

Gabriel looked inside the wallet again. Nothing but the ten-pound note. He read the message on the card again. Somehow the silver-haired man had known Gabriel was a thief.

Gabriel turned the card over and blinked. More writing, smaller this time.

USE THE NOTE TO BUY A TICKET TO MOORHEART STATION.
YOUR COIN WILL BE WAITING FOR YOU.
THERE IS A PLACE IN THIS WORLD FOR YOUR TALENTS,
GABRIEL AVERY.

Gabriel read the note a second time. Then a third.

My talents? Surely he can't mean . . .

Gabriel shook his head. If this man was a thief, chances were this was some sort of con. What the man hoped to gain from it, Gabriel hadn't a clue. But he certainly wouldn't be using that ten pounds to buy a ticket to Moorheart – a place he'd never heard of and which sounded, in Gabriel's opinion, entirely made up. The money would instead go towards something altogether more worthwhile.

'One bacon sandwich and one sausage, please,' Gabriel said to the rotund man at the Benson's counter. His name was Mr Hartley and he was one of the few people in Torbridge who didn't look at Gabriel as if he'd just done – or would at some point in the near future do – something unspeakably dreadful.

'I remember, I remember,' Mr Hartley said. He turned and shouted, 'One bacon and one sausage, Geoff. Careful with it, now. Burn one more sausage and yeh'll be out on yer bleedin' ear.' Mr Hartley turned back to Gabriel. 'Been a few weeks since I last seen you, Avery. What's kept yeh away?'

Money. The distinct lack of. 'Helping Grandma.'

Mr Hartley grunted. 'Yeh? And how is the old goat?'

Grandma had grown up in Torbridge. She and Mr Hartley had been friends/enemies in childhood and had picked right up where they'd left off when Grandma and Gabriel had moved back the previous year. To him, she was 'the old goat', while to her, he was 'that great ogre'. To be fair to Grandma, Mr Hartley did look a little like an ogre, except shorter, wider and a great deal hairier.

Gabriel said, 'She's all right. The sausage sandwich is a surprise for her, actually.'

Mr Hartley turned towards the kitchen. 'Geoff, burn the sausage a little—'

A gormless voice interrupted. 'But you just said—'

'I know what I said!' Mr Hartley thundered. 'But the old goat likes her sausages charred, so do it.' He looked back at Gabriel. 'You keepin' out of trouble?'

Gabriel nodded. ''Course. There's no trouble to be found in Torbridge.'

'And yet yeh always seem to find some.' Mr Hartley sniffed. 'September's comin'. What yeh doin' about school? Year Nine now, aren't yeh?'

A lanky, pimpled boy slunk out of the kitchen holding a plastic bag. Grease was already pooling at the bottom. He handed it over to Gabriel without a word.

'Thanks,' Gabriel said, and hurried out of the café.

'Oi,' Mr Hartley called after him. 'You didn't answer me question!'

Gabriel turned out of the train station and began the long, winding journey home.

That same question had been playing in his mind over and over for the last few weeks. Grandma was set on him going back to Torfalls for Year Nine. But he'd done one year at that grim place already and the idea of returning to a school where everyone hated or outright ignored him made him shudder. Worse still, most people who went to Torfalls ended up staying in this dreadful village. Gabriel wanted to go somewhere new and *exciting*. A town. Maybe even a city! Somewhere where people didn't look at him as if there was something wrong with him . . .

The OPEN sign hanging on the inside of the village shop's door flipped to CLOSED as he passed. Which, to Gabriel, was totally out of order – he'd never even stolen anything from them. In fact, apart from the occasional pie sitting on a windowsill just begging to be sampled, he'd never stolen from any local. The truth was that they disliked him because he was different. He'd lived in countless villages now and he'd learnt that people in villages didn't much hold with *different*. And in a sleepy Devonian village, a scruffy, olive-skinned boy who lived with his equally scruffy but pale-skinned grandma was a little too much *different* for most of them to bear. When people learned they weren't blood related, there were whispers, and then rumours, and then uncomfortable questions. Worst of all, it led to attention, and Grandma had always hated attention. Gabriel's wandering fingers only made things worse. So when the questions began, their time in a particular place ended. It always happened the same way.

As Gabriel crossed the famous boulder bridge, the line from the silver-haired man's note came back to him. *There is a place in this world for your talents, Gabriel Avery.*

Gabriel's heart began to race. How could that be true? His talent was picking pockets, and picking pockets was stealing, and stealing wasn't allowed *anywhere*.

Was it?

Lost in thought, Gabriel almost collided with a huge iron gate. Through the gaps in the bars he could see the white gravel driveway and the mansion looming large behind.

Gabriel sighed. *It's been ages and the Merciers still haven't done anything about the peeling white paint or the flipping ivy.* He dug into his pocket and pulled out a hairpin.

He'd left the key behind so Grandma wouldn't know he'd slipped out. Switching the sandwich bag to his left hand, he knelt, easing the hairpin into the gate's lock. After a little wriggling, he heard a familiar click.

The gate creaked open. Gabriel slipped through and shut it behind him. He walked up the driveway, taking care not to step on the freshly cut grass. Such neatness was a rarity for the stingy Merciers, but they'd had important guests to impress the night before, so they'd had it trimmed. Gabriel was sure they would now let it grow wild until the next VIP visitor.

Two fancy-looking cars – one black, one dark blue – glistened in the morning sun. He stopped for a moment beside the black one to glimpse his reflection. *Man, I need a haircut*. His curly light brown hair was nearly past his ears and—

'Planning on stealing the car next, are we?' a nasal voice said.

Gabriel tensed. He'd hoped coming back this early would mean he'd avoid *him*. 'Charlie—'

'You know very well it's *Charles*,' the boy cut in. The boy was leaning against the shaded side of the mansion, wispy black hair combed neatly to one side. The sharp features of his hawk-like face were completely hidden in shadow.

Gabriel shrugged. 'Yeah, right. I was just checking my hair out in the window. It's a bit wild at the moment, so . . .'

Charles slowly edged out of the shadows, ice-blue eyes narrowing. The rest of his face was slack, expressionless.

'Anyway,' Gabriel said, raising the plastic bag. 'I need to get this to Grandma before it gets cold—'

'Where's Father's fedora, Gabriel?' Charles asked coldly. The older boy took another step into the sunshine. Gabriel had always found that rich people moved far slower and smoother than everyone else, as if they had all the time in the world. Even when Charles leant down to pick up a piece of gravel, he did it with the kind of arrogant grace of someone entirely unused to the action. He straightened and began examining the gravel. 'It's gone missing, you see. And, to my knowledge, *you* are the only kleptomaniac in the immediate vicinity.'

13

Charles flicked the rock. It struck Gabriel's kneecap, hard.

Gabriel flinched. 'Then you don't know Grandma very well,' he said with a nervous chuckle, trying to diffuse the tension.

Charles tilted his head. 'Are you accusing *her* of theft?'

Gabriel gulped. 'No, not at all.' He slowly began backing away.

'Because if you are saying your grandmother is the thief,' Charles said, picking up another piece of gravel. 'Then I'm afraid we'll have to remove her from her position.' He flicked the rock at the other kneecap, but Gabriel lifted his leg just in time.

'It was a stupid joke, that's all,' Gabriel said. 'Tell your dad I haven't seen his hat. But I'll definitely keep an eye out. Promise.' Before Charles could say another word or flick another rock, Gabriel rounded the corner of the mansion.

With the sun glinting off the half-open glass windows, the summer house at the edge of the woods looked almost welcoming. But it leaked in a downpour, retained no heat in midwinter and there was a fifty-fifty chance that the water would run cold in the mornings. As Gabriel walked the last few steps down the softly winding path, he made sure to breathe in the sweet scent of the wildflowers growing in the woods behind, knowing full well that the overpowering smell of damp inside would soon steal it from him.

Gabriel peeked through the window and, seeing no sign of Grandma, slowly eased the front door open.

Uh oh.

Grandma stood just inside, arms crossed. She was dressed in her bleach-stained blue cardigan. Her luminous yellow cleaning gloves were already on. That was never good. 'I may not be quite as with-it as I once was, dear boy, but I'm afraid you're going to have get up a great deal earlier to pull one over on me.'

Gabriel really only had one move here. Smiling sheepishly, he held up the sandwiches. 'Hungry, Grandma?'

Grandma hesitated, torn between anger and hunger. Slowly, she uncrossed her arms and raised a thin white eyebrow. 'Sausage?'

Gabriel nodded.

'A little burnt?'

'Mr Hartley made sure of it.'

Grandma sniffed. 'Suppose there's one thing that great ogre's good for then.' As she took the bag from Gabriel, her eyes narrowed. 'And are you about to tell me that he just *gave* you these sandwiches for free?'

'I am,' Gabriel said innocently.

Grandma pursed her lips. 'And will it be the truth?'

Gabriel stayed quiet for a long moment, hoping to wait her out. But her light grey eyes held firm. So instead, he said, 'You know, Grandma, I think we still have some ketchup.' He quickly breezed past her and reached for the cupboard next to the constantly malfunctioning cooker.

The cupboard was bare but for salt, pepper and a quarter-full bag of spaghetti. Gabriel hazarded a glance over his shoulder. *She's still staring . . .*

'Tea then!' he suggested instead, closing the cupboard and filling the kettle. To his relief, she sighed and nodded. Tea *always* did the trick.

He and Grandma savoured every bite of the sandwiches and washed them down with mugs of tea. Grandma, as usual, left the last half of her sandwich for him. When Gabriel protested, she said, 'You're a growing boy. Besides, you'll need your strength for today. There's a great deal to do up at the Merciers'. Yes, a *great* deal.' Then with a smile, she added, 'But as a reward I'll be making casserole for tea.'

Gabriel returned the smile, though he knew what she meant by that. There would be no lunch today. Not if there was casserole for tea.

*

He worked alongside his grandma all day – deadheading the roses, dusting the banisters and cleaning the warzone that was the third-floor toilet, which was used exclusively by the careless children of the household – and all the while he was thinking about his stolen coin. And the silver-haired man who had taken it.

Slowly, a dangerous thought began to form. What if there *was* a place for him out there?

After he had finished with the bathroom, Gabriel wiped the sweat from his brow with his sleeve and poked his head over the banister of the spiral staircase. Grandma was sitting on a stool on the bottom floor, breathing hard and eyeing the first-floor steps with a defeated frown.

Gabriel took off his cleaning gloves, dug into his pocket and pulled out the white card. He read the message, then read it again.

THERE IS A PLACE IN THIS WORLD FOR YOUR TALENTS, GABRIEL AVERY.

What if this Moorheart place really did mean a chance at a better life? Not just for him, but also for Grandma. For that, and for her, there was nothing Gabriel wouldn't do.

*

As the sun was setting that night, a bone-weary Gabriel sank on to his bed with a satisfied sigh, his belly full. Was there a better feeling in the world than that?

Well, Gabriel thought, sliding a hand under his creaking bed and pulling something out. Wearily, he stood to peer into a small circular mirror on the windowsill. It was angled slightly up so he could see his torso, face and the rather large grey fedora now sitting lopsidedly on his head. *There may be one better feeling. But* only *one*.

CHAPTER THREE

The one benefit of living in a dead-end place like Torbridge was that there were no barriers at the train station. Which meant a ticketless Gabriel could stride on to the platform and board the 8.06 towards Penzance without so much as an inquiring glance.

But once he was aboard, well, that was when his problems started.

'Tickets, please,' the moustached conductor called as he shuffled through the busy carriage. Most passengers had found seats, but a few, like Gabriel, had been forced to stand in the aisles.

'Sorry about that, Miss,' the conductor said, bumping into a young woman who almost lost grip of her phone. 'Bit full on here this morning, isn't it?' The woman pulled out her ticket and handed it over without a word.

The conductor attempted to stamp the ticket, then shook the ticket machine. 'Damn thing's been playing up all morning. Just a second.' He tried it a second time and again it failed.

A grin slowly spread across Gabriel's face. *That's how I'm going to get out of this. I just need to . . .*

'Finally,' the conductor called, handing back the now-stamped ticket to the woman. 'Only took me four goes.' The woman nodded absentmindedly and returned to her phone. Gabriel edged closer.

The conductor continued up the aisle, staggering as though he was aboard a swaying ship in a storm rather than a gently rumbling train on a windless day. Next he came upon an older woman wearing a yellow raincoat and holding a brown tote bag that had seen better days.

'Mrs Davenport!' the conductor said cheerily, taking her ticket. 'All geared up for rain, are we? None forecast, I don't think.'

The older lady beamed. 'You can never be too careful, though, can you? It can get wild in the blink of an eye around here.'

'Certainly can,' the conductor said with a chuckle. 'Off to the market this morning, are we?'

As Gabriel watched, Mrs Davenport handed the conductor her ticket and received it back, *unstamped*.

The machine had malfunctioned again, and the conductor hadn't noticed.

Slowly, and without drawing the conductor's attention, Gabriel sidled up beside Mrs Davenport. Because he knew what was coming next.

3, 2, 1, he counted in his head. The carriage fell dark.

'Oh dear,' Mrs Davenport said. 'I always forget about this dreadful tunnel.'

Twenty seconds later, when soft sunlight filled the carriage again, Gabriel was already two people away from Mrs Davenport, her unstamped ticket sitting comfortably in his pocket.

When the time came, he handed it to the conductor with a smile and received it back, this time stamped. The conductor disappeared up the train.

'We will soon be arriving at Moorheart,' a pleasant voice announced. 'All those in the back four carriages, please move towards the front of the train to disembark as this station has a short platform.'

Gabriel began to move down the carriage. As he passed, a suited man leant over to his almost identically suited friend and said, 'No idea why they still stop at this place. No one ever gets off. It'd save us about ten minutes if the train company decided to skip it.' The train ground to a halt. 'I mean, look at it. The place is derelict.' Gabriel hid a smile as the train doors opened with a hiss. 'How much you want to bet that no one's gotten off here in five years? Go on, bet me.'

'I'll take that bet,' his friend said, smirking.

The first guy blinked in surprise. 'Really?'

'Yeah, because you've already lost. Look.' He pointed through the window at Gabriel, who was standing on the platform grinning and waving.

When the train and the gawping man had rumbled away, Gabriel turned to look at Moorheart station.

It wasn't like any station he had ever seen. Long fingers of ivy had overtaken the small building beside the rusting Moorheart signpost. Some of the vines were so thick, so weighty, that they were digging into the granite as if preparing to crumple the lonely-looking structure like an empty can of Coke. The windows were battened up, the blue paint on the door was peeling and the notice board had half-slipped down the wall. Only the high-pitched creak of the notice board could be heard now, swinging softly on the one remaining rusty nail from which it hung.

Nature, Gabriel decided, was well on its way to reclaiming this place.

He walked around the building once, twice, trying to peek through the boarded windows, even the keyhole, but saw only darkness. Eventually he gave up and leant against the ivy-covered wall.

So, the silver-haired man *had* done this to trick him. He'd robbed him of his coin and, as an even crueller prank, sent him to some abandoned station in the middle of the moors. But what Gabriel couldn't understand was *why*. Gabriel hadn't done anything wrong. Well, apart from steal his wallet. But the man had been ready for that. He'd *wanted* that to happen. The card that now sat in his pocket proved that. So it couldn't have all been for nothing . . .

Except it is, Gabriel thought, walking over and sitting on the platform edge. *Because it doesn't look like anyone has been here for years.*

The platform itself was short and overgrown – heather and gorse had swallowed the concrete and left behind a sea of purple and yellow flowers. Yet the train tracks below his feet still looked new. Trains did stop at Moorheart, he reminded himself, even if no one got off.

Strange, Gabriel thought. He had just made up his mind to take the next train back to Torbridge when something far stranger caught his eye.

A figure stood at the far end of the platform.

Gabriel gulped. 'Um, hello?' The figure stared in silence, unmoving.

Heart pounding, Gabriel wobbled to standing and took a half-step backwards in case he needed to run. 'I'm lost. Can you help me? I'm looking for a man with silver hair. He took something from me . . .' Gabriel trailed off.

A sliver of sunlight broke the thinning cloud cover, illuminating the figure.

'Scared by a *statue*,' Gabriel muttered to himself. 'Glad no one was around to see that.' Still wary – because who wouldn't be wary of a statue standing at the end of an overgrown platform on an abandoned station – Gabriel stepped closer. As he did, he thought something buzzed in his pocket, but decided he had imagined it. Then, in the distance, there was a faint whirring and a *click*.

Gabriel slowed. But the whirring stopped almost immediately. He moved closer to the statue.

It was made of bronze, with thin rivulets of turquoise

rust below the eyes and nostrils, though both were partially obscured by a top hat and the hand that was adjusting it. More patches of turquoise rust lined the edges of what looked to be a blazer. No, Gabriel corrected himself; a coat. Well, something in between the two. It was open slightly, as if the wind had blown it askew only for the figure to be frozen solid seconds later.

Gabriel grinned. 'Got anything for me?' he said, instinctively slipping searching fingers into the exposed inside pocket of the coat.

To his shock, his fingers touched something. He pulled it out and frowned. It was round and metal, but too small to be a coin. If anything, it looked like one of those small metal tokens you slid inside a bumper car to make them start. He rolled it around his fingers a few times, feeling its considerable weight, then looked around.

I wonder, Gabriel thought, *if this opens something.* He did another lap of the building, looking for any small opening where it might fit. Keyhole? Wrong shape. Window lock? Too large. The crack in the plastic-covered notice board? Too shallow to accept the coin.

It fit nothing.

Gabriel walked back over to the statue. 'You can have this back, mate,' he said to the statue grimly, dropping it back into the pocket. 'Doesn't open anything anyway.' He walked away and sat on the edge of the platform again, waiting for the train to come.

And yet . . .

Gabriel couldn't take his eyes off the statue. There was something that nagged at him about it. Something was definitely *off*. The clothes were weird, certainly. And the way that hand was adjusting the top hat was awkward, the fingers a little too straight to—

No way. Gabriel sprung to his feet and rushed over to it. With his eyes, he carefully followed the fingers on the statue's hand. Because, he now realised, it was *pointing*.

There, hidden deep amongst the overgrown ferns and the flowering gorse and heather, was a gate. And the gate, unlike everything else at Moorheart station, was in perfect condition. No rust, no ivy clinging to it, no black paint curling off the smooth metal bars.

Excitement swelled in his chest. 'Sorry,' he said to the statue. 'I think I'm going to need that after all.' He freed the token and, warily, walked towards the gate.

There was no ordinary keyhole in the gate, only a small slot for . . . well, a token. Gabriel slid it in. The gate swallowed the token with a clunk and, soundlessly, swung open. Behind, a well-worn path led up into thick woodland.

Gabriel looked over his shoulder at the train tracks that could, in just a few short minutes, lead him home. Then he took a steadying breath, nodded as if to convince himself, and strode into the woods.

All along the winding path, an army of lichen-covered trees huddled tightly together, mossy boulders at their feet. The purple of the heather and the yellow of the gorse were gone now, replaced by a thin blanket of blue bellflowers on either side of the path. Despite it not having rained for several days, the woods sagged with moisture. It even smelled damp. Heavy mists often covered the moors early in the mornings, leaving everything wet and glistening. But what was strange was that only specific patches of soil were wet, as if someone had been watering them that very morning.

This place, Gabriel began to realise, wasn't *wild* at all. Ivy had been pulled away from trees, squares of earth had been cleared beside the path and only the weeds that produced the most beautiful flowers had been allowed to flourish.

It was minutes before Gabriel began to notice the path was taking him in a slow, spiralling ascent. And a few more before he heard the sound of water. More still before he noticed shafts of sunlight breaking through the ever-thinning canopy.

Up ahead, the path dipped sharply out of view. Warily, he climbed the final few steps.

Gabriel's eyes went wide. 'What *is* this place?'

Below, dense woodland wrapped around an enormous lake, which was glittering in the sun like Mrs Mercier's diamond ring. In the centre of the lake sat a perfectly circular island with tall, thick trees of various types ringing it. Through the gaps between the trees rose a building that dwarfed even the Mercier mansion. It was pristine, too, with immaculate white walls and terracotta roof tiles. Ivy climbed up its walls, but here it grew in an elegant

S shape rather than in an untidy, crisscrossing mess. Other colourful vines and flowers Gabriel didn't recognise tumbled down its walls – from balconies, from window ledges, from walkways – towards the perfectly manicured lawn below.

Curved in a semi-circle in front of the main building were several smaller buildings, though all were still considerably larger than his summer house. It looked like a place out of the travel brochures he'd used to read to imagine himself somewhere other than the particular Nowheresville he was living in at that time. Somewhere in Spain or Italy or Portugal, where he'd travelled to in his mind but never in real life.

And inside, a silver-haired stranger with a stolen coin waited for him.

CHAPTER FOUR

abriel's descent through the woods was not nearly as slow as his ascent. Partly because he was going downhill, but mostly because his excitement made him pick up the pace, eyes fixed on the terracotta roof until he reached the water's edge.

Purple and yellow wildflowers grew along the bank, interrupted only by the odd cluster of blue bellflowers which had broken free from the dense woodland. A thin path led around the lake to his right, so Gabriel joined it. The water was calm and clear and so deep he couldn't see the bottom. He reached down and dipped a finger in.

If it's that cold in summer, Gabriel thought with a shudder, *what's it like in winter?*

Up ahead, a crooked wooden pier zigzagged out into the lake. A lone figure stood at the end, staring towards the island as if waiting for something. As he grew closer, Gabriel realised it was a girl, with light brown skin and thick, wavy brown hair that finished at the bottom of her black T-shirt. Strangest of all, the girl appeared to be speaking to herself. Repeating something with such intensity that her brow was crinkled.

Warily, Gabriel stepped on to the pier and followed the winding path towards her. He stopped a metre or so behind the girl, not wanting to startle her. She was murmuring words to herself in a language he did not know.

The girl tilted her head and removed one wireless earphone, still facing the lake. 'You shouldn't sneak up on a woman who knows ten different ways to render you unconscious.' Then, as if she hadn't just threatened him with extreme violence, she asked, 'So, do you speak Cantonese too?'

Gabriel looked around to check she was talking to him. 'Erm, no.'

'Mm,' the girl said, only now turning. She took out the other earphone and placed both in her shorts pocket. 'I'm not surprised. It's the hardest language I've ever learned.'

Gabriel blinked. 'How many languages *have* you learned?'

'Five fluently. But I understand another two. You?'

'If I'm really pushing it,' Gabriel said, feigning deep thought. 'Then one.'

The girl frowned. 'No French?'

'Je m'appelle Gabriel,' he said proudly. 'That count?'

She flinched. 'With an accent like that, it should count as a crime.' She turned and glared at the island, muttering,

'It's one o'clock. It should be here by now.'

Gabriel stepped beside her. Her unnaturally rigid posture made her look taller than him, though he suspected they were around the same height. 'What are we waiting for?'

'*We* aren't waiting for anything. *I* am waiting. I've no idea what *you* are doing.' She crossed her arms. 'Apart from bashing around in the woods like an elephant.'

'Were you spying on me?' Strange. He hadn't seen anyone on his walk.

'Very few people come the long route any more. Suppose I was just interested to see the type of fool who would.' She looked him up and down with a smirk. 'Now I know.'

'There's a shorter way?'

She raised an eyebrow. 'Obviously.'

'So what are *you* doing out here then?' Gabriel said, irritated. 'Looks like you came the long way too.'

'It does look like that, doesn't it?' the girl said, offering nothing more.

Standing side by side, they waited in silence for something to happen, though Gabriel had no idea what. He glanced at the girl again and saw now that her face and T-shirt were damp with sweat. 'What have you just been doing? Why are you so . . . sweaty?'

'After lunch on my free days, I listen to my Cantonese lesson and I do half an hour of HIIT – high-intensity interval training,' the girl said as if it was the most normal thing in the world. '"Fleet of foot, fleet of mind", Father always says. What?' she added, seeing the disbelieving expression on his face.

'It's just,' Gabriel started, 'people our age don't really do . . . that sort of thing. Exercising like that, I mean. That's more, you know, for adults. And you don't look much like an adult to me.'

The girl appeared wounded by this. 'What would *you* know about being an adult?'

'Me? Oh, nothing at all. Don't want to know either. Seems to me that becoming an adult is the real crime. No need for it, that's what I think.'

The girl gave Gabriel a disdainful look. 'I speak five languages, but I'm afraid *nonsense* isn't one of them.'

'I suppose that means I speak two then,' Gabriel said with a grin.

A flicker of a smile passed across the girl's face.

Moments later, a long, thin boat made of dark brown wood glided into view. A ghost of a man, tall and gaunt, stood on a flat platform at the back. Looking grumpy and off balance, he shoved an oar into the smooth surface of the lake, the ripples caused by his clumsy paddling reaching the pier a minute or so before he did.

'Couldn't even get me a half-decent oar, could they?' the pale man grumbled as he reached out, grabbed the edge of the pier and eased the boat to a shuddering stop.

'Who are *you*?' the girl said. (Rather rudely, Gabriel thought.) 'Where's Thomas?'

'Uncle Tommy's gone off on holiday,' the man said, hopping off the boat and wrapping a rope around a wooden stump on the pier. 'Just about half an hour ago, actually. I'm covering him until he gets back.'

'On *holiday*?' the girl asked, aghast. 'During the busiest time of the year?'

'Yeah,' the man said miserably. 'Just like him to conveniently forget to mention that little fact before he left. Now, are you two getting on or have I given myself another blister for nothing?'

'I'm not getting aboard until I see some credentials,' the girl said, crossing her arms.

Credentials? Gabriel thought. *This girl's thirteen going on forty.*

The gaunt man sighed, then reached into the breast pocket of his tattered dark blue shirt and pulled out a white card. 'Name's Mickey Jones. Was a student here once myself a long time ago. I've got clearance, all right. See.'

The girl snatched the card and examined it closely.

Frowning, Gabriel leaned closer to have a look. 'Hold on. That looks just like—'

'Mm,' the girl said, glancing up at the man. 'Everything seems in order.' She handed it back and hopped into the boat in one easy move. 'Shall we be off then? I'm painting a Matisse this afternoon and I need all the natural light I can get if I'm ever to master the brushwork.'

'Hang about,' Mickey said, glancing between the two of them. 'I've not even checked *your* bloomin' credentials yet.'

At that, Gabriel's hands began to sweat. Because, of course, he had nothing of the sort to show the man. 'I've never had to show your uncle anything like that before,' Gabriel bluffed. 'He knows me.' If English was his first language, and Nonsense was his second, then Lying was definitely his third. And he was fluent.

Mickey laughed. 'Rubbish. Tommy's a stickler for rules. He wouldn't let his own wife on his gondola without a clearance pass. Now,' he stepped closer, the amusement draining from his face. 'You got something for me or am I gonna have to call the Gardeners to escort you off the premises?'

Gabriel gulped. Mickey was between him and the shore. Jumping into the lake wasn't an option either – he was a hopeless swimmer. Maybe he could—

'His name is Gabriel Avery,' the girl called out, holding up a white card. 'And, while I can't quite believe I'm saying this, he does have the right clearance.'

'I do?' Gabriel stared at the card in her hand. He patted his pockets. 'Oi, that's my card!'

The girl stood and handed two cards to Mickey. '*Now* can we go? We are losing precious seconds of daylight.'

Mickey took both cards. He passed the first over a strange contraption attached to his wrist and grunted. 'Gabriel, yeah. A Merit, too. Like me. Good lot, Merits. Legacies are the – and pardon my Latin for this – toerags. Snooty lot, they are. Think that just because their parents were once-great cro—' He paused in the middle of swiping the girl's card and paled, staring at the contraption. 'You're . . . I didn't know . . . I'm sorry, miss. I didn't mean . . . I was just—' His eyebrows flew upwards. 'You won't tell him, will you?'

The girl smirked. 'If you get me back to the island in less than a minute, Mickey, I will forgive and forget every little thing I've heard. Does that sound fair?'

Mickey was already scrambling back into the gondola. 'Fairer than fair, I reckon.'

Merits? Legacies? What does any of that even mean? Gabriel thought, climbing aboard too. He slid into a seat opposite the girl, who was looking especially pleased with herself. 'Who are you then? Someone famous?'

The girl looked off towards the island. 'No. Not yet anyway.' Gabriel frowned. She did that a lot – half-answer a question. He was about to ask a follow-up, but Mickey spoke first.

'Now, I'm not strictly allowed to do what I'm about to do in daylight hours, Uncle Tommy said. But under the circumstances . . .' He tapped the contraption on his wrist as if it were a watch. Then he grabbed the oar, turning it around until he found a slightly darker patch of wood, which he tapped at lightly for a few moments. There was a hiss and a thin crack appeared in the platform he had been standing on previously. The two pieces of wood pulled apart, revealing a hole from which rose a brown seat and steering wheel. Mickey sat and clutched the wheel tight. He flicked a switch next to the wheel and a gurgling began at the rear of the boat.

'If I were you,' Mickey said, more to Gabriel than the girl, 'I'd hold on tight.'

There was a roar and the front of the boat suddenly rose in the water. Gabriel clung on as the boat lurched forwards and took off across the lake. The girl, on the other hand, looked comfortable, happy even, her long hair rippling in the wind.

They reached the island in less than a minute. Gabriel's eyes watered from the speed, his stomach still flip-flopping as Mickey tied the boat to another crooked pier. In one graceful move, the girl leapt on to the pier and started towards the treeline. 'Your secret is safe with me, boatman!'

Clumsily, Gabriel clambered on to the pier and took off after her. 'Hey! My card.'

She smiled and walked on, Gabriel's card dancing back and forth across her knuckles.

Despite the odd way she talked and acted, and her annoying habit of never answering a question directly, Gabriel was a little in awe of this strange girl. So when he caught up with her, he didn't immediately snatch back his card. Instead, he fell in step beside her, and together they silently followed the path through the tall trees that ringed the island.

'Here,' the girl said eventually, handing over his card. 'You'll need that if you're ever to get back into the grounds.'

Of course, Gabriel thought. He remembered the brief buzzing in his pocket on the train platform – and then the statue had released the token. It had been the card. 'Thanks.'

When they broke through the treeline, they found themselves on the huge, circular lawn. In the distance loomed the villa with the terracotta tiles. In between, more or less in the centre of the lawn, stood an easel with a half-finished painting mounted on it. Gabriel had never seen anything quite like it, but he had certainly seen the silver-haired painter before.

'You!' Gabriel's voice echoed around them as if held in by the wall of trees.

The man laid his paintbrush down and turned slowly, as if he had all the time in the world. When he saw Gabriel, a smile spread across his face. 'Gabriel Avery. As I live and thieve!'

Gabriel marched across the lawn towards the man. 'Where's my coin? I want it back.'

'And you shall have it back,' the man said cheerily. He picked up a paint-stained rag and wiped his hands. 'Tell me of your journey. I do so love to hear of a Merit's first encounter with the station. The woods. The lake! But first you must tell me – what do you think of our disreputable establishment?'

Gabriel stopped a metre or so away. *Merits. Legacies. Security cards. A mansion hidden away on an island.* He didn't know whether he was still queasy from the boat ride, but his mind was muddled. 'I don't understand. What is this place?'

'This,' the man said, sweeping a hand towards the building behind, 'is Crookhaven. A school for wrongdoers, swindlers and thieves. And, if you so choose, your new home.'

CHAPTER FIVE

'This is a . . . *school*?' Gabriel said eventually.

'Why, of course!' the silver-haired man said with a laugh. 'And a rather selective one, come to that.'

The girl breezed past Gabriel. 'Father, how can *he* possibly be one of the forty-eight students who got into Crookhaven this year?'

Father? Gabriel thought. *So that's* why the boatman had gone wide-eyed at the sight of her name.

The girl carried on. 'He only speaks one language, he thinks HIIT is only for adults and, to him, Matisse may as well be a type of cheese! Have our recruiting standards slipped so drastically that—' The girl stopped. A grin broke across the man's face. 'What, Father?'

The man nodded towards Gabriel, who was at that moment juggling the girl's earphones and whistling. 'You are skilled in several methods of crookery, Penelope, but you have yet to learn humility.' He tutted as he swept past her. 'You *must* come to understand that what you don't know will always outweigh what you know. Even at my age. Skill is no substitute for modesty.'

Penelope rifled through her pockets, face crimson with embarrassment. 'Father, I—'

He raised a hand to cut her off. 'By my watch, it is already ten past one. Which means you are ten minutes late for painting with Palombo. And if there is another person in all the world who loathes lateness as much as Palombo, I am yet to meet them. So I suggest you dash off before he makes you hold his canvas all afternoon again while he paints.' The man shook his head, then lowered his voice so only Gabriel could hear. 'Hell on the arms, that.'

Penelope looked like she wanted to say something else but clearly thought better of it. Instead she turned and started towards the villa.

'If you're going that way,' her father called after her, 'be a dear and take the easel and painting with you.'

Penelope stopped, her jaw clenching tightly. She returned for the easel and her father's supplies. With the easel under one arm, the painting under the other and the brushes and paints spread between her left and right hands, she staggered towards the house. Every few steps she would drop something and have to reposition everything to pick up the fallen item. After this had happened for a third time, Gabriel made to go help but felt a hand on his shoulder.

'Don't, Gabriel. My daughter is exceptional and I'm afraid she knows it. Confidence is the holy union between self-belief and skill, while overconfidence is a trait which has led nations to ruin and individuals to make mistakes from which they can never recover. But repeated failure humbles even the most brash. So let her fail.'

Penelope, sweating now, allowed the easel to slip through her fingers again. Without looking back at her dad, she also dropped the rest of the items on the grass and stared at them for a moment, considering carefully. Then she picked up each item in a different order – easel first, held horizontal in both hands, the painting on top of that and, finally, the painting supplies. This time, she walked smoothly, no items tumbling from her grasp, until she rounded the corner of the villa out of view.

The man let out a satisfied grunt and held out a hand to Gabriel. 'Caspian Crook.'

It was the smoothest, softest hand Gabriel had even shaken. 'Crook? Is that your real name?'

Caspian laughed. 'Oh yes. I come from a long line of Crooks, all of whom also happen to be crooks.' Caspian leant closer. 'You know, some say my family are the reason the word *crook* is associated with criminality.' He straightened, chuckling again. 'But I've never been one for speculation.'

Gabriel looked around again. 'If this is a school, then where is everyone?'

'Well, you, young man,' Caspian said, 'are early. It usually takes two or three days for a Merit to summon the courage to follow the instructions on the card we give

39

them. Don't worry, they and the Legacies will all arrive before term begins, six days from now.'

'Merits?' Gabriel asked. 'Legacies?' He was getting sick of hearing these words that he didn't understand.

'Mmm, yes,' Caspian said, turning on his heel and walking towards the villa. 'I will explain all. But first I think a tour is in order, don't you?'

Gabriel followed in a sort of daze. They crossed the lawn, passed the three smaller buildings that sat in front of the villa, and rounded the eastern side. Gabriel examined the main building as they walked, counting five floors, with balconies on every level.

Trailing Caspian back into the woods that ringed the villa, Gabriel soon found himself in a clearing. A shaft of light broke through the canopy, illuminating a building made of dark wood and glass. The windows were large and square and so clean that even Grandma would've been impressed.

Gabriel followed Caspian inside.

'This is our Forgery wing,' Caspian said, gesturing to the left where easels were set up in neat rows of six, then to the right where large chunks of rock sat on sturdy tables. 'Painting, drawing, sculpting – we teach it all. If you look at the back, you'll see pottery wheels and kilns, then just over there you might spy an oven for ageing paintings. We have paints from every decade in the twentieth century and most of the nineteenth; chisels that Michelangelo himself would recognise; photography equipment from—'

Caspian cut himself off. 'Ah, but I see this is all rather overwhelming for you.'

Gabriel held up a hand as if to shield his eyes. 'It's just a bit bright in here, that's all.' A quick, clumsy lie. In truth, Gabriel still felt a little queasy. Maybe from the boat ride or more likely from the downright craziness of this place.

'Bright, yes!' Caspian said excitedly, gesturing for Gabriel to follow him as he began walking towards the back of the building. 'By design, of course. The natural light on this side of the island is perfect for the delicate art of Forgery.' He paused as he passed the last row of easels. 'Speaking of delicate art . . . Penelope! For goodness sake, smooth out your strokes. You look like you're swatting a fly.'

Gabriel peered around an enormous canvas and saw Penelope, a paintbrush in her hand and a white painter's jacket covering her black T-shirt. A tanned man, small, with deep frown lines stood behind her, his arms crossed. He was looking at the painting as though it was deeply displeasing to him. Palombo, Gabriel guessed.

'I tell her already, Caspian. She come in angry and start chop-chop-chopping at the canvas as if was piece of wood.'

Penelope frowned but refused to look at her father or Gabriel. Instead she slowed her strokes; Palombo visibly relaxed with each dab.

'Let us go,' Caspian said, sweeping out of the Forgery

wing. 'There is a great deal more to see.'

Next up was a building that housed all manner of exercise equipment, though not the type Gabriel had ever seen before. Climbing walls covered half the building, strange items that looked as if they were to be leapt over or leapt through sat in the centre of the room, and there was a large, padded area at the far end. Small, dark droplets of something that looked suspiciously like dried blood dotted the padded floor.

'This is our centre of Crimnastics,' Caspian explained, vaulting a waist-high object with the grace of a man half his age. 'Here, we work on functional fitness. Do you know what that means?'

Gabriel shook his head, secretly wondering if he could leap over the object too.

'It means that we work on activities and exercises that will aid you in your criminal pursuits. Climbing instead of rugby, parkour instead of tennis, Krav Maga instead of football.'

Gabriel's heart soared. *There really is a place for someone with my talents after all.*

*

That afternoon Gabriel saw all kinds of wonders – rooms, large and small, filled with familiar items that should not, strictly speaking, have been on the island. Hanging on a wall in the lunch hall, just beside a flaking map that read *Alcatraz Blueprints*, was a painting that looked suspiciously like the *Mona Lisa*. Though it couldn't possibly be the *real* version.

Could it?

The entire top floor of the main villa was a library, packed with books that looked to be hundreds of years old. One thick, tattered book sat in the centre of the room under a glass casing. Something called the *Crimina Carta*. Despite its glass protection, large sections seemed to have been torn out of it.

Stranger still was the fact that, growing through the centre of the villa, was an enormous, curved oak tree.

'Ah, yes,' Caspian had said, when Gabriel stopped to look up at it from the second floor landing. 'The Crooked Oak has been here for as long as I can remember. The family legend goes that we Crooks bought this plot of land and sought to create a lake with a large island at its heart, so that no one could ever stumble upon our school for wrong'uns. But they couldn't decide where to build the villa. Then we happened upon this old oak, bent by the moorland winds but still upright. Still standing its ground despite all life had thrown at it. So when we shaped the island, we thought it only fitting to keep the Crooked Oak at our heart.'

Gabriel's eyes followed the tree from its roots up through all the floors and out of the roof. As they passed through each new room, with their endless oddities pinned on walls or spread across tables, Gabriel fizzed with questions. Caspian seemed to anticipate every one and answer them either with entertaining stories or a promise to explain another time. To a connoisseur of crime like Gabriel, this place was Disneyland.

The school had bewitched him to the point that he'd almost forgotten why he'd come. But it was getting late now, and Grandma would be worried. Gabriel cleared his throat. 'My coin. Can I have it back now, please? That's all I've come for.'

Caspian raised an eyebrow. 'Certainly, Gabriel. It's in my office. Though something tells me that your coin isn't the *only* reason you came here today.' With that, he turned and strode out of front door of the main building, down the stairs and across the lawn into the dense treeline. Gabriel followed.

Here, the trees were older and larger than on the eastern side of the island, with sunlight barely able to break through the thick canopy. Nearly at the water's edge, they came upon a wooden building about the same size as Gabriel's summerhouse, though in far better condition. It, like some of the other smaller buildings dotted around the island, was built from wood and glass.

'In you go,' Caspian said, holding the door open. Inside, it was warm and cosy, with a fireplace at the far end and two enormous wooden desks side by side in centre of the room. 'I'm afraid my co-Headmaster is currently . . . elsewhere. Over the summer holidays there have been a number of disturbances in the Underworld that have required her attention. She—' He shook his head. 'Anyway, never mind that.'

Gabriel pulled out the wallet he had taken from Caspian at Torbridge station. 'Here. Sorry I took this.'

'Nonsense,' Caspian said, taking the wallet and placing it on the table. 'It brought you here, to Crookhaven, didn't it?'

'So this is really a school for criminals.' It was meant as a question, though it came out more as an accusation.

'We are so much more than that,' Caspian said, sitting in a plush leather chair and gesturing for Gabriel to sit in a similar one across the table. 'We are a home for the forgotten, a sanctuary for the lost and, yes, a training ground for the greatest crooks of the future.'

Gabriel shook his head. 'But I'm not a . . . crook. I just steal what I need for me and Grandma. That's all.'

Caspian nodded as if he'd heard countless similar protests, his slender fingers moving to his shaven chin. 'The word *crook* is misunderstood, I think. You steal for the same reason we at Crookhaven steal – to put the world back in balance. Tell me, do you know how the Merciers acquired their fortune?'

Gabriel flinched at the name of the family whose mansion he cleaned daily.

Caspian continued. 'By selling cars with cheap, faulty parts they knew would probably fail within two years. They don't care about those who are harmed in the process – one family even died in an accident, but the

Merciers' expensive lawyers kept them out of jail. They sit in their mansion, roundly praised for their business nous, all the while turning a blind eye to the damage they have caused.' Caspian leant forward and, for the first time since Gabriel had met him, anger flickered in his grey eyes. 'Do you want to know the great secret of the world, Gabriel Avery? The real criminals aren't wearing stripes and balaclavas, they're wearing suits and smiles. And most are too wealthy, too *powerful*, to be made to pay for their evildoing.' Caspian leant back. 'That is, in essence, what we do here at Crookhaven: we do wrong to put the world right.'

'Still, even when we have nothing to eat, Grandma hates it when I pick pockets.'

Caspian nodded seriously. 'She's an honourable, hardworking woman, and she wants you to follow in her footsteps. Every parent does. But what you do for her is honourable too, Gabriel. You don't want to see your grandma go hungry, so you steal just enough to feed her and no more.' He sat upright. 'Let me ask you something – if you made something beautiful, something truly invaluable to you and your family, and then someone came along and took it, would you try and take it back?'

''Course.'

'And if you caught fish from a nearby river, only to one day see the water blacken and the fish die because someone was dumping waste upstream, would you try to stop them?'

The answer was obvious, wasn't it? 'Yeah, I would.'

'And if Grandma put every penny she'd ever saved into a scheme suggested to her by a man who earned her trust, only for it all to disappear the next day, what would you do?'

Even the thought made Gabriel's skin prickle. 'I'd get it back.'

Caspian smiled. 'Of course you would. But if you had to break into someone's house to take back that invaluable item, is that a crime? If you had to hack into the company who was dumping waste in your river in order to stop them, would that be wrong? And if you found the man who stole your grandma's life savings, is there *anything* you wouldn't do to get them back?'

Gabriel fell silent, thinking. 'But why me?'

Caspian nodded, as if he'd been expecting this question. 'We have been watching you for the last few years, following you from Milesden to Barrow-on-the-Hill and now Torbridge.' Caspian gestured around the room, to countless photographs of men and women – young and old, alone or in small clusters, in colour and in black and white – who all possessed the same knowing smile. 'Crookhaven's alumni network are always watching, you see. Their collective eye is trained to spot young talent. Merits, we call them. The Merits who are brought to our attention by our alumni are then looked at more closely, often by our teachers themselves.'

'Like you?' Gabriel asked.

'Well, not ordinarily, no. Neither I nor my co-Headmaster can go for a wander around the country when we feel like it, even during the summer holidays. Particularly me. In some unsavoury circles, I'm rather ... well ... *known*.' He cleared his throat as if he had no intention of clarifying. 'But as it happens, you were only a single train ride away, so I decided to recruit you personally.'

'Recruit?' Gabriel said, with a chuckle. 'By letting *me* pick *your* pocket?'

'By showing you an irresistible mark – distracted by my phone, wearing baggy trousers with large pockets that showed a wallet – and seeing whether you took the bait. Many don't, and so they are never offered a place.'

Gabriel thought for a long moment. This was what he wanted, wasn't it? A place where his talents were valued. Where he could be himself and be celebrated for it. This magical, crooked place was all he'd ever dreamed of and more. And yet ...

He held out his hand. 'I think I'd like my coin back now, please.'

Caspian sighed. Reluctantly, he slid the coin out of his top drawer and placed it in Gabriel's waiting palm. Gabriel flipped it to the burnt side and smiled. 'Thanks.' He looked up. 'I'm sorry, but I don't speak five languages or do Crimnastics or know who Matisse is. I don't belong here, sir. Not really.'

'Ah, but Gabriel,' Caspian said, eyes lighting up. 'It is

those who feel like they don't belong who are most welcome at Crookhaven. Do you know why?'

Gabriel shook his head.

'Because it is the outsiders, the forgotten, the ones who've always felt like they *don't* belong, who end up changing the world.'

That was all well and good, but Gabriel had a life to get back to. 'Sorry, sir. I don't want to change the world.' Gabriel stood. 'It's getting late. Grandma will be worried.' He slid his coin into his pocket and pulled something else out. 'Thanks for showing me around Crookhaven. I promise I won't tell anyone about it. Oh, and these are Penelope's. She'll need them for her Cantonese lessons.' He dropped the EarPods on to the desk. Gabriel walked towards the door and opened it.

'Here at Crookhaven, Gabriel Avery, your talents can lead you to places you cannot yet dream of,' Caspian called after him calmly. 'Whereas out there, untrained, I fear they will only lead you to prison.'

Gabriel paused halfway out the door. Prison. That was what Grandma had always said. That one day he'd be caught and he'd not be able to lie or charm or squirm his way out. Then she'd be all on her own.

Gabriel's grip tightened on the door handle. 'Grandma's so tired every day. And most days she goes hungry. Everything I steal . . . it really is all for her. Always has been.' He turned, glanced up, tears in his eyes. 'I didn't lie before: I don't want to change the whole world, only *our* world – mine and hers.'

Caspian stared for a moment. Then, slowly, he rose from his seat and walked around the desk. He placed a hand on Gabriel's shoulder and smiled warmly. 'If we all had such dreams – to better the lives of the ones we love – how wonderful a place this world would be.'

Gabriel wiped his cheeks. 'But I can't help Grandma if I'm here.'

'Not at first, no,' Caspian said, face growing serious. 'You won't be there with her every day any more. But you can talk to your grandma once a week and visit during the holidays. And while you must inform her that you have accepted a place at a boarding school and arrived safely so that we don't have the police knocking down our door, you won't be able to tell her where we are located, who your classmates are or, most importantly, what it is that we *do* here. To protect our world, you will be forced to lie to the person you hold most dear. In return, you have this place. You will not pay a penny to us until you graduate, whereupon we will only take a five per cent cut of your lifetime earnings. And *most* importantly . . .' Caspian bent down to Gabriel's level, eyes softening. 'If you truly want to build a better life, for you *and* your grandma, there is no better place in all the world than Crookhaven.'

Not visit Grandma for *three months*? Gabriel couldn't do that. She'd worry herself half to death. Besides, she needed him there in Torbridge to help her clean and garden. No, he'd just have to go to the village school, with all those kids that hated him, and then he'd clean the mansion with Grandma after school and at weekends.

A sinking feeling came over Gabriel. For how long? Until the end of school? *Five years* of that? Picking pockets at the train station so they could afford a bacon butty. Being forced to live in that leaking, crumbling excuse for a house. Cleaning that disaster of an upstairs toilet in the Mercier mansion. Seeing Grandma get up tired and go to bed bone-weary. Watching her miss breakfasts and lunches and dinners . . . Stuck in rotten Torbridge *for ever* – or until Grandma couldn't do the work any more and they had to move to an even worse place.

Nothing would ever change, Gabriel realised then, unless he *made* it change.

'Actually,' Gabriel said, stepping back into the office and closing the door. 'It's probably best that I stay. I don't have enough money for a ticket home.'

CHAPTER SIX

Dear Grandma,
I'm sorry I disappeared like that, but it's for a good
reason. The thing is, I got accepted into a school
for criminals—

Gabriel stopped writing. Well he definitely couldn't say *that*. Grandma would worry herself sick. She'd probably call the police and report him missing before she'd even finished reading. Besides, the Headmaster had forbidden him from saying a word about Crookhaven to her anyway. No, he had to come up with something more believable.

Frowning, he scrunched up the paper and threw it into the bin in the corner of his new room. After he'd accepted Caspian's offer, he'd been shown into one of the three smaller buildings that sat in front of the main villa. It was nothing like where the final year students stayed in the main building. He'd seen their floor on Caspian's tour.

It was spacious and lavish and, because they were deemed skilled enough at Crookery to venture out into the real world, the spoils of their outings were pinned on every wall, positioned in every corner, even proudly displayed on their hanging uniforms.

Gabriel's building, on the other hand, was cramped and basic. All that was in each bedroom was a single bed, a rickety-looking wooden desk, a plastic chair and a temperamental desk lamp that was either blindingly bright or pathetically weak.

Still, it was larger than his room at home, it didn't leak and, best of all, it was warm. The only times Gabriel remembered being warm the previous winter were when he'd broken into the mansion while the Merciers were away and set a fire in their enormous fireplace. He'd only ever done it on those midwinter nights when the glass of water Grandma always placed on his bedside table froze over, and he always cleaned up the embers when it was all burned out. But those few hours in the early morning, curled up on the soft carpet beside the roaring fire like a cat, were blissful. Grandma never scolded him for it, though she must have known what he was doing because he always laid his own duvet over her before sneaking out.

He missed Grandma, then. Longed to be back in that leaky house, sitting across from her after a hard day's work. Talking about nothing and everything across an empty dining table and laughing so they didn't end up crying. But he couldn't leave. He had to stay – for Grandma.

For a chance at a better life for them both.

Gabriel shook himself from his daydream and started writing again.

Dear Grandma,

I want to start this letter by telling you that I'm safe. I haven't run away from home, so please don't think that. I'll be back for Christmas, I promise. The thing is I got accepted into a boarding school. I didn't tell you I was applying because I knew you wouldn't let me go. That's also why I left without saying goodbye. But I did get in, and they've given me a full scholarship too. So you don't have to pay for anything.

I know you'll be mad at me, and that's OK. But I've made sure that you won't have to clean the mansion on your own. I called Mr Hartley and he's agreed to come by on weekends and help. On weekdays, he'll send his nephew along in the afternoons instead. Mr Hartley's an ogre but he's kind.

Sorry I couldn't call you, but I know that on the phone you'd convince me to come back and I can't do that yet. This new school is different to Torfalls. Better. Here I have a chance to learn things that will mean we don't have to live in the summer house any more. I want us to have a proper home, with heaters and a roof that doesn't leak and enough food so that you never have to miss a meal for me. And, most of all, I don't want you ever to have to clean another toilet. That's why I'm here, and that's why I have to stay. I just hope you can forgive me.

See you at Christmas.

Gabriel

P.S. I'm sending my jumper along with this letter so you know it's really from me. There are too many holes in it anyway. Besides, I have a uniform now.

Gabriel put the pen down. *Yes*, he thought, rereading it. *That's better.*

CHAPTER SEVEN

Over the next few days, as he waited for the rest of the Merits to arrive, Gabriel explored the island. It was bigger than he'd thought, and there was much more to discover than he'd imagined. Nothing was entirely as it appeared. He'd spent several minutes one afternoon marvelling at a small tree that appeared to have grown crooked, much like the Crooked Oak itself, only for a third year Merit to come along, pick it up as though it weighed nothing, and walk off. What a crook could possibly need a lifelike papier mâché tree for, Gabriel hadn't a clue, but the replica was faultless.

Some aspects were even more baffling. For instance, all the toilets – every single one – were locked from the outside so that anyone wanting to use them had to pick the lock to get in. Forget to lock the secondary lock while inside and an uninvited guest might just burst in mid-pee. When Gabriel asked Caspian why he'd done this, the

Headmaster had said, 'Isn't it obvious? We are never more desperate, more stressed or more under pressure than when bursting for the loo. If you can pick a lock when your bladder is threatening to explode, you can pick one at any time.'

But worst of all, items that were in one spot in the morning could, and often would, be in a separate corner of the island by the afternoon. Caspian got the Gardeners – adults dressed in loose-fitting grey overalls who seemed to be Crookhaven's security guards – to move them around to test the students' memories. He also had a habit of stopping one of the newly arrived Merits and quizzing them about a nearby item. If they answered correctly, he lavished praise upon them; if they didn't, he would say the same line: 'Try to pay closer attention to your surroundings. Once term begins, it will matter a great deal.'

Gabriel, thankfully, had managed to avoid such questions so far. He wasn't nervous he'd fail the test. Quite the opposite. Part of what made him a skilled thief was that he remembered things – almost everything, really. Which was wonderful . . . and also terrible. Gabriel remembered every failed attempt to pick a pocket down to the style of jeans the mark was wearing that day. He also remembered every hurtful word from a classmate, every cold shoulder from a villager, every single night his grandma had gone hungry so that he could eat.

Sometimes Gabriel wished he could simply . . . forget.

Forgetting wasn't something other people were ever grateful for, but they should be. It was a blessing. Gabriel would give up every treasure he'd ever picked from a pocket in exchange for forgetting the worst times in his life. But they were forever burned into his memory. Every detail as crystal clear as the day they'd happened. Perfectly, harrowingly the same.

On the day before the Legacies were to arrive, Gabriel set out to walk around the entire island. Staying close to the water's edge but near enough to the treeline that he could hide should a stranger appear on the shores of the mainland, he trudged on. It had rained the night before and parts of the shoreline were saturated, pools of muddy water blocking the well-worn path and forcing him to jump over or swerve around them. He was just coming up to the crooked pier when he saw two figures standing on the rocks beyond. They were grinning and pointing out into the lake. Ten metres or so from shore, a small fin sliced through glassy water.

Gabriel almost stumbled into a puddle. The fin was far too small to be a shark or dolphin. And in a lake? It didn't make sense. Something else was going on.

Gabriel passed the crooked pier and climbed the rocks towards the two boys. Up close, he could tell they were around his age, with round smiling faces and dark skin which glistened faintly with sweat as if they'd been running. One held something with his left hand and tapped at it with his right. The other was calling out instructions Gabriel couldn't make out. Navigating his way around rock pools, he moved closer.

'Anything down there?' the one on the left asked.

'Sonar's picking something up,' the one on the right said excitedly.

'How big?'

'Oh, it's big, man. *Big* big.'

They went for a high five but missed wildly. It didn't seem to bother them at all.

'Um, hello?' Gabriel called.

They turned at the same time and bumped heads. Gabriel winced.

'Why you always have to get so close to me?' Left said, holding his forehead.

'What you talking about? *You* bumped into *me*,' Right said, rubbing his temple.

'Are you Merits?' Gabriel asked. They both started as if, in the few seconds since he'd spoken, they'd forgotten he was there.

Twins, he thought, *identical twins*. And he would have been unable to tell them apart but for two things – the boy on the left had a shaved head and a silver skull-and-crossbones earring hanging from his right ear, whereas Right's hair was about two centimetres long and his own skull-and-crossbones earring hung from the *left* ear.

'Merits?' Left asked, confused for a moment. Then his eyes widened. 'Oh, yeah. That's us. Earned our way in and all that. You?'

Gabriel nodded. 'Me too. I'm Gabriel by the way.'

'I'm Ade . . .' Left began.

'. . . and I'm Ade,' Right finished.

Left turned to Right. 'No, you're not . . .' He sucked his teeth. 'Come on, man, why you doing that foolishness again?'

The second frowned. 'I was just having a bit of fun. Now we just look weird.' He raised his voice. 'Bet you think we're weird now, don't you?'

Gabriel didn't know what to say, so he said nothing at all.

'Don't listen to him,' Left said. '*I'm* Ade and *he's* Ede. Okoro.'

Ede shrugged as if to say, *Fine, whatever.*

'And that,' Ade said, pointing out towards the fin which bobbed softly on the surface of the water, 'is Sneaks. We made her ourselves. She can dive underwater, roll across land and even fly. Plus, listen.' He cupped his hand around his earring-less ear.

'I . . . don't hear anything,' Gabriel said.

'Exactly!' Ade cried, startling Gabriel. 'Silent as a mouse. That's why, you know, she's called *Sneaks*.'

'Oi,' Ede said to his brother. 'First off, we decided Sneaks was a *he*. Second, mice aren't silent. Remember the old house? Their horrible little nails scraping the floorboards . . .' He shuddered. 'Sneaks is more like a leopard.'

Ade was about to interrupt but Gabriel cut in first. 'Is that what you do then? Make stuff? Is that how you earned your way to Crookhaven?'

Ade snorted. 'Nah, Sneaks is just a bit of fun. We're white hats.'

Gabriel stared blankly.

Ede crossed his arms. 'You have heard of white hats, right?'

Gabriel shook his head, cheeks growing warm.

'Well,' Ade said, 'they hack into systems and, for the right price, tell the people they've hacked how they got in so they can fix their security and stop anyone else from doing the same. Other times, they expose the evildoings of the horribly corrupt.'

'Can't forget that part,' Ede chimed in. 'So yeah, that's what we do. And we're good too.' Ede shrugged. 'We're pretty well known online. But it's not something you ever get to boast about. People not knowing who you are is kind of the name of the game. Anonymity and all that. Now we're here, though, I don't suppose it matters any more.'

'So,' Gabriel said. 'What are you known *as*?'

The brothers shared a wary look.

'We're known as—' But Ade was cut off by his brother.

'Rah,' Ede said, frowning. 'Why do you get to say it?'

'I'm older. That's how it works.'

'You're older by *three minutes*, Ad. That doesn't even count!'

'Who ironed your school clothes all of last year?'

Ede frowned. 'You, but—'

'And who made dinner for all of us when Mum

was too tired?'

'You, but Ad—'

'Ex-act-ly,' Ade cut in. 'Means I deserve to introduce us.'

Ede thought about this for a long moment. 'Nah, let's say it together.'

Ade rolled his eyes. 'Fine.'

Ede seemed pleased by this. He held up three fingers and began counting down to one but stopped short at two. 'Nah, we can't say it together. That's so cringey. Just let me do it—'

'We're the Brothers Crim,' Ade finished.

Ede turned to him, mouth agape.

Ade shrugged. 'Older brothers don't hesitate.' He turned to Gabriel. 'That name mean anything to you, Gabe?'

Gabriel was about to admit, with further embarrassment, that it did not. But before he could open his mouth, an excited shriek came from behind, making them all swivel sharply.

Penelope Crook crashed out of the thick treeline and, with the nimbleness of someone who'd been doing Crimnastics all their life, dashed across the moss-covered rocks. 'I knew it! I knew you were the Brothers Crim the moment I set eyes on you.' She was dressed in her all-black running gear, her long dark hair tied into a ponytail. The only splash of colour on her was the tatty violet ribbon which held her hair in place.

'You know them?' Gabriel asked.

She looked at Gabriel and blinked, as if only now

noticing him. 'I don't *know* them. But I know *of* them. Everyone does.' She turned to the brothers. 'Your Con-Oil job was a masterpiece. You were in and out of their system in minutes and the dirt you found put them out of business for good. And – and—' She was having trouble breathing, she was talking so fast. 'And the Hydro-Cell – the ones who were dumping toxic waste off the coast of – you exposed that too. And – and—' Penelope paused to gulp down air. Then she started again. 'I heard you got into hacking because of your dad. He was badly injured – because his company were using faulty equipment – and you wanted to expose them—'

Ade kissed his teeth. 'Ed, why's she telling *us* our *own* story?'

Ede grinned at his brother. 'Oi, I think we've got a fan.'

Ade, though, was frowning. 'Hackers shouldn't have *fans*. Means someone knows what we're up to. And if someone knows what we've been up to, it means we left a trace.'

'Only enough of a trace that our Headmaster could find you,' Penelope said. 'There's no shame in that. There isn't a better hacker in all the world than Whisper.'

'Your dad's a hacker too?' Gabriel asked Penelope, feeling as if the conversation had suddenly moved into another language. One he couldn't understand.

The colour drained from Penelope's face and she shot Gabriel a vicious look.

'Hold on a sec,' Ade said. 'The Headmaster's your *dad*?

You a Crook then?'

'Uh oh,' Ede said, eyes narrowing. 'We got ourselves a Legacy.'

'Yes,' Penelope said, raising her chin defiantly. 'I'm a Legacy. So what?'

'Oh, nothing,' Ade said, in a tone that suggested it was definitely something.

'Does that matter?' Gabriel asked. 'That she's a Legacy?'

The twins gaped at him. Ede spoke first. ''Course it matters. Some of us earned our way here, while others, you know, *didn't*. Each year, us students compete against each other to win the ultimate prize. But a Merit hasn't won it for *eleven years*.'

'What's the ultimate prize?'

'The Crooked Cup,' Penelope said. 'We compete the whole year, in all manner of crooked activities, and finish with the Break-in. Each year, the teachers choose a single room to fortify – pressure sensors, thermal cameras, extra Gardener guards—'

'So everything, basically,' Ede said.

'*Not* everything, no,' Penelope snapped. 'It's meticulously set up to replicate a security system which has been previously bested by one of our alumni. And Break-ins get more challenging the older you get.'

'So this year will be easy for us?' Gabriel asked.

Penelope raised a disdainful eyebrow. 'Of course not. Most years, not a single student in any year succeeds.' Slowly, a smile spread across her face. 'But if they do, they win fifty points, which is *always* enough to win them the Crooked Cup. There's more, though. Whoever succeeds at the Break-in also wins—'

'What all us crooks want most,' Ade interrupted, eyes hungry. 'Information.'

'They get to ask one question,' Ede continued. 'Which Crook himself must answer truthfully—'

'So long as answering it wouldn't put Crookhaven or its alumni in danger,' Penelope cut in. 'Most people waste their question. Father can't give out information like the location of the real Crown Jewels—'

'What do you mean the *real* Crown Jewels?' Gabriel asked. Penelope ignored him.

'—without the consequences of such a revelation casting a light on parts of the Underworld that he'd rather remain in shadow.'

Ede tilted his head. 'Why do you talk like that, eh?' He mimicked her accent. '"*Without the consequences of such a revelation . . .*"' He burst into laughter, unable to finish.

Ade nudged his brother and leaned in conspiratorially. 'It's the silver spoon, man. Does something to their tongues and—' They bumped heads. Gabriel had never seen two less in-sync people than Ade and Ede.

They grumbled at each other, giving Gabriel a chance to turn towards Penelope. 'Your dad is a hacker as well as a pickpocket?'

'No,' Penelope said. 'Whisper is my father's co-Headmaster. Her identity was exposed a few years ago, meaning that nowhere was safe for her but Crookhaven. In the wrong hands, someone of her skill could be the most dangerous weapon in existence.'

'But your dad told me that she was away?'

Penelope nodded, preoccupied. 'Yes, she is. But that was unavoidable . . .'

Why did she always answer a question without really answering it? It was infuriating.

Ade looked up. 'Hey, did you say Whisper was a she?'

Penelope nodded.

Ade raised his hand, palm up. 'I told you Whisper's code was too beautiful to be a man's. Come on, pay up.'

'Whatever,' Ede said, handing over 50p. 'As long as Whisper is a teacher here at Crookhaven, I couldn't give a rat's knuckle what she is.' They went to bump fists but missed entirely. A little embarrassed, Ede turned to Penelope. 'So when's she back?'

'She'll arrive at the same time as the Legacies,' Penelope said. 'Tomorrow night.'

CHAPTER EIGHT

All those on the island of Crookhaven gathered on the shoreline to await the arrival of the first year Legacies. The older Merits and Legacies, who had arrived on staggered trains earlier in the day, huddled in small groups at the back, whispering excitedly about their summer holidays. Gabriel and the first year Merits stood shoulder-to-shoulder at the front, in silence, their eyes glued to the other side of the lake. Caspian Crook, the Forgery teacher Palombo and several other teachers Gabriel hadn't yet met were dotted throughout the waiting crowd. The torches they had used to escort everyone safely through the trees hung at their sides, now turned off. The only light came from the moon and stars. Even the usual winds, the ones that blew across the moors with such ferocity that they had forced the Crooked Oak to bow, had stilled. And into the frigid night rose the warm breath of the onlookers.

Then a single light began to bob through the woods on

the far bank. Not a beam like torchlight; something softer, like candlelight. It made the trees nearby glow warmly and the older years behind Gabriel fall silent. It drifted along the bank until it was opposite them, then stopped. Slowly, a woman's face appeared in the orange light. Tight ringlets of chestnut brown hair framed a round and youthful face. Even at that distance, Gabriel could see her slanted smile and mischievous dark eyes.

'Hey, Crook!' she called playfully, voice echoing. 'Do me a favour and get that platform up, would you? It's freezing out here. And if I lose my fingers, I'm as good as useless.'

Gabriel snatched a glance at Caspian, who was trying to hide a grin. 'Of course, Headmaster Whisper.' Ade and Ede shared a wide-eyed look and began to nudge each other excitedly. Caspian spoke again. 'Please stand back a little. We wouldn't want you or your charges getting soaked, now, would we?' Caspian held up a small, black remote and pressed a button. For a moment, nothing happened.

Then bubbles began to form on the surface of the lake. A line of them, stretching from the island to the other bank where Whisper waited. As one, the first years leant forwards to peer into the water. Deep in the black depths, something began to glow. It was a strange sort of glow, like pinpricks of unnaturally blue light which . . . Gabriel blinked. Were the lights *rising*?

The bubbling grew into a frothing. Then something broke the surface. The crowd gasped but no one took a step back. Only Gabriel and Penelope took a step forward. They looked at one another for a moment, giddy with excitement, then back towards the lake. The water had settled now, revealing a long black path which stretched from them to the far bank. Luminescent pebbles lined it, lighting the way from one side to the other.

Gabriel leaned over to Penelope and whispered, 'You didn't tell me there was a *path*.'

'They don't raise it for just anyone,' she said. 'I've only seen it brought up twenty times in my whole life.' She paused. 'Well, twenty-one now. But I've never walked across it.' For a moment she looked sad. 'I thought today would be the day but . . .'

'You're a Legacy. Shouldn't you be over there with them?'

'I should.' She set her jaw. 'But Father says that it would be ridiculous for me to be officially welcomed to a school I've lived at my whole life.'

'Did you tell him you wanted to?'

She sighed. 'It doesn't matter now.' Her eyes widened. 'Look, they're crossing.'

Whisper strode along the path first, her mane of curly hair bouncing with each step. Her voice carried over to them across the water. 'Right, first years, follow me. When you're halfway down the path, pick up two pebbles. Once across, give one to a first year Merit – they're the ones at the front looking like they might faint.' Someone behind asked a question and Whisper raised a hand sharply. 'Ah, ah, ah! Never ask a question to the back of someone's head. It can't answer. Don't worry, all will become clear in just a moment.'

Whisper strutted across the bridge and smiled at Caspian as she stepped off the path. 'Miss me, Headmaster? Bet it's been dull as anything.' She turned and beckoned the waiting first year Legacies to follow her across the bridge.

Caspian grinned. 'Refreshingly dull, Headmaster.' He lowered his voice so that even Gabriel, who was standing closest, could barely hear him. 'And your . . . travels?'

Whisper's smile flickered and she too whispered, 'Not in the least bit dull, I'm afraid. It's worse than we thought, but we'll talk about that later.' She paused and looked around. 'Where's the brains of your family then? I thought she'd be with the other first year Legacies.'

Caspian nodded at Penelope, who was oblivious, too focused on the first year Legacies about to cross. 'She's with the first year Merits, but she won't appreciate it if you go over and embar—'

Whisper tutted. 'Me? Embarrass her? I think you've already beaten me to it by putting her with the Merits.'

The Legacies' eyes were wide and their mouths were open, though with fear or anxiety or wonder, it was impossible for Gabriel to tell. They were all dressed in smart shirts and dresses and coats, their shoes so polished they reflected the stars. Though most appeared to be strangers to one another, they edged along the path in

70

clusters, as if the mere presence of someone close by was enough to keep them moving.

Beside Gabriel, Penelope stiffened and her hands began to tremble. Then a hand fell on her shoulder, snapping her out of her trance.

'I've got a little something for you, Miss Crook,' Whisper, who had slipped unseen through the crowd, said in a tone that was unmistakably one of a teacher to a student, but leaked a warmth that the dark-skinned woman couldn't mask.

Penelope looked up. 'For me, Headmaster?'

Whisper reached up to her ear, unclipped something and placed it into Penelope's hand. 'I think you'll find that useful . . . for your studies.' With a wink that no one but Gabriel saw, Whisper walked away.

Ade and Ede shuffled over. 'What is it?' Ade asked, then gasped when he saw. 'That's sick.' A small, slender USB drive with a mother-of-pearl coating sat in Penelope's palm. Ade gave his brother a look. 'Her earrings are USB drives. *Her earrings are USB drives.*'

Penelope shushed him but there was a smile on her face as she turned back to face the illuminated path.

When the first years were about halfway across, they began to pick up the pebbles. Some put them into their pockets, but most held them out in front, clearly unsure of what to do. Then all were across and not a single pebble remained on the path. Nervously, the Legacies left the safety of their clusters and spread through the crowd in search of a first year Merit to give their spare pebble to. No less than four boys approached Penelope to offer her their pebble. She tried to explain that she too was a Legacy and therefore shouldn't be taking one, but eventually gave in and accepted the one from a floppy-haired, sharp-faced boy who smirked at her and then swaggered away through the crowd. Gabriel had known boys like him at school and he'd wanted to snatch the pebble and toss it into the darkness.

Meanwhile, a small girl wearing a bright red and gold hijab offered Gabriel her pebble. She had copper skin and eyes that glittered a warm green in the pebble's light. Gabriel accepted it, thanking her. She nodded once, turned left, realised there was nothing but woods in that direction, and scuttled off to the right.

The crowd began to turn towards the co-Headmasters when a voice shouted, 'Wait!'

They all turned to see a girl walking across the unlit path from the shore. The pebble that sat in her hand bathed her pale, rounded face in an otherworldly glow, which made her ice-blue eyes glisten in the darkness.

'Is that a first year?' Gabriel asked, more to himself than anyone else.

'Must be,' Penelope said. 'She's got a pebble. But only one, which is strange.'

But where did she get it? Gabriel thought. *There weren't any left. I'm sure of it.*

'She looks older with those clothes,' Ede said. And he

was right. The girl's smart white coat was at least two sizes too big and so were her black trousers, though somehow neither looked altogether wrong on her. Maybe she meant for it to look oversized. Maybe it was *fashionable*. It wasn't as if Gabriel had the first clue about fashion . . .

The girl drifted across the bridge like a graceful ghost, her eyes scanning the watching crowd. She certainly knew how to put on a show, and everyone there seemed happy to watch. But there was something about the way she smiled that sent shivers down Gabriel's spine. It was carefully practised, and that, in his experience, always spelled trouble.

The girl stepped off the bridge and, without breaking stride, walked into the crowd as if expecting it to part for her. It did. Only when she stopped did the rest of the students close in around her. When, finally, everyone had stilled, Caspian walked up on to the raised bank, cleared his throat, and began to speak.

CHAPTER NINE

'Welcome, all, to Crookhaven,' Caspian began. 'Most of you are returning to this crooked isle for another year at our world infamous school. Some of you, sadly, are returning for the last year.' He looked over at the first years, his eyes sparkling mischievously. 'But for some, this is your first time. It is to you I extend my warmest welcome. I would implore you to look around. Take this moment in. There are precious few magical moments in a lifetime, and taking your first step on to this island and into a new world is, undoubtedly, one such moment.' Caspian paused. 'Now, as you all know, this is no ordinary school. Whether you caught the eye of our alumni network or are following in the footsteps of your ancestors, you are here for a reason – you are crooks. And here, away from the prying eyes of the world, crooks are not shunned or vilified. They are welcomed.' He pulled a luminous pebble out of his suit jacket pocket and held it up. 'Crooklings – that means you first years – hold up your pebbles for me, please.'

Gabriel lifted his hand and unfurled his fingers, freeing the pebble's light. Around him, all the other Crooklings did the same.

'I want you to think of each pebble as a Crookhaven alumnus,' Caspian continued, gesturing towards the lake. 'And the lake-bed as every country of the world.' He paused again, the blue light dancing in his eyes. 'This next part is important, so listen well. Take what I say into your heart and let it give you courage.' He paused for a moment, and it felt as if he was looking each of them in the eye. 'Wherever you may go in life, however far your adventures may take you once you leave this great school, understand that you will never again be alone.'

Caspian leant back and threw his pebble in a looping arc. It plopped into the lake about halfway out and began to fall through the black waters towards the bottom.

Then something strange happened. A pinprick of blue light appeared less than a metre away from Caspian's pebble. Then a second, on the other side this time. Soon there were ten, twenty, thirty pebbles alight in the depths. Before long, the whole lakebed was aflood with light. In every direction Gabriel looked, pebbles glittered. There had to be thousands of them down there . . .

'You may not notice us at first,' Caspian said, and everyone turned to face him again. 'Indeed, if we teachers do our jobs well, you won't. But we, Crookhaven's proud alumni, *are* out there, in the world beyond this place. So every time you feel alone, picture this sea of pebbles and remember that we – the outcasts, the misunderstood, the reviled – are many. And the moment you cast your pebbles into that lake, you become one of us.'

The people around Gabriel were still and silent, their breath held, their eyes unblinking. Penelope was the first to move. Gabriel felt her swivel beside him and heard the *whoosh* of air as her arm flew past his ear. Then, in the distance, there was a slight *plop*.

He curled his fingers around his own pebble and, in one clean movement, launched it high into the sky. He didn't see it land in the lake, only heard it. He and Penelope smiled at one another.

There was a collective *whoosh* as the other Crooklings tossed their pebbles into the air and then a rippling of the glassy water as they landed.

Silence fell again.

'Merits, there is one last thing I want you all to know before I let my dear co-Headmaster take over,' Caspian said, his warm breath hanging in the cold air like a cloud. 'You have not been chosen to attend this infamous school solely for your crooked talents; you have been chosen because of what you were doing with your talents when we found you. Those of you who we found stealing were not stealing out of greed, but to survive or to give your loved ones a better life.' Caspian's eyes touched on Gabriel, then slid away. 'Those of you who were hacking did not hack for profit, but to expose the wrongdoings of corrupt companies or individuals. Those of you who were picking locks or scaling walls did so only to reclaim what was yours or recover that which once rightfully belonged to another. That is to say – you are good people. Honourable people. And those are the *only* type of students we accept at Crookhaven. Here, we will teach you to do wrong, but only so that one day you will put the world right.'

Gabriel looked at the upturned faces of the students around him, knowing full well that he would forever remember every one of them, and allowed a smile to spread across his lips. *Can we really do it?* he thought, excitement churning within him. *Can we put the world right?*

'Right then,' Whisper said eventually. 'Time to get inside, I reckon. It's flippin' freezing out here.' She spun on the spot and looked over her shoulder. 'Crooklings, follow me. The rest of you, follow Headmaster Crook. Everyone know what they're doing? Wonderful. Let's get to it!' Whisper took off up the bank, a tall, dark-skinned female student trailing her, and the Crooklings following them both. Only one Crookling stayed behind, now deep in conversation with Caspian Crook. It was the unnerving blonde girl.

Gabriel and the remaining Crooklings zigzagged through the dark woods until they came out on to the lawn where Gabriel had first seen Caspian.

'Come on, come on,' Whisper called out to the stragglers. 'I need to get you all settled so I can get back to my keyboard. It misses me if I'm gone for too long.' She let out a chuckle and walked on, her curly hair swaying with each long stride.

'You reckon she knows who we are?' Gabriel heard Ade whisper to his brother.

''Course she does,' Ede snorted. 'Must've been her who recruited us.'

'She recruited the Brothers Crim,' Ade corrected. 'Not us. She probably doesn't have a clue what we look like.'

Ede blinked. 'You're right. Think we should wear a suit to her class or something? You know, to make a good impression.'

'A suit?' Ade kissed his teeth. 'You've never owned a suit in your life. Where are you going to get one now?'

Ede squinted, thinking hard. 'A few delivery companies are using drones these days. Maybe we hack into one, find a drone that's delivering a suit and redirect it here!' He said this so triumphantly that Gabriel had to turn away to stop from grinning.

'A drone!' Ade said. 'Good one. Why don't we, on our first day here, redirect a drone to probably the most secret, most off-the-grid place in the whole world? I mean, yeah, we'd have revealed the exact GPS coordinates of Crookhaven, but at least we'd have our *suits*.' Ade sighed. 'Sometimes I wish I'd eaten you in the womb, Ed. Serious.'

'It was just an idea,' Ede muttered. 'I never said it was a *good* idea.'

Whisper stopped in front of the smaller buildings which

sat at the feet of the main villa. 'Three buildings. The one on the left is yours, Crooklings. Girls will have the second floor – the view from up there is incredible, you can thank me later – and boys will be on the first floor. The Merits will know this already, but each of you has a room, and inside that room you will find a bed, a desk and the belongings the Gardeners liberated from you earlier. You will also find your new uniform. There are bathrooms on every floor and a common room on the ground floor.' Whisper finally exhaled. 'Any questions?'

Hands flew up.

Whisper pinched the bridge of her nose. 'All right, let me take care of a few of these real quick. Yes, you're allowed on to the other floors, but only until 6 p.m. After that, anyone found where they shouldn't be will have to deal with the Headmasters. Yes, everyone in your house is allowed in the common area. Yes, there is a uniform; yes, you have to wear it; and yes, there is a very good reason for it. Yes, the lessons begin tomorrow at 9 a.m.' She looked skyward for a moment, muttering to herself. 'That everything? I think that just about . . . ah, 'course! Yes, you will be fed – all your meals will be served in the main villa. Legacies, I'll take you up to dinner once you've all settled in. Merits, you can wander up to the main villa now. You already know where to go.' Whisper turned and made to walk into the Crookling building but paused. 'Knew there was something I was forgetting.' She whipped around. 'Right, I need you all in one line. Come on, come on.'

Feet shuffled as the Crooklings obeyed.

'Dela,' Whisper called to the tall girl at her shoulder. 'Make a note of this for me.' Whisper then summoned the first Crookling, the green-eyed girl who had given Gabriel her pebble, forward.

The Headmaster pulled out a small torch. 'Raise your hands for me, palm-up.' The girl obliged. Whisper clicked on the torch and shone it on the girl's palms.

'That's a UV torch,' Ade whispered to his brother in the queue behind.

'Look,' Ede whispered back, 'the pebble has left a colour on her hands.'

Gabriel squinted. In the centre of the girl's hand were two distinct patches of colour from the two pebbles she had picked up on the bridge. Both red.

Whisper looked up. 'There are forty-eight of you this year, Crooklings, so that will mean four classes of twelve people. Once we've sorted you into those classes, Dela will pin the class timetable in the common room.' She glanced at the green-eyed girl. 'Class 1B for you, Miss Dhawan.' She gestured towards the building. 'Next.'

Five others were quickly sorted according to the colours the pebbles had left on their palms – two into 1A (blue), one into 1C (green), one into 1D (yellow) and the lanky, floppy-haired Legacy into 1B.

'1B, Mr Avery,' Whisper said when he eventually made it to the front – an outcome Gabriel had already anticipated because the girl who had handed him the pebble only had red on her palms. Up on the bank, the green-eyed girl gave him a shy smile and disappeared inside. To Gabriel's relief, Ade, Ede and Penelope were all placed in 1B too, though Ade and Ede had clearly tampered with their own readings by aggressively shaking hands, leaving their palms an ugly and indistinguishable combination of red and blue. Whisper had rolled her eyes and, clearly too weary to argue, put them both in 1B.

The twins cackled as they ran over and threw their arms around Gabriel and Penelope.

'Ah, man,' Ade said. 'This year is going to be *sick*.'

CHAPTER TEN

Gabriel awoke on Monday morning giddy with excitement for the day's classes. In truth, he'd barely slept. He'd actually gone to bed so nervous that he felt sick. But somewhere around 3 a.m. something had changed in him and he'd begun to feel an unfamiliar warmth of excitement bubbling up. It reminded him of the few seconds before he picked a pocket. But that wasn't really the same. Afterwards, he either had a wallet or he didn't. Either way, by then the feeling had melted away.

But this feeling, he thought as he pulled on his new uniform, *is different*. This really was a fresh start, in a place where his skills would be praised rather than shamed, with a Headmaster that had personally recruited him. Here, at Crookhaven, he was wanted. And here, at Crookhaven, he might just belong after all.

Gabriel looked at himself in the small mirror that hung on the back of the door. The trousers and blazer – could it really be called a blazer if it went past the knees? – were a deep maroon. The blazer had multiple different sized inside pockets, with little wooden coin-like things sitting in each. The shirt he wore was black and, when done up, fit snugly around his neck. According to the pamphlet in his room, it was called a 'grandad collar', which was altogether strange as he'd never seen any old men wear such a thing, nor could he picture it. The shoes, too, were black, and a good fit. The look as a whole was, if Gabriel was honest with himself, quite odd. Unlike every other uniform he'd ever worn, it was impossible to wear it in a cool way.

But unlike every other uniform he'd ever worn, this one was comfortable.

The material of the trousers and blazer was soft and didn't chafe when he moved; though the grandad collar was snug, he didn't feel as if he were being choked like he usually did wearing a tie; and the shoes were smart but didn't feel as if they'd give him blisters for the first couple of days.

I look weird, Gabriel thought, *but I feel great.*

The common room was already abuzz when he walked in at 8 a.m. Gabriel walked towards the timetable on the wall.

'Oi,' a voice called before he'd even had a chance to look. Ade and Ede rushed over, blazers rippling behind them. 'We've already checked – we got Deception first. 9 – 10.30 a.m.'

Gabriel grinned. 'Deception?' *That's my kind of lesson.*

'Yeah,' Ede said. 'But first it's time to *eat*.'

'Not yet, it's not,' came a familiar voice from behind them. They turned to see Penelope with her arms crossed and a mischievous smile on her face. '*First*, it's time to learn which room we will be breaking into this year. That's right – they're announcing the Break-in.'

*

The co-Headmasters met them by the entrance of the Crookling building and led all forty-eight of them out into the cold, drizzly morning. They traipsed through the trees, huddling together under the large black umbrellas the Gardeners who accompanied them held. To Gabriel, it felt a little like a funeral procession. Except, of course, for the excited murmurs that rippled through the crowd. The Break-in, it seemed, was *the* event of the year, and whilst almost no one ever succeeded, the prospect of doing so had them fired up. None more so than Penelope, who walked at the front of the crowd, her steps purposeful and eyes alight.

Eventually they found themselves outside the co-Headmasters' office. A steady ribbon of smoke billowed from the chimney and an orange-yellow glow from inside promised warmth. But Caspian stopped at the entrance and turned; it appeared that no one would be invited inside.

'Today is your first day as a student of Crookhaven,'

Caspian Crook said with a smile. 'And as your Headmaster—'

'*Co*-Headmaster,' Whisper reminded him. She stood at his side in an all-white tracksuit, holding a matching white umbrella.

'You're quite right,' he said, holding up a finger. 'As your *co-Headmasters*, we wanted to give you all a personal welcome.'

Whisper grimaced at the water trickling off one corner of her umbrella. 'If I'd known it was going to rain I might not have been so generous.'

Chuckles passed through the crowd. *She's good at that*, Gabriel thought. *Putting people at ease.*

'But there is another reason we are both here with you this morning,' Caspian continued. 'The Break-in.' At his words, all the Crooklings fell silent. Caspian smiled. 'As some of you may already know, each year, the teachers choose a single room here at Crookhaven to fortify for you Crooklings – pressure sensors, thermal cameras, extra Gardener guards, and much, much more.'

'The security set up is carefully chosen,' Whisper cut in. 'We mimic the security systems which have been bested by Crookhaven alumni out in the real world. The Louvre, the Tower of London, even the Vatican – suffice it to say that no student conquered any of *those* Break-ins. You won't be told which security system we're basing your Break-in on until afterwards, or one of you nosy lot would look up how it was bested.'

'Naturally,' Caspian chimed in, 'we will require the room in question for its intended use during the daytime, but during the night-time,' he grinned, 'the defences will be activated. Using the skills you've learned so far, you are tasked with finding a way into that room and stealing an item – any item at all – without being caught.'

Chatter began amongst the Crooklings again, at once nervous and excited.

'This isn't going to be easy,' Whisper said flatly. 'So let's get that out of the way right now. I'm going to be outfitting the place myself this year. And just because the first person to successfully steal something gets fifty points, doesn't mean we're allowing you to wander the grounds at all hours. Got it? If the Gardeners catch you *out* of bed when you should be *in* it, you're out. If you set off any of my defences, you're out. If you find a way in, but can't find a way out, guess what? You're *out*. And if we can easily discern which item you've stolen? You're *out*. This isn't meant to be easy. Most years *no one* wins those fifty points.'

And there was something else. Something that interested Gabriel far more than the points. *That question for Caspian*, Gabriel thought, *don't forget that. Because I haven't.*

Whisper let out a sigh, her breath a white cloud. 'A word of advice – this first term is solely for recon, so use it, eh? No Break-in attempts are permitted until term two, and even then you don't *need* to be first to try your luck.

Why do I say that? Well, most of you are going to ignore me and be out within those first two weeks of the second term, that's always how it goes. Too eager. Not nearly patient enough.' She shook her head. 'Any words of wisdom from you, Crook? Or are you finally wisdomed out?'

Caspian nodded his thanks. 'As it happens, I do.' He turned towards the huddled Crooklings. 'Remember this – anyone can steal . . .'

Beside Gabriel, Penelope whispered, *'But only the most skilled crook can steal without their mark ever learning something is missing.'*

Sure enough, Caspian echoed her words.

'Told you,' she whispered. Gabriel grinned.

'But *where* will you be trying to steal from this year, hm?' Caspian asked. 'Well, here, of course.' He swept a hand behind him. 'The office of the co-Headmasters.'

Whispering began again, this time frantic. But Gabriel had closed his eyes tight and was piecing together every fragment of memory he had of the first afternoon he'd stepped into that office. The smoky scent coming from the fireplace, the alumni pictures and paintings on the walls, the two heavy wooden desks sitting side by side.

When he eventually opened his eyes, Penelope was smirking, her dark eyes flickering from the windows to the roof to the front door. If she had been alone at that moment, Gabriel was certain she would have already tried to break in. Rules or no rules.

'As I've said, phase one of the Break-in is recon and it

begins today,' Whisper said. 'You've got one term to scope this place out before phase two – heist – begins. Make it count.' She shifted and, glancing at Caspian, blew into a gloveless hand. 'Right. We all sorted, then? I'm flippin' freezing.'

CHAPTER ELEVEN

PERIOD 1 & 2 9 – 10.30 A.M.	PERIOD 3 & 4 11 – 12.30 P.M.	LUNCH 12.30 – 1.30 P.M.	PERIOD 5 & 6 2 – 3.30 P.M.	PERIOD 7 & 8 4 – 5.30 P.M.	DINNER 6 P.M.
DECEPTION	HISTORY OF CROOKERY		TRICKS OF THE TRADE	CULTIVATING A CROOK	

G abriel had never been in a classroom as unnerving as the Deception classroom. Every part of every wall was covered in mirrors. Some old and circular, some square and modern, some rectangular and partially cracked, some diamond-shaped and filthy, and some which looked very, very valuable.

In their first class, on their first morning, wearing *that* uniform, a room of mirrors was the last thing the Crooklings of 1B needed.

The desks were set up in a circle, leaving a large space in the centre of the room. In it stood a tall, clean-shaven man with light brown skin and dark brown eyes which, every so often, flickered to one of the mirrors as if he were inspecting himself. He wore bright clothes with intricately threaded designs on the collar and sleeves, and the way he moved in them was so fluid it was almost a dance.

'Welcome, Class 1B, to Deception,' he said, arms outstretched as if ready to embrace them all one by one. 'My name is Mr Khan and I will be your teacher this year.' His accent was thick, though Gabriel couldn't pin it down. 'I expect you're wondering what a class with such a name holds in store for you?'

There was murmur of agreement.

Mr Khan laughed. 'I will get to that soon. But first I want something from all of you.'

Gabriel's heart sank. This sounded like some awful icebreaker activity, where they had to share an interesting fact about themselves.

Gabriel glanced at Penelope. She was sitting four desks to his right wearing an exhaustingly eager expression. The blonde Legacy from last night sat across the room from him, her eyes frighteningly blue, the corner of her lips ever so slightly upturned in a smile that wasn't really a smile at all.

Gabriel turned back to Mr Khan, who spoke again. 'Tell me, 1B, where do you think I'm from?'

People glanced at one another, confused.

'It is not a trick. I am simply asking a question. Any guesses?'

Gabriel stayed quiet. If there was one thing he'd learned in all the schools he'd ever attended, it was to let those who were over-eager to impress go first. Their answers could then shape his own.

'India, obviously,' said the tall, floppy-haired Legacy who'd given his pebble to Penelope the night before. Penelope had told him his name was Edgar Decome.

'Incorrect,' said Mr Khan delightedly.

'Sri Lanka?' guessed an oval-faced girl to Gabriel's right. Her answer was shot down with another 'Incorrect!' and she paled and sank into her chair.

'Pakistan?' called an enormous boy with a thick neck and even thicker gold-rimmed glasses.

'Incorrect!'

'Iran?' tried a scrawny girl, the fingers of her right hand moving nimbly and shaping a red hairband into ever more intricate patterns. *That's Mona Moriarty.* Penelope had told Gabriel that Mona's parents had been legendary—

'Incorrect.'

'It's definitely India,' said Decome, grinning stupidly as if he knew he'd been right all along and was waiting for Mr Khan to admit it. When the teacher cried, 'Still incorrect, Mr Decome!' the boy crossed his arms and narrowed his eyes.

Gabriel looked at Penelope. She was sitting on her hands, glowering.

She can't answer because she already knows where Mr Khan is from. Gabriel smiled. Living at Crookhaven all her life, of course she would. This must be torture for her.

91

'I see someone is smiling,' Mr Khan said, and with horror Gabriel realised the teacher was looking right at him. 'I presume that means you know the answer, Mr Avery?'

Gabriel flinched. The way his new teacher addressed him – eager, excited, expectant – made him nervous.

Gabriel met his eyes. 'Sorry, sir, but I don't know where you're from.'

Slowly, something strange happened to Mr Khan's face. Gabriel couldn't work out what, exactly. But it started in the eyes. As if, in a split second, one person left and another returned.

'Now that,' Mr Khan said, his thick accent melting away to one very similar to Gabriel's own, 'is the correct answer.'

The classroom fell still. Stunned.

'This is the first and most important lesson of this world,' Mr Khan continued, his shoulders squarer, his eyebrows now lower over his eyes. 'Never assume. If a heavy accent is all it takes to deceive you, this world and those in it will continue to deceive you at every turn. Begin, instead, with one single assumption: that you don't know *anything*. From there, you can scratch away the lies until all that's left is the truth.'

Mr Khan smiled then. A playful grin that made Gabriel lean in slightly. 'But I am not here just to help you unravel the layers of lies that make up each of us. No, no. I am also here to show you how to *become* a living lie. To walk and talk differently, to disappear so deeply into the mannerisms of someone else that your own mother wouldn't recognise you. Or, if you so choose, to be seen in a crowd, as if a spotlight is shining upon you.' At this, Mr Khan's eyes lingered on the blonde Legacy girl. He tilted his head slightly as if he didn't quite know what to make of her. Then he moved on, hand gesturing to all the mirrors on the wall. 'I can teach you to become anyone. To become *everyone*.'

Gabriel had never heard something so wonderful. To become anyone at all? Who would he choose to be? Not someone anything like the real him, that was for sure. Someone rich who wore fancy clothes and drove fancier cars. Maybe an explorer, a great traveller who knew more than the collective cruelty of the sleepy villages the real Gabriel was used to. Or perhaps Mr Khan could teach him to be the kind of person who went unnoticed, who faded effortlessly into the background. Maybe Gabriel could become that very thing himself – a living lie.

Mr Khan observed each of class 1B in turn. When he got to Penelope, he sighed. 'Yes, Miss Crook, you've been very restrained. Please go ahead, do tell them where I am *really* from. I can tell you're about fit to burst.'

'Harrow!' she called and breathed a long sigh. 'You're from Harrow in London.'

'That I am,' he said. 'But thank you for remaining quiet and not revealing what you knew. That would really rather have ruined the point I was trying to make.'

'If that's the most important lesson you have,' Decome said smugly, 'do we have to stay for the rest of class?'

'Not at all,' Mr Khan said cheerily, gesturing to the door. 'Please, be my guest.'

Decome shifted in his seat, smile faltering. 'Actually, I'm all right.'

'Mr Decome, I insist,' Mr Khan said, and there was a sharpness to his voice now.

Decome frowned. 'Am I being kicked out? Because my mother will—'

'Certainly not.' Mr Khan chuckled. 'You are very welcome back *next* class, when I will be teaching a new lesson. One that I hope you will not have already learned.'

After Decome slunk out of the class, Mr Khan asked, 'And what lesson did that young man just learn?'

Penelope's hand flew up. 'Overconfidence is the enemy of the crook.'

Mr Khan raised a thick eyebrow. 'That's certainly a favourite lesson of Headmaster Crook, but no. If anything, I advocate for overconfidence. To become another person, you must be overconfident to the point of delusion. You must truly believe you are them for however long you are wearing their skin. No, the lesson here is simple really: a lesson lived is a lesson learned. Do you think young Mr Decome will ever forget the words "never assume"? No, no. It will be ingrained in his subconscious for ever.'

I wouldn't be sure about that, Gabriel thought. He doubted Edgar Decome even had a subconscious.

'Now,' Mr Khan said, walking into the centre of the room again. 'We've already spoken about how my accent misled you, and you can see that I wore my shalwar kameez for the very same purpose, but can anyone tell me how else I deceived you today?'

CHAPTER TWELVE

Gabriel's next lesson, History of Crookery, was equally strange. Rather than taking place in a stuffy room filled with dusty old books as he'd imagined, the lesson was in an immaculately clean room with polished wood floors, no books and, incredibly, no desks either. The teacher was not old or bearded or remotely as bespectacled as Gabriel had expected. She was young and pretty and had wide unblinking eyes that bounced off each of the Crooklings of 1B as they stepped in.

'The first thing you will notice is that there are no desks,' the young teacher said, without any kind of official welcome. Her voice surprisingly low and rough. 'I assure you that this is not some first day prank. I simply loathe clutter.' She gestured around the empty room. Nothing on the bookshelves, nothing on the walls, nothing but a standing desk with a surface no bigger than one of those trays Gabriel used to get at school lunches. On it sat only a pencil, a notepad and a small black remote control.

The teacher walked behind the standing desk and lowered it slightly. 'The reason is simple – we cannot hope to have clear minds if our surroundings are cluttered.'

'Not even . . . desks?' Decome asked. He'd returned to third period and was looking sheepish, though clearly still brave enough to speak up first.

'Each of you will have a standing desk like mine brought in for lessons in which it is *absolutely necessary*. But today is not one of those days. All you need today are these,' she said, pointing at her ears, 'and these,' she pointed to her lips. She tapped a small device fixed to the back of her desk. A beam of light exploded from it, illuminating the entire wall at the far end of the room. Class 1B turned to see the Crookhaven crest projected on it.

'Now,' the teacher continued, 'let us begin at the beginning. Who can tell me when Crookhaven was founded?'

Hands flew up. But all of them, Gabriel noticed, belonged to Legacies. He and the other Merits had stuffed their hands into their pockets.

The teacher nodded. 'If anyone would know, it's you, Miss Crook. Do go on.'

'September 30th, 1829, Miss Jericho,' Penelope said proudly, then looked around at the other Crooklings as if to say 'Now you have her name. You're welcome'. Her attention back on Miss Jericho, she said, 'It was just one day after the founding of the Metropolitan Police Service, the first modern and professional police force in the world.'

Miss Jericho nodded. 'Not even a whole twenty-four hours later! I must admit, that's still staggering to me.' She sighed and stared at the crest for a few moments, lost in thought. Then she went on. 'But do not misunderstand *why* that was the case. Crookhaven was not set up to oppose the police, far from it. It was created because there is only so much the law can do to keep the true criminals of the world in check. If the police fail to serve justice lawfully, Crookhaven's alumni use unlawful means to serve it. Not that the police would thank us for it, mind you.' She chuckled. 'Of course, the crooks of the world – good and bad alike – were conspiring and competing with one another for *centuries* before the founding of Crookhaven. The history of Criminalkind does not begin in 1829. The history that you all are becoming a part of is older than you can possibly imagine. Older even than the Crimina Carta itself.' A few Legacies gasped, and the teacher smiled. 'But I'm getting ahead of myself.'

She straightened her waistcoat slightly. 'Now tell me, what are the three principles upon which this great school was founded?'

Again, hands flew up. Again, none belonged to Merits. The teacher nodded to a petite Chinese girl named Lulu Cheng.

Ede elbowed Gabriel in the ribs and whispered, 'Word is she's descended from Ching Shih, the Pirate Queen herself.' That didn't mean much to Gabriel, but he raised his eyebrows as though impressed all the same.

'Lie,' Lulu said, her voice low and even. 'But never lie to yourself. Cheat. But never cheat your friends. Steal. But never steal from those in need.'

'Exactly so,' Miss Jericho said, pressing a button on the remote to reveal a slide with the three principles laid out in full. 'I'm sure Mr Khan has already given you his spiel about how you must *become* your chosen character, that you must *believe* that you are them. But in my class, I will not ask you to disregard our first principle. *Never lie to yourself*. Instead, I intend, with a great many examples, to reinforce its importance.

'But before all of that, it is my duty to educate you on these hallowed halls of holduppers.' She pressed a button again and a new slide appeared, split into two sections – Tier One and Tier Two. 'The most accomplished crooks of Crookhaven, past and present, are organised into two Tiers. But who can tell me what each Tier represents?'

More Legacy hands flew skyward. Miss Jericho frowned and, for a moment, looked slightly embarrassed. 'It appears I have done the Merits a disservice. To expect you to know such things is unfair and foolish. Forgive me. No more questions for now.' She cleared her throat and looked again to the projection. 'The Tiers represent a crook's standing in the chronicles of Crookery. Tier Two is for the most famous crooks ever to live. Honourable crooks who did exceptional things in the world without ever harming a soul. Crooks that even the

Merits will know.' She pressed the remote and several faces familiar to Gabriel appeared on the screen.

Gabriel straightened. *Now this I can do. There's no one who knows more about the most notorious thieves than—*

'But we don't need to linger on what you all already know,' Miss Jericho continued. She pressed the remote again and the faces melted away. Gabriel deflated.

'On Tier One, however, you will find the *greatest* crooks ever to live. The ones who were so skilled that the wider world never even learned their names, whose exploits are known only to those inside our crooked little world.' More faces appeared on the wall, all unfamiliar to Gabriel. Were there really crooks he didn't know? He was at once furious and exhilarated.

'Only nine names have ever made it to Tier One,' Miss Jericho continued.

'Nine?' Decome whispered. 'I thought there were ten?'

'Nine names,' went on the teacher firmly. 'Four individual crooks and five crews. Three of those crews were formed right here at Crookhaven.' Class 1B looked at one another, daring for a moment to dream. The teacher laughed. 'Of course, none of you will ever make it to Tier One.' She said this with such certainty that Gabriel flinched.

'Who says?' the slender blonde girl said. It was the first time since the welcoming ceremony that Gabriel had heard her speak and her voice was nothing at all as he'd imagined – it was smooth and high-pitched and sickly sweet.

'I do, Miss Harkness,' Miss Jericho said flatly. 'As I mentioned, I am not like my dear friend Mr Khan. I refuse to teach you to disobey our first principle. So it follows that I cannot possibly encourage you to aspire to Tier One. If I do, some of you will believe that it is possible. You will repeat that lie to yourselves over and over. Then you will be devastated when you inevitably fail.' She wagged her finger. 'No. Instead I will only tell you the truth. You will all aim high and fall disastrously short. That, I'm afraid, is just how it is.'

The Harkness girl was smiling again. 'Forgive me, miss, but didn't you say that three of the crews in Tier One were from Crookhaven?'

'Three crews, yes,' she said. 'And then, out of the four individual members, two crooks attended Crookhaven. Between them, they recovered and returned the Carsus Diamond to its rightful home in Sierra Leone, infiltrated and then exposed the company responsible for the Kilmore Water Crisis and broke an innocent woman out of Marasev High Security Prison to reunite her with her daughter.' Miss Jericho tilted her head. 'You may be wondering why I included that final example. The answer's simple – that woman was my mother.'

The blonde girl's smile widened. 'If three crews *and* two individuals from Tier One came from Crookhaven, getting there doesn't seem so impossible to me.'

It was Miss Jericho's turn to smile. 'I don't suppose it will just yet, Miss Harkness. But one day soon, you will understand.'

Gabriel glanced at Penelope, surprised that she hadn't joined in the protest. But she was staring up at the projection of Tier One, her gaze glued to someone – Gabriel thought it was the copper-skinned woman in the bottom left with the wavy brown hair and a charming smile. As Gabriel watched, he heard Penelope murmur the phrase: '*Much is expected of a Crook*'.

Did Penelope recognise that woman? Who was she?

Miss Jericho clicked the remote and then quickly clicked again, skipping a slide.

'What about the last Tier?' a voice said. With horror, Gabriel realised it was his own. Miss Jericho had skipped past a slide headed 'Tier Three' before he could see what was on it, and his curiosity had gotten the best of him.

Miss Jericho's eyes turned hard as stone. Then she let out a resigned sigh. 'The unofficial third Tier – more commonly known as the Blacklist – is for the crooks who . . . go astray. And by astray, I mean everything from stealing from crooks-in-arms, to kidnapping, to . . .' She swallowed. 'Murder.'

She clicked the remote and hundreds of faces appeared. 'You will recognise some very famous figures in this Tier. Bonnie and Clyde, Jesse James, Dick Turpin—'

'Ching Shih,' Decome said, smirking at Lulu who paled and lowered her eyes.

So even amongst the Legacies there's a pecking order, Gabriel thought.

'The point is,' the teacher said, shooting Decome a glare, 'there are more crooks on the Blacklist than the other two lists combined. Why? Well, because it's far easier to use the skills we teach to do wrong than to do right. But if we create the monsters, then it's also our job to hunt them. Most of the faces you see here were caught by us and handed to the authorities on a silver platter.' She turned around to face the blonde girl. 'Now if you were to aim for the Blacklist, Miss Harkness, *that* would be realistic.'

The girl tilted her head and pursed her lips. 'Should I really do that, miss? Maybe I will. And then I could join the Nameless.'

The Legacies gasped. The Merits looked at one another, lost.

'What . . . what did you just say?' Miss Jericho stuttered.

Harkness giggled. 'I mean, they were probably Tier One once, weren't they? Maybe they were even the tenth name on the Tier One list, like Edgar said. But after everything they've done, they *must* be on the Blacklist now. I'm right, aren't I? So if I can't join the best of the best in Tier One, miss, then it might be fun to join the best of the worst.'

The teacher's mouth hung open. 'F-fun?'

Gabriel elbowed Ade. 'What's going on?'

But it was Ede who replied. 'That one's lost the plot.'

'Villette Harkness is her name,' Ade said. 'I'm not sure

she ever had the plot, but she has *definitely* lost it now.'
He shuddered. 'Ah, man, I just got the chills.'

'Who are the Nameless?' Gabriel asked Ade. Far too
loudly. The whole class turned towards him.

The teacher raised her hand, eyes still locked on
Harkness. 'We are *done* for today. I'll see you all for
periods five and six tomorrow. Everyone but Miss
Harkness, please make your way to the door.'

CHAPTER THIRTEEN

The students of Crookhaven were fed well, in that there was a great deal on offer, which was all that really mattered to Gabriel. The large circular tables scattered across the high-ceilinged dining room were covered with brightly coloured foods – red peppers, purple sprouting broccoli, roasted plantains, pan-fried salmon, baked sweet potato. All of it steaming and glistening and giving off a smoky-sweet scent that made Gabriel's mouth water.

The older years were already seated and happily shovelling spoonfuls into their mouths. But most of the Crooklings hovered by the door, unsure where to sit now that all the older years had arrived. That suited Gabriel just fine. He strode forward and sat next to the roast chicken and sweet potato. Seconds later, he had piled his plate high and was inhaling forkful after forkful. Healthy or unhealthy, delicious or vile, to him it only mattered that his belly was full. What it was filled with was unimportant.

His grandma had always said, 'Eat what you can, can what you can't.' And the leftovers in those cans had gotten them through some tough times. So, when he was done, Gabriel walked up to the old man who had just deposited a plateful of steamed green beans on a different table, and asked, 'Could I have an empty can, please?'

The man stared at him blankly. 'Eh?'

'A can,' Gabriel repeated. 'Like from a can of baked beans?'

The man snorted. 'Does it look like we do baked beans here, lad?'

He had to admit it didn't. 'Tinned tomatoes? Chickpeas?'

The man shrugged. 'I'll have a look.' He started to walk away but stopped, turned. 'Hang about. Why? You looking to save some food for later? If they find food in your room, you'll be for it, you know.'

'I won't keep food in my room,' Gabriel said. *I'll keep it safely hidden away at the bottom of the common room fridge.*

He nodded and walked away. Gabriel looked over his shoulder and saw Penelope and the twins sliding their trays on to the table where he had set up. A minute later, the man came back and gave Gabriel an empty can that had once held red beans. Gabriel thanked him and tucked it inside his jacket.

'Oi,' Ade said, as Gabriel got back to the table. 'Miss Jericho's lost it, you know. No desks? Are you serious, man? My legs are dead.' Penelope was smiling along until

Ade turned to her and added, 'Don't tell her I said that. I know you're tight with the teachers.'

She blushed. 'You think I'd . . . I would *never* . . . I don't even really *like* Matilda—'

'Matilda,' Ede said, nudging his brother. 'Reckon we could get away with calling her that? "Oi Matilda, I beg you 'low us a proper desk".'

Penelope's fork trembled in her hand.

'The Nameless,' Gabriel said, purposely changing the subject. 'What do you know about them?'

All three of them turned towards him, wide-eyed.

'You heard what Matilda—' Penelope broke off, then started again. 'You heard what *Miss Jericho* said. The Nameless are secretive, and dangerous, and we just . . . don't talk about them on this island.'

Ade tutted loudly. 'You've lived here all your life, in the only place in the world that might actually hold the truth about the Nameless, and you've never even thought to look? Seriously?'

'I never said that—'

'Brainwashed,' Ede said, shaking his head. 'You hate to see it.'

Gabriel wasn't much in the mood for teasing; he wanted answers. If there was something he didn't know about the criminal world, he wanted to find out. He *needed* to find out. The way he saw it, the more he knew about this world, the better chance he had of excelling in it. The more he excelled, the better the chances of freeing Grandma from her miserable life. 'What about you two?' he countered, addressing Ade and Ede. 'You're hackers, you must know something about them.'

Ade raised an eyebrow. 'I mean, we're *good*. Maybe the best thirteen-year-old white hats to ever live—'

'Maybe?' Ede interrupted. 'Nah, def-in-it-ely the best.'

Ade nodded in agreement. 'Right. But even *we* have nothing on the Nameless.' He looked embarrassed for a moment. 'Truth is, we aren't really looking too hard.' He leaned forward. 'That crew is bad news, man. And you know what's worse? They're good at it too. There are a whole lot of bad people out there, but it's the ones who are good at being bad that are the worst.'

'Isn't that what we're here for though?' Gabriel asked. 'To get good at being bad?'

'Nuh uh. Not like them,' Ade said. 'Those people kidnap. They hurt and kill. All for a payday.'

'I mean, a payday does sound nice,' Ede said. 'Think about the upgrades we could make to Sneaks – ah! What was that for?'

Ade lowered his fist. 'You know the house rules, man. Every time you chat rubbish, you get a smack. Mum made them, not me, so take it up with her.'

'I wasn't *saying* . . . it's not like I would . . . ah, whatever, man.' Ede crossed his arms and sunk into his chair.

But Gabriel was thinking about something Villette had said in class. 'The Nameless were once Tier One, right?' He leant in closer. 'Which means they are *seriously* good.'

'I wish you would all stop talking about—' Penelope tried. But Gabriel wasn't done.

'So good that nobody even knows what their crew is called?' he pressed.

'Nah, it's not like that,' Ade said. 'Their crew don't have a name. Never did, not even when they were Tier One. If they did, someone in the Underworld would've opened their big mouth about it by now. So that's the problem right there – how do you track a crew who have no name, whose members don't use codenames and who never run the same con twice? You can't. They're just . . . ghosts.'

'No,' Penelope hissed, suddenly furious. 'Because people believe in ghosts. But a lot of people at this school don't even acknowledge the Nameless exist. They're the Underworld's version of the Bogeyman.'

'Do *you* believe they exist?' Gabriel asked.

Penelope's jaw tightened. 'I know they exist.' She fell silent, seemingly lost in thought. Then she blinked and seemed to remember herself. 'We shouldn't be talking about this.' She stood and picked up her tray. 'See you in Tricks of the Trade.'

Ade followed her to the door with his eyes. 'Legacies are weird, man.'

Even Gabriel found himself nodding at that.

But even as he sat there, listening to the twins debate the various quirks of the Crookling Legacies, Gabriel could not stop thinking about the Nameless and why no one wanted to talk about them. Which, in truth, only made him that much more determined to learn the truth behind the Bogeymen of the Underworld.

CHAPTER FOURTEEN

'There is a reason you're all wearing these blazers,' the Tricks of the Trade teacher, Mr Velasquez, said as he shrugged a matching blazer over his crisp black collared shirt. 'And I'm sure the Legacies already know what that reason is.'

The maroon of the blazer against the black of his shirt looked somehow stylish on him, something Gabriel hadn't thought was possible. Most of the girls in 1B seemed to agree – they were leaning forwards on their desks, unblinking. Only Villette was unaffected, her unnerving eyes instead carefully scanning the walls, which boasted hundreds of small, seemingly unrelated items: rusted coins, brand-new watches and glittering rings. Gabriel knew exactly what they were.

These are all the items this man has ever picked from pockets.

'I was once a Merit myself,' the teacher continued,

smoothing down the blazer, 'so I am well aware that the first few weeks at Crookhaven are especially challenging for us. We do not come here knowing the Underworld's history or its customs, and we certainly have no idea about what goes on at Crookhaven. So Legacies, I ask for your patience as I cover a few things that you may well already know.' He bowed slightly, long brown hair sliding off his shoulders.

'You will no doubt have already noticed that inside each blazer pocket is a circular wooden token.' Mr Velasquez pulled one out and let it dance across the tops of his fingers. 'But while all the tokens may appear the same, they are not.' He showed the class the inside of his blazer. There were three columns of three pockets, each slightly closer to the body. 'The tokens inside the pockets of this far column are worth a mere one point. The second column is worth two, and the third, you guessed it, is worth three. Each token's worth is marked on it clearly.'

'Points?' Ede asked. 'For what?'

The teacher smiled. 'The Crooked Cup, of course. Each year has one. You Crooklings will be competing against each other all year, earning points in various ways. The one with the most points at the end of the year wins the infamous cup. Every year above you does the same.'

'Legacies have won the Crooked Cup for the last eleven years straight,' Penelope chimed in proudly. Then she blushed and looked sharply away. Gabriel rolled his eyes. *Seriously? Her too?*

'True, Miss Crook,' Mr Velasquez said in his slight Spanish accent. 'In total, the Legacies have won *fifty-five* Crooked Cups since a Merit last won, if you count every win for every year group across those eleven years. But all it takes is one Merit win and the balance will shift.' His eyes scanned the room. 'Only one.'

Gabriel's grip tightened on the side of his chair. *Only one.*

'One of the ways to earn points for your team,' Mr Velasquez continued, 'is by picking the pocket of one of your fellow Crooklings and returning the token to one of the Gardeners. But there's a catch: if your target feels your attempted attack and, within ten seconds, presses this button here' – he pressed firmly on the blazer's middle button – 'then it's the *target* who gets the point. So if they catch you trying to pickpocket a token worth three points, then those three points are awarded instead to them.' He tilted his head and wagged a finger. 'But if you press the button and someone has *not* attempted to take one of your tokens, then one point will be deducted from you. We have a name for this – Crying Crook.' He leaned in and, grinning, whispered, 'A word of advice – those who Cry Crook are not exactly popular. It's far better to have a three-point token picked than to Cry Crook.' He winked. 'Trust me on that.'

Many of the girls nodded eagerly. Ade tutted and nudged Gabriel. 'Look at them all. You'd think Idris Elba had walked in here or something.'

Ede yawned and leant back in his chair. 'He looks a bit like you actually, Gabe. You both got that Mediterranean thing going on.'

Ade looked from Mr Velasquez to Gabriel, then blinked. 'Nah, that's creepy, actually. Your eyes are kind of . . . even your hair colour . . .' He narrowed his eyes. 'What talent did you get recruited for again?'

Gabriel smiled and raised a three-point token. 'Pickpocketing.'

Ade patted his blazer. 'Oi, are you mad?'

Gabriel flicked the token back to Ade, who quickly tucked it inside his blazer pocket.

'I want to make myself clear,' Mr Velasquez was saying, as Gabriel turned back to the front. 'Not every Crookling has had this explained to them yet, so this competition doesn't begin until tomorrow morning. Is that understood?'

'Yes, sir!' the class answered as one.

'Excellent. Now, who wants to try and pick my pocket?'

The question caught 1B totally off guard. Gabriel knew what they were thinking. *Pickpocket a person who knew you wanted to pickpocket them? Was that even possible?* But not him. This was the one area of Crookery he knew. For most of his life, his fingertips had practically lived in other people's pockets. So it was only right that he stand up and volunteer—

'I'll give it a go,' a voice called from behind him. He turned to see Edgar Decome stand and lope through the desks towards Mr Velasquez.

'Excellent! What's the scenario?' the teacher asked Decome excitedly. 'Tourists in a crowded street? Rush hour on a London tube? Or are *you* trying to plant something on *me*?'

Decome shrugged. 'Doesn't really matter. The tourist one, I s'pose.' The tall boy flexed his fingers. Gabriel winced. They looked slow and, worst of all, clumsy.

'Perfect.' Mr Velasquez rubbed his hands together and took a step back. 'Before we start, Mr Decome, you should know that I only have three tokens hidden in these twelve pockets. So choose wisely.'

Decome licked his lips and nodded.

Mr Velasquez started to walk forward, playing a tourist, face upturned as if mesmerised by some non-existent monument. Decome approached from the front.

Decome bumped into him hard. There was a ruffling of clothing and some exaggerated apologies. Then they were past one another. After a few steps, Mr Velasquez whirled around.

'So? Any luck?'

Decome opened his hands and frowned. 'Nothing.'

Mr Velasquez turned towards the class. 'Can anyone tell me what Mr Decome did wro—well, well, someone's eager! Avery, is it?'

Gabriel nodded. 'He approached you too fast, sir. And too front-on. If he had picked a token, you might have seen his face and been able to describe him to the police. He also didn't consider his surroundings. Nowadays, there are "beware of pickpockets" signs on crowded tourist streets, so if someone feels a stranger bump into them, the first thing they do is check their pockets. If something is missing, they'll know straightaway that it was the person who bumped into them.'

Decome crossed his arms and glared. The teacher, on the other hand, stared for a long moment. Then laughed. 'Good. Very good. Anything else?'

'Yes. He made an even worse mistake,' Gabriel said.

The teacher raised his eyebrows. 'Is that so?'

'He didn't keep an eye on what *your* hands were doing, sir. Even now, I don't think he's realised that his ring is in your right hand.'

Decome raised his now-ringless hand and looked up at Mr Velasquez. 'When did you . . .'

The teacher raised his own hand and unfurled his fingers to reveal a large bronze ring. 'Excellent, Mr Avery.' He rolled the ring in his hand and caught it between his index finger and thumb. 'Never wear a ring when you are picking pockets, particularly a loose-fitting one such as this, that slides off without so much as a tug. It might catch on a zip or a button or slip off. It might even end up in the possession of the very person you were trying to pickpocket.'

At that, Gabriel thought of his coin, that nauseous feeling of having his pocket picked by Caspian Crook momentarily returning.

Decome stepped forward to reclaim the ring but Mr

Velasquez closed his fingers around it. 'Ah, ah, ah. You will get it back when you can *take* it back.' He reached into his jacket and dropped the ring into the top one-point token pocket.

'That's my family ring,' Decome said in disbelief. 'I need—'

'To improve your skills?' Mr Velasquez finished. 'Yes, Mr Decome. You do.' The class chuckled, but the teacher quickly turned on them. 'You may laugh now, but these pockets will be filled with rings and bracelets and watches from each and every one of you before long.'

Not from me, Gabriel thought. Not out of arrogance, but because he'd only come to Crookhaven with the clothes on his back. And his coin of course, but that was now hidden inside his right shoe. He had nothing else at all worth stealing.

As if Mr Velasquez had read his mind and wanted a chance to steal something from him, he said, 'Up you come, Mr Avery. Now we know you can pick apart someone else's performance, but let's see if you can pick a pocket.'

As Gabriel stood, he heard Ede whisper to his brother, 'What is this, man? *Oliver Twist* or something?'

Gabriel strode forward. As they passed one another, Decome nudged him and whispered, 'Should've kept your big mouth shut, Avery.'

'Same scenario?' Mr Velasquez asked when Gabriel reached the front, rubbing his hands together excitedly.

Gabriel nodded. And so it began.

Again the teacher looked up as if he was a distracted tourist. But instead of approaching him straight on like Decome had done, Gabriel took a piece of paper out of his pocket and approached from Mr Velasquez's blind side. 'Excuse me!'

The teacher started, then looked around. 'Yes?'

Gabriel sidled up to him, paper outstretched. 'I'm meant to be meeting my mum near Buckingham Palace, but I think I'm lost. My parents are waiting for me on this corner over here.' Gabriel gestured towards the top right of the paper. 'No, that's wrong. I think it was down here. Just a second, Mum wrote the street name down somewhere. Can you hold this for me?' Mr Velasquez took the piece of paper in both hands as Gabriel rummaged around in his own pocket. 'Here it is! Ah, no. That's a sweet wrapper.' After a while, he feigned frustration and took back the paper. 'Never mind. I'll keep going this way. Sorry for bothering you. Enjoy the rest of your day.' He turned and walked a few steps, then stopped.

Mr Velasquez said, 'Get anything?'

Gabriel shrugged. 'Three.'

'*You* got all three?' Decome called from the back of the room, a mixture of disbelief and accusation in his voice.

Gabriel unfurled his fingers to reveal two one-point tokens and one three-point token. For a moment, Mr Velasquez looked stunned. Then his face softened into a grin. 'Impressive. Care to tell the class how you did it?'

'Misdirection,' Gabriel said matter-of-factly. 'I showed you a map, which kept your eyes busy. I talked a lot, which kept your ears busy. Then I gave you the map, which kept both your hands busy. With one hand, I rifled through my own pockets, and with the other, I rifled through yours.'

Mr Velasquez tilted his head, considering Gabriel carefully. 'Merit?'

Gabriel nodded.

'And were you recruited because of your pickpocketing, by any chance?'

'I was.'

The teacher laughed then turned to the rest of the class. 'That's it for today, 1B. I'll see you all on Wednesday.'

Gabriel started to walk back to his desk but Mr Velasquez, in a soft, firm voice, said, 'Stay a moment, Mr Avery.'

When everyone else was gone, the teacher gave him an amused look. 'So you picked all three of my tokens, then?'

'Yes, sir.'

'That's a truly remarkable achievement. Especially considering I only hid two in my blazer.'

The blood slowed in Gabriel's veins. 'But I found three.'

'Do you know what I think?' Mr Velasquez asked, perching on his desk. 'I think you found both the tokens in my pockets. But I think you picked the third from Mr Decome when he nudged you as he was going back to his desk. Does that sound about right?'

Why do you always go one step too far? 'Sir, I can

119

explain—'

Mr Velasquez held up a hand, the fingers long and slender – perfect for picking pockets. 'You don't need to. You were trying to impress your class, and, by the looks on their faces, you succeeded. I don't fault you for that, especially if this is the area where you excel. But by picking that boy's pocket before the Crooked Cup has officially commenced, you have broken the rules.'

What did that mean? Points deducted? Would he be disqualified? No, there was no way. He needed to win. He already knew the question he wanted to ask Caspian Crook . . .

'What's going to happen?' Gabriel asked, and he could hear the tremor in his own voice.

'It's simple,' the Tricks of the Trade teacher said, taking back the two tokens that belonged to him and leaving the third with Gabriel. 'You must return that token to Edgar Decome's pocket before 9 a.m. tomorrow, when the competition officially commences. Do that and no one need ever know of this. Fail, and there will be consequences.'

CHAPTER FIFTEEN

Gabriel hadn't been sure what to expect from a lesson called 'Cultivating a Crook'; but it certainly wasn't walking through the woods with a scary-looking escort. Four Gardeners in their uniforms, loose-fitting grey overalls that a regular gardener at the Mercier mansion might have worn, walked alongside class 1B. Two at the front, two at the rear. However, anyone causally observing the strange collection of individuals would have found their eyes drawn not to the Gardeners but another person: Mr Sisman.

In some ways, he was perfectly ordinary – elderly, slightly hunched, with a tattered, off-white sack hanging from the crook of his bent right arm. But in every other way he was the most wonderfully odd person Gabriel had ever seen.

His shoulder-length hair was lilac, his fingernails were painted all the colours of the rainbow and his long robes, though maroon to match everyone else at Crookhaven, were covered in misshapen patches of different materials. When Lulu Cheng had asked if the patches were because he'd often caught his clothes on branches or thorns in the woods, Mr Sisman had said, 'Oh, my dear, no. Whatever gave you that idea?'

The woods 1B trudged through glistened in the afternoon sun, the earthy-sweet smell of a recent downpour still hanging in the air. They had taken the gondola to the far bank and, from there, cut up into the dense treeline. Penelope was blazing the trail. Or, rather, the two Gardeners were blazing the trail and she was pretending not to notice them. Every thirty seconds or so, she would turn around and gesture for the rest of the class to hurry up, eventually prompting a sweaty Ade to mutter, 'Is she a gazelle or something?'

'Nah, I swear I'm having a heart attack. Feel this.' Ade grabbed Gabriel and Ede's hands and placed them on his heaving chest.

'Rah,' Ede said, wide-eyed. 'Don't die, man. The *Brother* Crim sounds rubbish.'

Ade laughed. 'If I die, you definitely have to change your tag. How about *Brainless*? Bet that's not taken.'

They started to bicker breathlessly, which gave Gabriel a moment to look around for Edgar Decome. He was near the back, deep in what appeared to be a one-sided conversation with Villette Harkness. As usual, she was smiling sweetly, but Gabriel could tell she was bored.

How am I going to get his token back to him? As light

as it was, it felt heavy in his trouser pocket, and he just wanted to be rid of it.

But when they were forced to tiptoe around a puddle that blocked half the narrow path, another thought intruded.

I hope Grandma remembered to close the window in the bathroom or the floor will be flooded. She was only a short train journey away, but he couldn't visit. And he hadn't yet been able to bring himself to call her. He was too scared that he would hear the pain in her voice and jump straight on the first train home, leaving Crookhaven behind for ever. But he couldn't. He just wished he knew if she was doing OK without him. He had no idea whether she'd even received his letter . . .

'Right, my dears!' Mr Sisman said pleasantly, coming to a rickety stop beside a large oak tree. Beneath it sat a huge patch of tilled soil. 'Who fancies a little gardening?'

1B looked at one another, completely lost. Only Villette seemed unfazed, that permanent look of amusement still plastered to her face.

Ede shook his head and whispered, 'Gardening? I'm not about that life, man.'

'Mr Sisman,' Penelope called, frustration seeping into her tone. 'Surely we're not out here to *garden*.' Her eyes fell to his sack. 'Are we?'

'Well, of course we are, Penelope my dear. Didn't I just say so? Whyever else would we be wandering the woods in the late afternoon?'

Penelope blinked. 'To learn about the flora that may be

of use to us in the future. Herbs that render someone unconscious, fungi that cause temporary paralysis.' She shrugged. 'That kind of thing.'

'*Render someone unconscious*,' Ade mocked quietly.

'*Temporary paralysis*,' Ede joined in.

She shot them a ferocious look.

'My dear,' Mr Sisman said, shaking his mane of lilac hair. 'Crooklings don't cover such things. You'll be a Miscreant – possibly even a Lower Delinquent – before you ever go near such subjects.'

'Two more *years*,' Penelope mouthed, crestfallen.

'For this year,' Mr Sisman said, 'you will learn the king of all crooked traits: patience.' He raised a hand and closed his eyes. 'For it was Geoffrey Chaucer who said, "*Patience is bitter, but its fruit is sweet*".'

'Actually, sir,' Penelope said, forcing Mr Sisman to crack open an eye, 'it was Aristotle who said that. Geoffrey Chaucer said, "Patience is a conquering virtue".'

Mr Sisman looked skyward again, deep in thought. 'Hmm. I'm not sure about that, my dear. Not sure at all. We'll have to look it up.'

Penelope started to retort but Mr Sisman held up a hand. 'Patience,' he said, 'is the single most useful trait for a crook. And the second most useful trait, I hear you ask? Well, one that holds patience's hand for dear life, of course. Discipline! And how do you learn about patience and discipline? Why, through what else but gardening? Because if you don't have the patience and discipline to cultivate a garden, you certainly don't have the patience and discipline to pull off a long con. Both need to be well cared for if they are to bear fruit. Or – in the case of the latter – loot!' Mr Sisman laughed then. And it was a laugh that Gabriel hadn't thought existed outside of a cartoon. It was squeaky and shrill and sounded like *tee-hee-hee*.

Gabriel wasn't convinced that he should be taking lectures on discipline from a robe-wearing, lilac-haired goon. But if it made him a better crook, he'd try it.

Mr Sisman rubbed away tears of laughter and bent down to pick up his sack from a nearby rock but stopped short with a wince. He looked over his shoulder at the youngest of the Gardeners. 'Jonathan, would you be a dear and pick that up for me? My back's not what it was.'

The young Gardener did as he was asked and then quickly fell back into formation.

'Does he know that Gardener?' whispered Gabriel to Penelope.

'Of course. Mr Sisman was Jonathan's teacher.' When she saw the perplexed look on Gabriel's face, she added, 'The Gardeners are all Crookhaven alumni, you do know that, right? Some of the best it's ever produced.' She shook her head, amused. 'Do you really think we'd have *outsiders* protecting Crookhaven? Certainly not. We only trust our own.'

'Some of the best? So you'd be a Gardener then?'

'Of course, for a short while at least. You know how

125

some countries call their citizens up to serve in the military for a while?'

Gabriel nodded.

'It's the same for the Gardeners. You either volunteer to protect the school for a year or the school calls you up before you turn forty.'

'Really?' Gabriel asked, shocked. 'Every crook? Even the best ones?'

'*Only* the best ones. Why would we want the likes of Decome as a Gardener?' She chuckled cruelly.

'Heard that, Crook,' Decome whispered.

'You were meant to,' Penelope shot back. She looked at Gabriel. 'Ask any of the Gardeners and they'll tell you it's an honour to protect the school. As for famous crooks who came back . . .' She blushed a little, then. 'Mario Deserio was a Gardener two years ago – some of the women here were pleased about *that*, I can tell you. Hector Van der Camp was here last year. And Jonathan Mason . . .' Penelope jerked her head towards the young Gardener who'd helped Mr Sisman. 'He's part of a crew that stole back *The Leopard* by Silvio Sansa, a painting that had been taken from the Kunsthalle in Munich and replaced with a forgery.' She lowered her voice. 'Which was all the more impressive because it was the Nameless who stole it to begin with.'

Gabriel raised an eyebrow. 'Woah. Does anyone stay a Gardener for longer than a year?'

Penelope shrugged. 'Sometimes.'

'Would you?'

'No.'

'Why not?'

She looked at Gabriel with such intensity that he almost took a step backwards. 'Because I intend to be the greatest crook ever to live.'

If Gabriel hadn't been looking her in the eye then, he might have laughed at that. But he had been, so he found himself believing every word. And in that moment, Gabriel found himself thinking, *If I can hold on tight to this girl's coattails, I just might get where I need to go.*

Mr Sisman emptied his sack on to a portable table and ran a hand over the items. 'Please take some seeds, a hand trowel and claim your spot. Remember, you will be cultivating your garden for a whole year, so choose every detail with great care.'

'What does he mean by that?' Ede asked.

'Your patch of soil, your seeds, your equipment – choose it all carefully,' Penelope said, making a beeline for the seeds.

Ade and Ede followed her. But Gabriel instead turned and made his way to the carefully outlined patches of soil just beyond, grabbing a hand trowel from one of the Gardeners as he passed. He'd had his eye on one spot from the moment they'd arrived. It was in the north east corner, where the canopy was thinnest, allowing both plenty of rain and sunlight through. It was also the patch farthest away from the enormous oak tree, so its thick roots wouldn't steal any nutrients from his own little garden.

All those years of helping Grandma garden might just pay off after all.

He drove his hand trowel into the dirt, claiming the patch for himself. Then he turned and saw Decome approaching. The sharp-faced boy was juggling three packets of seeds in one hand and holding a spade in the other. His blazer was unbuttoned and the pocket Gabriel had picked was *right there*. It would be as simple as—

'Clever, Avery,' a voice said, as its owner brushed past him. Penelope placed her trowel in the patch next to his. 'I was going to pick that square myself.' She turned. 'But I guess I'll have to make do with picking this instead.' She held up a token.

Gabriel's heart stopped. He didn't need to feel his trouser pocket to know she'd picked it.

She narrowed her eyes at it. 'Care to explain why there's a token in your trouser pocket?'

Gabriel said nothing. *Come on, think. Think!*

'Did you keep one of Mr Velasquez's tokens for yourself?' She furrowed her brow. 'No, that wouldn't make any sense.'

'It's one of mine,' Gabriel explained, holding out his hand. 'I was playing with it in my pocket to keep my hands busy.' The best lies, he'd found, were the ones grounded in truth. Playing with a coin or a pen was something he always did, to keep his fingers nimble. That hadn't been the case this particular time, but she didn't need to know that.

Penelope didn't even look at his outstretched hand. 'You know, Avery, each token has the owner's initials engraved into it.' Gabriel's heart sank. 'Shall I check if there's a GA on this one?' She raised an eyebrow in challenge.

'Are you talking to a Merit, Crook?' a voice called from behind. Decome.

She looked at him, then at Gabriel, then eyed the microscopic initials on the edge of the token, the ones Gabriel hadn't even known were there. Slowly, her eyes widened, as if recalling their run-in during the Tricks of the Trade class. Suddenly it all clicked. 'Only because Avery here has very kindly offered to switch spaces with me.' She gestured to their trowels, side by side in the dirt.

'No, I didn't—'

Penelope flicked the token into the air and caught it.

Gabriel worked his jaw. *This was not how this was meant to go.* 'Fine. Yeah, let's switch.'

'Sounds about right,' Decome said in a superior tone, patting Gabriel on the back as he walked past. 'Let a Legacy show you how it's done.' Thankfully, after shooting Penelope a smarmy smile, he chose a doomed-to-fail patch on the far side, well clear of them.

Gabriel held out his hand again. 'The token.'

Penelope flicked it to him. 'I bet Mr Velasquez found out and is making you return it, isn't he? That's why he made you stay after class. How do you plan on doing that by tomorrow morning? Are you going to ask the chatterbox twins for help?'

Gabriel caught the token and quickly stuffed it in his pocket. 'Don't worry about it.' He took off towards Mr Sisman and the seeds.

'I'll help you.'

Gabriel stopped, swearing he'd misheard. He looked around. 'Why would you do that?'

She shrugged. 'Partly to make up for taking your spot, I suppose. But mainly because, if you fail to return the token, you will face a points penalty and that means you will have an excuse when you lose.' She stepped forward, eyes alight. 'And I don't want there to be any excuses. When I beat you to the Crooked Cup, I want it to be *fair*.'

Gabriel considered her for a long moment. 'Is this a trick?'

She jabbed her thumb towards Ade and Ede, who were jostling over two equally appalling patches of dirt a metre or so away. 'Would you rather ask them for help? Online, they may end up becoming the most skilled tag-team in Underworld history, but in person they are the human equivalent of two left feet.' Just then Ede threw a caterpillar at his brother, who squealed and bolted in the opposite direction.

She wasn't wrong. 'Fine.'

She smiled. 'Shall we come up with a plan then?'

'Actually,' Gabriel said, looking over at the Brothers Crim again, 'I think I already have one.'

CHAPTER SIXTEEN

Dinner was chilli con carne with brown rice and mixed roast vegetables.

Gabriel finished his plateful in less than two minutes. While the others – particularly the Legacies – complained that it was too cold or that they didn't like onions, he and Penelope watched Edgar Decome. The floppy-haired boy was laughing along with a freckle-faced boy from 1B called Dorian MacArthur. Dorian was a Scottish Legacy descended from Rory MacArthur, who had, over a century ago, broken into Edinburgh Castle and stolen back several priceless treasures that had once rightfully belonged to his ancestors. So Penelope had told him, anyway. Gabriel wasn't much interested in what people had done in the distant past – only what they were doing now.

'You eat like a robot,' Ede said, eyeing Penelope carefully.

Ade nodded, then looked at Gabriel. 'Both of you do.

I've never seen anyone enjoy food less than you lot.'

Penelope shoved in another mouthful. 'Food is fuel. Nothing more.'

The brothers looked at one another, appalled. 'Food is one of the best things in life,' Ade said at last.

'One of?' Ede said, horrified with his brother. 'Nah, it's *the* best. Even breaking through a supposedly impenetrable firewall can't compete.'

Ade nodded. 'And the food's good here, too. So you lot and your blank-faced chewing are disrespecting the chef. Oi, Ed, should we bring the chef out here and see what they think?'

'Hold up,' said Ede, eyeing Penelope suspiciously. 'Maybe we should check whether she really is a robot in a uniform first.'

Ede went to poke Penelope's shoulder, but before he even got close, Penelope had grabbed his wrist and, still eating, wrenched it into an unnatural angle. 'It's rude to touch.' He whimpered and she released him.

Ade laughed. 'Now you know what happens when you try and touch a robot!'

At the other end of the table, Decome stood.

Gabriel went to tap Penelope on the shoulder but immediately thought better of it. Instead, he whispered, 'It's time.'

She nodded, stood and walked away. After a few seconds, Gabriel stood too, leaving Ade and Ede with confused looks on their faces, and followed Decome like a shadow towards the counter, where students deposited their dirty plates and cutlery.

'I heard your mum pulled off a big one last month,' Penelope said, approaching from the other side and placing her plate down beside Decome's.

'Yeah,' he said proudly. 'Nice score. But it made the papers, so she's not too happy about that.'

From his left pocket, Gabriel pulled out a large seed packet and held it close to Decome's blazer. Out of it crawled a large, hairy spider. Gabriel sidled to his right and waited.

Man, that guy can really talk, he thought as Decome rattled off the different newspapers his mum's crime had been covered in.

Then, 'Spider! There's a spider on your back!' Penelope squealed.

'Where?' Decome started to squirm and writhe. 'Where!'

Gabriel stepped up. 'It's on your sleeve. I've got it.' He flattened it with his first slap. The second and third were just for fun. 'It's gone. Look.' Gabriel pointed at the floor where the creature lay unmoving. 'You alright?' he asked, wiping Decome's blazer.'I'm fine,' Decome said, shrugging Gabriel off. 'Where did *you* come from anyway?' He didn't wait around for the answer. Penelope, too, was long gone. And so was the token – safely back inside Decome's blazer.

'Bold,' a voice said. Gabriel turned to see Mr Velasquez smiling down at him knowingly. 'Very bold indeed.' He turned to leave but paused. 'Don't forget that if you, as a Crookling, know a move like that . . . everyone else in this room does too.' The Tricks of the Trade teacher placed a hand on his shoulder. 'There is a fine line between being bold and being foolish. You will do well to remember that.' With that, he left.

Their operation had been a success. But, as Gabriel watched the tall man leave, for some strange reason it didn't much feel like it.

*

It was a little after 5 a.m. the next morning when Gabriel gave up trying to sleep and snuck into the dark woods which surrounded the co-Headmasters' office. The Gardeners were patrolling the island, their torches cutting through the crisp autumn night like the beam of a lighthouse. He looked at them differently now he knew how skilled each of them truly was.

But tonight, he could see that their attention was mostly on the lake and the far bank, not the island itself. So Gabriel kept to the shadows and eventually settled beneath a large pine tree that had a natural nook at its base. He squeezed inside and wrapped his Crookhaven winter jacket tight around his torso and knees, leaving only his eyes and nose exposed to the cold.

For a while, he watched the office in the clearing, silent and dark and vulnerable. It looked empty, unguarded, as if he could walk right in through the front door, pluck an item at random and disappear into the night. But the closer he looked, the more he noticed. A soft red light flickered in the corner of the room, announcing the presence of a night vision camera. The neatly trimmed grass around the edge of the building was ever so slightly uneven, which told Gabriel that something – though he didn't know what – was underneath. And a Gardener patrol cut through the clearing every four-and-a-half minutes, like clockwork.

This isn't going to be easy.

To the east, through a small gap in the treeline, the crescent moon glittered on the perfectly calm waters.

It looks just like our old pond, Grandma. Two years before, Grandma had found herself a job as a live-in maid at a rundown hotel just outside Plymouth. 'People want to hire experienced people,' Grandma had said. 'Then you reach my age and all that experience counts against you. I've worked in some of the best hotels in this country, but when they don't believe you can still push around a hoover, none of that matters. So I'm afraid this will have to do for now, dear boy.'

There they had lived in a windowless attic which got so frigid in winter that sleep was near-impossible. So, in the early hours of the morning, when the world was coldest, the two of them would wrap up warm, fill a flask with hot tea and walk around the lake the hotel backed on to. When they were warm from moving, they would sit and watch the moon dance on the lake. And when it froze solid, they would walk out on to it and Gabriel would slide around until he was weary. Then they would go back to that attic and try to sleep until sunrise.

When Gabriel came back to himself, nestled inside the pine tree, he was shivering. Tears filled his eyes, making the reflection of the moon on the lake a fuzzy blur.

He missed home so badly. No, that wasn't it; Gabriel had never really had a home. What he missed was Grandma. Her every wrinkle and smile-line, every chuckle and well-meant nag – they were all as alive in his cursed mind as if he had left her moments ago.

She would be so worried about him. But after the last few days, he knew he couldn't just go back to his old life. There was a whole new world at the tips of his fingers. Caspian had been right – there *was* a place for someone like him: Crookhaven.

Just then, something caught his eye. It was white and feather-light and floating towards him from above. He opened his coat and let it fall into his waiting palm.

Is that . . . a tissue?

Gabriel shuffled out of his nook and peered up. For one crazy moment, he could have sworn a blue shape darted from one branch to the next. But when he blinked, it had vanished.

Spooked, Gabriel stuffed the tissue into his coat pocket and clambered to his feet. He waited breathlessly, watching the Gardeners' torches pass by before scampering from one tree to the next. And all the while he was thinking, *It will all be worth it, Grandma. I promise.*

CHAPTER SEVENTEEN

'**Y**ou look like death warmed up, Avery,' Penelope said, smirking. She was leaning against the wall of the Centre of Crimnastics in her jogging gear, her long brown hair held in a ponytail with that same shabby violet ribbon.

Gabriel gave her a weary grin as he and the twins approached. 'Morning to you too.'

Ade glared at Penelope as he swept past. 'Nah, no one should be that upbeat this early in the morning.'

'I just get adequate sleep,' Penelope snapped. 'Eight hours every night without fail.'

'See,' Ede said, jabbing a thumb in Penelope's direction as he followed his brother inside. 'Robot.'

'For your information,' Gabriel said, 'I'm tired because I was scouting the Headmasters' office last night.' Gabriel yawned, then blinked as Penelope fell into step with him. 'Hold on. Don't tell me you were *waiting* for me?'

She forced a laugh. 'Certainly not. Friedrich asked me

to make sure everyone in our class finds this place safely.'

'Miss Crook,' a low rumbling voice called from inside. 'How many times do I need to tell you? Come in and *sit down*.'

Penelope paled.

Gabriel chuckled. 'I get it – you're just looking out for your partner in crime. Makes perfect sense to me.'

'Don't call me that,' she hissed, following him inside. '*Partner*.' She almost spat the word. 'I don't need a partner. I don't need anyone. You'll see.'

Gabriel shrugged. 'Whatever you say, *partner*.'

Friedrich was not a man but a woman, and the single scariest-looking person Gabriel had ever seen. Arms crossed, she waited for them at the base of a climbing wall. She was incredibly short, but stocky, with powerful shoulders and tree trunks for thighs. Her greying hair was pulled up into a topknot so tight that it forced her eyebrows high up her forehead and made her grey eyes glitter with the kind of silent fury of someone in permanent pain.

'You, the tired one,' she said, pointing at Gabriel. 'Here.'

The rest of 1B were already sitting down. They shuffled back, leaving a corridor for him to walk through.

'Yes, miss?' Gabriel said warily.

'Not Miss,' she said firmly. 'Or Mrs, or Ms, or Professor or any other such title. Call me by my name: Friedrich.'

Villette giggled in that high-pitched way of hers. 'Isn't that a boy's name?'

'Yes, it is,' Friedrich said matter-of-factly. 'My dad wanted a boy. So instead I gave him a girl who could outdo any boy. Turns out he didn't like that very much.' She turned on Gabriel. 'Do you run?'

'Only when I'm being chased.' The moment the words were out, Gabriel regretted them. But to his surprise, Friedrich let out a short, sharp laugh that sounded like a car backfiring.

'Good,' she said. 'Running is a waste of time. What we teach here is functional fitness. Meaning that everything you will learn within these four walls will be of use in your future crooked pursuits.' She turned to 1B. 'So tell me – what do you need to know if you are attacked?'

'Self-defence,' said the oval-faced girl, who Gabriel had discovered was called Oh Ji-a.

Friedrich nodded. 'And what do you need to know if the only point of entry is through a third-floor window?'

'How to climb,' Villette answered, smirking. 'Or how to abseil, depending on where you're starting.'

Friedrich nodded again. 'And if a plan has gone wrong and you are being pursued through the streets and across rooftops, what do you need to know?'

1B looked at one another. *How to run* seemed the obvious answer. But Friedrich had already said running was useless, so what could she mean? Gabriel had a guess. He had only heard the word once but thought he might as well give it a try: 'Parkour.'

She looked over her shoulder. 'That's right.'

'Parkour?' Decome scoffed. 'Isn't that just a bunch of weirdos jumping over bushes?'

Faster than lightning, Friedrich was past him. She sprang over a piece of equipment, cartwheeled over another, then leapt into the air and used a wooden beam to swing herself up on to a two-metre-high platform jutting out from the wall. She landed gracefully, then turned to 1B. '*That* is parkour.'

1B stared, wide-eyed and open-mouthed. Only two people remained unmoved.

'Swear down, I'm tired just *watching* that,' Ade whispered to his brother.

Ede shook his head. 'My body doesn't bend like that, man. Did you see when her back was like . . . and her feet did this . . . rah.'

Friedrich backflipped off the platform and landed on the floor with the kind of casual elegance of someone who had done it thousands of times. 'Everyone in this room will be able to do that before they leave Crookhaven. And much, much more besides.'

'If they last that long,' Decome said, shooting Gabriel a look.

'But today I merely want you to get a feel for all of this equipment,' Friedrich said, gesturing at all the odd-looking padded shapes that grew out of the ground and jutted from walls. 'I want you all to feel completely comfortable in here. If you don't know the name of something, ask. If you don't know how it should be used, ask. Today, you can ask me anything. But from tomorrow on, anyone who doesn't know the name of a particular piece of equipment does ten press-ups.'

'Knee press-ups?' Villette asked.

Friedrich snorted. 'Do I look as if I've done a single knee press-up in my life?' Gabriel had to admit that she did not. 'No, *full* press-ups. For everyone.' She walked over to the wall and, with her back to it, slid down. 'From tomorrow, every time a piece of equipment is used incorrectly, you will do wall sits like this for one minute.' She stood. 'Don't misunderstand me. I expect you to fail hundreds of times while performing these moves, but I will not tolerate *misuse* of equipment. That's how people get hurt.'

'Wall sits,' Ede said, giving his brother a knowing look. 'Mum's been training us for this our whole lives.'

'What's your record again? Six minutes?' Ade asked.

Ede shrugged, looking smug. 'Nah, longer. I actually fell asleep in that position once.'

Ade shook his finger at his brother. 'See you went too far with that nonsense. You *always* go too far.'

Friedrich turned her attention to the talking twins. 'Lastly – and this is the rule that will ensure you don't lose a finger or an earlobe – no jewellery is to be worn inside this building.'

The twins reached for their skull-and-crossbones earrings. Frowning, they unclipped them and stuffed them into their pockets. Ji-a, Villette and some of the other girls took off rings, necklaces and earrings. Much to Gabriel's amusement, Decome automatically reached for his bronze ring but found nothing. He had not yet managed to steal it back from Mr Velasquez.

'Psst,' Villette said to the girl beside her. It was the girl who'd given Gabriel her pebble on the first night. 'You might want to take that off too. What if it gets caught on something?'

The girl ran her hand over her blue hijab self-consciously and looked away.

This only spurred Villette on. 'No? Mm, I guess it isn't exactly *allowed*, is it? I'm just trying to look out for you, Amira.'

The girl sat quietly, arms wrapped tightly around her matching blue trousers. Gabriel thought he saw tears welling in her green eyes, then. But she blinked and they were gone.

They spent the lesson exploring the huge room and asking Friedrich about the equipment. There were tricking hoops and steps, blocks, asymmetric bars and large wedges, vaults and springboards. At each piece, Friedrich demonstrated the many different ways they could be used. It made Gabriel's head spin, and by the end, one thought was playing over and over in his mind: *So many people are going to be doing wall sits this year.*

'Before we finish,' Friedrich said. 'I want to have a little competition.' She whirled around and bounded up the climbing wall with the grace of a cat. On the top hand grip, she stuck a red dot. Then she leapt on to a nearby platform and sat cross-legged, facing 1B.

'You, tired one,' she said, pointing at Gabriel, 'and you, knee press-ups.' She pointed at Villette. 'You two are team captains. One by one, your entire team must climb the wall, touch the red mark and climb down. Think of it as a relay race. I will keep time. The winning team leaves early. The losing team helps clean this place up. Knee press-ups, you pick first.'

Villette stood slowly. She ran a painted nail along her chin as she considered the class. 'I think I'll choose . . . Crook.' Penelope sprang up like someone used to being picked first. Villette slid her smiling eyes to Gabriel as if to say, 'Oops, did I take your pick?' But Gabriel hadn't planned on picking Penelope first anyway.

'I pick Amira.'

'He's been with us for days now,' Ade said to his brother. 'How does he still not know . . . my name is Ade, man. *Ade*.'

'I know. But I'm picking Amira.'

The green-eyed girl looked up as if startled from a daze. Gabriel nodded at her.

'But . . .' Villette began. 'Why would you—'

'Can't I?'

Amira gave him a nervous smile and joined him.

'She's a Legacy,' Villette said. 'She belongs with us.'

'In my class,' Friedrich said impatiently, 'there is no such thing as Merit and Legacy. There is only *good* at

145

Crimnastics or *bad* at Crimnastics. Now hurry it up.'

Decome, Mona, Dmitri and Dorian joined Penelope and Villette. While Ji-a, Lulu, Ade and Ede joined Gabriel and Amira's team.

Ever the show woman, Villette went first. She was quick and nimble and completed the climb in 34 seconds. On Gabriel's team, Ade went first, finishing in 45 seconds and Ede second, getting an embarrassing 51. In between them, Penelope had unsurprisingly managed it in just 32 seconds. Gabriel's 33 delighted Penelope and infuriated Villette. Decome lumbered to a 49. Ji-a dashed to a 44. Mona flew to a 43. Lulu scampered to 40. Dorian made it in just 39. That left Dmitri, the thick-necked Russian boy, from Villette's team, and Amira from Gabriel's.

Amira stepped up slowly, her eyes closed.

'She's not even ready,' Decome said, shoving Dimitri forwards. 'You go first.' The large boy stumbled and crashed into Amira who staggered sideways but caught her balance with surprising ease.

'Sorry,' Dimitri said to her, hands up. 'I didn't mean . . .'

Amira nodded and took a shaky step back. Dimitri took her place and, despite his size, climbed in an impressive time of 36 seconds.

Then it was Amira's turn. As she was standing there, her eyes closed once again, Gabriel had the sudden realisation that he should have let her go first. Or at least in the middle. He had left her with an impossible burden – they were too far behind. Even for a draw, she would have to get a time of 21 seconds. Nobody had even gone below 30 seconds.

Guilt swirled in Gabriel's stomach. He should have gone last.

Amira launched herself on to the wall, her fingertips delicately closing around the first grip. Then she began to climb. No, everyone else had merely *climbed*. Their movements purposeful but clumsy, their breathing heavy and erratic. This was different. Amira *floated* upwards. Her hands and feet barely grazed the grips before she was reaching for another. Some she skipped entirely. Her breathing was controlled and even.

She was a bewitching blur in blue.

When her feet touched the floor, Friedrich stopped the clock and sprang up on her platform. She blinked in disbelief at the time. Then turned it towards 1B. '17 seconds. Tired boy, your team wins.'

*

'That was incredible,' Gabriel said to Amira after class. Ade and Ede had grown impatient waiting for her to finish talking with Friedrich, so it was just the two of them now, cutting through the woods towards the main villa.

She smiled up at him, but continued walking. He followed. 'Where did you learn to climb like that?'

She furrowed her brow and said, 'Sorry. My English is . . .' She waved her finger. 'I understand a lot. But

147

speaking . . .' She waved her finger again. Then her eyes brightened, as if she'd been struck by a wonderful idea. 'But I speak Italian, Arabic . . . do you speak?'

'Ah, no, only English. Sorry.' They walked side by side in silence for a while. Ivy covered the whole eastern side of the villa, and Gabriel absently found himself wondering whether Amira could climb it. 'Well all I wanted to say is that I'm very glad you were on my team.'

She beamed.

'And I also wanted to say thank you for this.' He reached into his pocket and pulled out the tissue. When she saw it, her eyes went wide and she looked quickly away. 'When I saw a flash of blue in the trees last night, I thought I was seeing things. But after watching you climb . . .' He came to a stop beside the marble fountain of the Crooked Oak. So did Amira. 'It was you who gave me this last night, wasn't it?'

She fiddled with a delicate bracelet on her left wrist. 'Sorry.'

'Don't be. Next time you can't sleep, you can come and sit with me, if you want. There was plenty of space and I don't mind sharing ideas about the Break-in.'

'I get up to pray.'

'Oh. Well, after you pray, then.'

She nodded and they fell in step together again. There was something else Gabriel had been wanting to ask Amira. 'Your pebble. Why did you give it to me, that first night?'

148

Amira looked up at him again. 'You have kind eyes. Like my brother, Ishaan.'

Gabriel blinked. No one had ever said anything like that to him before. He was used to hearing, 'He's got a shifty look about him, that one' and 'You can see the Devil himself in that boy's eyes'. But *kind* eyes? He didn't know what to say. And thankfully, he didn't have to because Amira gave him one last shy smile and then walked speedily away.

CHAPTER EIGHTEEN

Of all the teachers Gabriel had seen so far, Palombo was the one who most suited his subject – Forgery. The small Italian man had a delicate moustache that twitched whenever something displeased him, and something *always* displeased him. From the way 1B entered the Forgery ring in a disorganised cluster, to the way some of them sat at the wrong easels, to the way most of them picked up a paintbrush to inspect it despite him instructing them not to. Ten minutes into the class and a sheen of sweat already covered his tanned face.

'Stand!' he suddenly cried, striding into the middle of the room. 'All of you.'

So they did.

'In this room,' he said in his rhythmic, musical accent, 'I have taught crooks to mimic Michelangelo's masterpieces, shape diamonds like the world's finest cutters and paint like Picasso himself. But I never,

never had to stop a lesson ten minutes in because my students refuse to listen!' He spun around, glaring at each member of 1B in turn (even those, like Decome and Dimitri, who were taller than him). 'Now, we begin again or I have you stand in complete silence for next two hours?'

'We're ready to start again, sir,' Penelope said. She was sitting on the opposite side of the room to Gabriel, but the icy glare she gave her classmates made him shudder even from a distance.

'Excellent,' Palombo said. 'Now, as you can see, your own easels are empty. But the two behind me hold something. Step back and tell me what you see.' Soles scuffed polished wood as they took a step back.

'Two identical paintings,' Decome said.

'No!' Palombo said, pointing a paintbrush at him accusingly. 'Anyone else?'

Penelope frowned, yet again forced to restrain herself from answering.

'An original and a forgery,' Ji-a said. The way she was carefully considering each of the paintings made Gabriel think that this class, Forgery, was why the Merit girl had been recruited to Crookhaven. She had a short bob of jet-black hair, clever dark-brown eyes and, when she smiled, which was almost all the time, she had a dimple in her left cheek.

'Excellent, Miss Oh. Which is original and which is forgery?'

Gabriel squinted. *There's . . . no difference.*

'Left is . . . the original,' Ji-a offered. 'Right is the forgery.'

Palombo's moustache twitched as he smiled. 'I am flattered, but no.'

Ji-a raised an eyebrow. 'Sir, did *you* paint the one on the left?'

His attempt at a humble shrug was so awkward that it looked more like a flinch. This was clearly a man for whom humility was an entirely foreign language. 'Guilty. Though I admit that painting this piece did take up most of my morning . . .'

Ji-a gaped. 'A *morning?*'

The same insincere shrug again. '*Mio dio.* Sounds like I am boasting!' *You are.* 'I did not mean for it to come off like that.' *Yes, you did.* 'Anyway, we get on with the class?' *Yes, please.*

Gabriel looked to his right at Ade and Ede. They had hidden paintbrushes in their sleeves and, when Palombo's back was turned, were flicking each other on the backs of the knees with the wooden ends.

'Do you know why forgery is greatest of all art forms?' Palombo pulled up a red velvet chair and sat in the centre of the room. 'Because we master how to imitate a Master of their craft. Most of them – painters, sculptors, jewellers – spent their entire lives perfecting their art. And we learn the style and technique of not just one of these Masters, but countless. So what, then, does that make us?'

'A master who's mastered the Masters?' Gabriel said.

'The Swiss army knife of the Underworld?' Villette added, smirking.

'A crook of all trades?' Ede chimed in.

1B snickered. Even Palombo smiled. 'Laugh, yes, but you are all correct. It make us a master of the Masters, a Swiss army knife *and* a crook of all trades. In other words, it make us *adaptable*.' He leant back in his chair and pressed the tips of his fingers together. 'But all we speak about so far is *art* forgery. But we cover so much more than that here. Anyone tell me what else falls under the term "Forgery"?'

The class talked about forging documents and signatures, banknotes and coins, jewellery and even stamps. Gabriel absorbed all the information. But he'd known from the moment he saw it on his timetable that Forgery would be his least favourite class. Sitting still, working on something delicate like a painting or a sculpture, would never be interesting to him. His hands, now so agile from years picking pockets, would mean that he could get good enough, he thought. But he would never be great, like Penelope or, he guessed, Ji-a.

Just then he remembered a conversation he'd heard the day before between two final years – more officially known as Robins or Robin Hoods.

'When we get out of this place,' one of the boys had said to the other, 'who do you reckon is gonna do the best?'

'Probably Theo,' the other had said.

153

'Theo? Hmm. He's good at everything but not *great* at anything. He's like an ocean that's an inch deep.'

Like an ocean that's an inch deep. That phrase had stayed with Gabriel like a warning. He didn't want to be good at everything; he wanted to be *exceptional* at a handful of things. But what were those things?

Pickpocketing, of course. But what else? Well, that was exactly what he was at Crookhaven to find out.

*

It was between the Forgery building and the Tech-nique class that Caspian Crook caught him. The Headmaster had once again been in conversation with Villette Harkness when he'd looked up and their eyes had met. He said a quick goodbye to Villette and then stepped into the sunlight.

'That's the third time I've seen your dad and the villainess talking,' Ade whispered to Penelope, as Caspian approached. 'What's that all about?'

Penelope stayed silent, but *I don't know* was written all over her face.

'Gabriel Avery,' the tall man said, ducking under a low branch and sauntering over to Gabriel, Penelope and the Brothers Crim. 'How is it that, amongst the Crooklings, only you have managed to avoid playing my little game? Mm?' Mischief glittered in his dark eyes.

'I don't know, sir,' Gabriel lied. In truth, every time he'd seen the Headmaster, he'd found a way around him.

He'd hoped he'd be able to put this moment off for at least another week. But here he was . . .

'Not to worry,' Caspian said. 'Now that school has officially begun, you get to play for real points.'

Gabriel nodded. He turned to the others. 'I'll catch up with you.'

Penelope eyed her father warily. 'We can wait if you want.'

'Penelope, must you *glare*?' her father said. 'If you worked half as hard at your brushwork as you do at glaring, you'd be top of your class in Forgery. But I hear Oh Ji-a is quite the talent there. And a Merit as well.'

Gabriel couldn't bear to watch Penelope squirm any longer. 'You three should go or you'll be late for Headmaster Whisper's class.'

'Whisper's class, eh?' Caspian said. 'You two will certainly be in your element.'

Ade looked at his brother. 'We've been waiting all our lives for this, sir. Can't believe we're about to be taught by *Whisper* herself. Rah . . .' They went to high five and ended up entangled.

'Careful what you wish for, boys. My co-Headmaster is one of a kind, that's for sure.'

The twins waved their goodbyes. Penelope followed, though she kept looking back until she had disappeared around the corner.

'It appears as if you've already won my daughter over, Gabriel. I've been trying for years and . . .' He shrugged.

'What's your secret?'

Gabriel shuffled awkwardly. 'I don't have one, sir. I think she only hangs around with us because the rest of our class are either too shy or too . . . awful.'

He tilted his head. 'No. She likes the three of you. I can tell.'

'She likes those two, sir, because they're the Brothers Crim. She knows just about every hack they've ever pulled off. She only hangs around with me because they're my friends too.' *Friends*. The word came out so easily, so naturally. Moving from town to town, he'd never had a good friend to speak of. And now he had two. Three, if he included Amira. Which he thought he could now.

Maybe even four, if Penelope—

'I'm glad she finally has friends her own age.' Caspian looked over to where Penelope had rounded the corner. 'Living here all her life, surrounded by students so much older than her . . . not to mention everything else that's happened to her.' Caspian shook himself, then smiled. 'Well, she's grown up too fast is all.'

Caspian clapped loudly, forcing Gabriel to flinch. 'Now, to my game!' He began to walk in a slow circle around Gabriel. 'Our dear Gardeners moved three objects around the grounds earlier this morning. You will get a point for each item that you can name correctly. Providing, of course, that you can also tell me where they moved *from* and where they now lie.'

Gabriel looked at the ground for a long moment, trying

to decide what to do.

'Sir, I'm going to be late for—'

'Whisper will understand,' Caspian said. 'Learning to hone your memory is just as important as learning how to navigate a firewall.'

Gabriel looked to where the others had disappeared. If only he'd walked a little faster . . .

'I don't know what was moved, sir,' Gabriel said.

Caspian narrowed his eyes. 'Then why do I feel like you do?'

Gabriel pretended to think. 'Wait. Is it the marble statue of—'

'I think you know very well that it's not,' Caspian said, crossing his arms. 'Now why would you lie when points are on offer, hm? What are you trying to hide, Gabriel Avery?'

Unable to lie his way out of the test, Gabriel sighed and closed his eyes. *Fine.* 'The oak bench,' he said. 'Yesterday it was outside the front of the Crookling house. Today it's by the back door of the main villa. The rope swing that's usually beside the Forgery wing is hanging from an oak tree close to the crooked pier today. There's also the painting of a cherub which I saw in your office that's now hanging in the dining hall.' Gabriel raised an eyebrow. 'And while the Gardeners were moving it yesterday, one of them accidently broke off a piece of the Crooked Oak fountain and fixed it with superglue.'

When Gabriel opened his eyes, Caspian's arms were

uncrossed and he was staring wordlessly. Then, after a long moment he said, 'Follow me.' They made their way around the side of the villa towards the Crooked Oak fountain. 'Show me the piece that's been glued on.'

Gabriel pointed. Caspian squinted at the seam of glue that was still just visible, then turned.

'You've got an eidetic memory.'

Gabriel shrugged. 'I struggle to forget things.'

'What a curious way to put it.' Caspian narrowed his eyes. 'Are there things you wish to forget, Gabriel Avery?'

So many that I've lost count. 'I don't know. Maybe.'

'Most would think it a gift, you know. Possessing a memory that never fades. But it's not, is it?'

Gabriel shook his head.

Caspian looked over his shoulder and smiled. 'You sent your friends away because you didn't want them to witness this. You don't want to lose whatever advantage it might give you in the future.' Caspian rocked on to the soles of his feet and laughed. 'Oh, that is truly devious. You're thinking like a real crook now.'

That isn't it at all, thought Gabriel; it was that knowing the truth had always changed things. People thought it was cool at first, of course, until they remembered the secrets they had told him. From then on, they watched what they said and tiptoed around him in case he one day used what he knew against them. Eventually, they started looking at him like a vault that hid all the worst parts of themselves. Not for one moment did they consider that all the best parts of them were tucked safely within him too. No; to them it was like he had broken some unwritten rule of nature, and they could never forgive him for it.

'Congratulations,' Caspian said, 'you have just won the first four points of the year.'

'Four?'

'You named all three items correctly, plus a fourth that even I didn't know about. That doesn't happen very often. So yes, four points. Now off to Whisper's class you go.'

CHAPTER NINETEEN

Whisper didn't even acknowledge Gabriel when he entered class late and panting. She was standing by a circular table littered with devices, which she was pointing at and naming. 'In-ear receiver, signal jammer, wireless headset, military-grade drone and a standard listening device, also known as a bug. What do all these items have in common, eh?'

'They're cool,' Decome said. Dimitri snickered at his side.

Whisper tutted. 'There's always someone who does their best to crown themselves the class clown. But it's never the funny ones, is it?' Whisper's gaze lingered on Decome accusingly for a moment. 'No. What all these items have in common is that you won't be using them for at least two years.'

In amongst 1B's general muttering of confusion, Gabriel heard Ade whisper to his brother, 'What did she say?'

'Two *years*,' Ede whispered back. 'Then what are we—'

'Ah, ah, ah,' Whisper said, holding up a hand for silence. 'Just because you won't be *using* them doesn't mean you won't be learning about them.' She picked up the drone and, hands moving terrifyingly fast, began to take it apart. Within seconds, the pieces sat in neat rows on the table. 'You can't master this equipment until you know how their pieces fit together. Only when you can disassemble and assemble them *with your eyes closed* will I teach you how to use them.'

'Why, miss?' Mona asked, in her soft Irish accent. After showering at the Crimnastics Centre, her blonde hair had dried into a mane of soft curls.

'A doctor doesn't go poking around inside someone without knowing what they'll find, do they?' Whisper asked. ''Course not. They know exactly what they'll find, and they know exactly how to fix any problem they may come across. How? They spend years *learning*, that's how.'

The co-Headmaster had a way of speaking, in her low, gruff voice, that made everyone in 1B huddle closer.

'I found my first computer at a dump at the bottom of my road,' Whisper said, leaning against a dusty wooden table that had seen better days. 'Whoever had owned it before probably assumed it was busted and threw it out. But *everything* can be fixed. Learned that from my dad, bless 'im. He was a car mechanic for forty years. Never said no to fixing one up. If the price was right, of course!' She laughed. 'So when I found that computer, I set out to fix it. I had no idea what I was doing, so I went to the library and learned. It took me a whole year, but I did it. When I turned it on for the first time . . .' She trailed off and closed her eyes, a smile breaking across her face as she revelled in the memory. 'Nothing like it. And every time it's gone on the blink since, I've taken it apart and fixed it.' She tapped the large black PC on the desk beside her. 'There's no Whisper without her.'

'That's the *same* computer?' Villette asked, sounding more amused than interested.

'It is,' Whisper said proudly.

'But it's so . . . ugly.' Villette giggled.

Whisper frowned. 'Point is, Harkness, before you can master a piece of equipment, you need to learn what makes it tick.'

'So everyone should know how to take apart their phone before they use it?' Villette asked, a challenge in her tone.

'Not everyone,' Whisper said. 'But *you* should. You're not at Crookhaven to be ordinary; you're here to be extraordinary. You're here, I hope, to become the great crooks of the future. And I can tell you something for nothing – every one of the great crooks of the *present* can assemble and reassemble the items on this desk in seconds. Hand any one of these to a Gardener and they'll take it apart with one hand and make you a cup of tea with the other. So wipe that smirk off your face and watch me closely.'

One by one, Whisper took apart each item and,

explaining as she went, put them together again. 1B copied. Gabriel's nimble fingers helped him follow along reasonably well, but next to Ade and Ede he looked like a baby stuffing square toys into round holes. They didn't need to copy Whisper because they easily kept pace with her, their fingers a blur. Even more surprising was that they worked together on every item. Silently, yet in perfect harmony, they moved and pulled and adjusted, their movements so in step with one another that their hands never once touched. And suddenly Gabriel became very aware that he was no longer looking at his clumsy friends Ade and Ede Okoro.

No, these were the famous Brothers Crim.

*

In every lesson so far, Gabriel had been watching Villette and wondering whether the blonde Legacy with the unnerving smile had an area of specialty, like he did. Or whether, like Decome, she had been admitted solely because of her family. She was good at most things, that was true, but she hadn't yet excelled at anything. By the end of Infiltration class though, Gabriel wasn't wondering any more.

Their teacher, Ms Locket, a miniature woman with greying hair and a kindly face, had set up a series of locks on 1B's desks. Some were large, some small, others appeared as if they had been smashed with a cricket bat or savaged by a bear.

'Are we all in and settled, my lovelies?' Ms Locket asked cheerfully. 'Wonderful! Now, I'm sure several other teachers have started off with great long speeches about how their subject is unique and blah, blah, blah. But not me. I will simply say this: once I am finished with you, there will be no lock or safe or device that will be able to stop you. You, my dears, will be human lockpicks.' She gave a cheerful clap.

'Sorry, miss,' Ji-a suddenly called, eyes bulging at something she'd seen engraved on her desk. Gabriel craned his head, trying to get a glimpse. The letter M, it looked like, carved into the wood. 'Is this . . . can this really be . . .'

'Maravel?' Ms Locket chuckled. 'Yes, he was a dear – always sat at the back, cried whenever he met a lock he couldn't pick. You'll find countless signatures of well-known crooks on these desks. I had asked that we get new desks this year, but dear Caspian feels engravings like these are an integral part of Crookhaven's history. And as you can tell by the sheer number of engravings, I'm all for a bit of doodling when you're stuck on a difficult lock. Clears the mind. Caspian also said that they charm budding young crooks like yourselves. By the looks on all your faces, it appears he was right.'

When there was an excited squeak from two desks to Gabriel's right, he was astounded to see that it was Villette. 'SS. Does that mean . . . Samson Sorensen?'

Ms Locket pursed her lips. 'Awful grouch, that boy.

But had a way with safes such as I've never seen.'

'Miss,' Penelope called. 'This A overlapping the M . . .'

The tiny teacher nodded. 'Annabella Mariano. The girl could read a room of lasers like a children's book! Though she always had to listen to heavy metal music to get her thinking.' Ms Locket winced. 'Made a dreadful racket.'

'And ID is India Duvalle?' Decome asked, pointing at the leg of his own desk.

A storm broke across Ms Locket's sunny face. 'No, Mr Decome. *Not* India Duvalle. India is on the Blacklist for a reason – we do not teach our students to use explosives at Crookhaven. Only those who lack skill need to resort something as barbaric – and dangerous, I might add – as explosives. Had she attended this infamous school, she would know that.' Her face softened. 'But as luck would have it, there is someone in here who knows the person who etched that ID into your desk.' Ms Locket turned slowly towards Amira. 'Hello, my lovely.'

Amira looked up.

'Do you know that of all of his siblings, Ishaan was most excited for me to meet you, Miss Dhawan. Though I heard that until recently you were enrolled in our sister school in Sicily, so I didn't think I would get the chance. But here you are.' She paused, smiling warmly. 'It's a true pleasure. And I wouldn't worry about what people are saying about him – I'm sure it's all complete nonsense.' She smiled again, but this was a strange, sad sort of smile that Gabriel didn't understand.

'*She's* Ishaan Dhawan's sister?' Decome scoffed. Amira looked sharply to the floor.

Ms Locket tutted. 'Careful, Mr Decome. Within the walls of this room there's rumoured to be a cupboard so dark that, after only a short while inside, you may begin to believe you have ceased to exist.' She smiled sweetly. 'At least, that's what those unfortunate few who purport to have experienced it say. Personally, I think it's just a nasty rumour. But if such a place existed, what type of person do you think would be sent there? A bully perhaps? Hmm?'

Decome swallowed and fell silent.

'Dear, oh dear,' Ms Locket said, putting her hands on her hips and looking around at 1B. 'Listen to me blabbering on. And after all my talk of keeping it short too!' Ms Locket launched into an explanation of the exercise for the day, but Gabriel kept watching Amira. Her right hand, he noticed, had gone to the bracelet on her left wrist. She was trembling.

Ms Locket started her timer and 1B began to pick the first of the seven locks, but Gabriel was still watching Amira. His hands were moving automatically – he'd picked enough doors and gates to know the feel of a lock as it gave in – but his eyes remained elsewhere. Even as he fought his way through the fourth lock, he was thinking, *Did something happen to your brother, Amira? And did he give you that bracelet?*

'All done,' called a high-pitched voice. Villette Harkness was spinning the seventh lock around her finger and giggling. 'Any more? This is fun!'

Gabriel looked around. He and a few of his classmates had picked the first four locks. Only Penelope had picked the fifth, and the fury pouring from her eyes was practically molten.

No one other than Villette had even begun the sixth lock, an ugly square thing that looked as if someone had recently taken a sledgehammer to it.

'How thrilling, Miss Harkness,' Ms Locket said. 'It isn't often that Legacies excel at Infiltration. Picking locks and cracking safes aren't skills that are seen as very . . . refined.'

'How silly,' Villette said, throwing her head back in a delighted laugh. 'Aren't all of the best things locked away?'

CHAPTER TWENTY

The rest of the first week flew by in a blur of new classes and old problems. Specifically, Gabriel still couldn't sleep. But he hadn't dared to sneak out to the Headmasters' office again because the Gardeners had changed their patrols and Gabriel hadn't yet worked out their new pattern. Instead he stood at his window watching their thin beams of torchlight criss-cross through the tall trees and cast long, ugly shadows on the lawn.

Now Caspian knew his secret, he made sure to stay clear of Gabriel. It was obvious why. Gabriel would beat his memory game, and that meant easy points for a Merit. Caspian couldn't be seen to be biased, of course. But if there was a person in all the Underworld that screamed Legacy louder than Caspian Crook, Gabriel would eat his stolen hat.

By the third week at Crookhaven, the favouritism was really starting to annoy Gabriel. When a Legacy like

Dimitri wore his ring or when Villette wore her glittering earrings, the teachers said nothing. But when a Merit did it, it 'attracted too much attention' or 'got in the way' or, worst of all, looked 'tacky'. Only Ade and Ede had been allowed to keep their skull-and-crossbones earrings in. Gabriel suspected that was solely because, without them, now that Ade's hair had grown out a little, teachers couldn't tell the twins apart. When Gabriel had asked why they chose skull-and-crossbones, the twins had looked at him blankly. Then Ade had said, "Cause when we sit at our keyboards, we're hunting for treasure. Obviously.'

Ede shook his head as if disappointed. 'There's a reason they call it online *piracy*, Gabe.'

Ade clipped his brother around the back of the head. 'That's not what we *do*, man.' And so began another Okoro row.

In classes, Legacies continued to shine because of their inborn knowledge of the Underworld. In one particularly awful History of Crookery class, not a single Merit spoke for two hours. Gabriel had tried once, but Penelope had been chosen to answer the question instead. Good thing, too, as his answer had been wrong.

As his own personal act of defiance, Gabriel began to pick pockets. Mostly those of Legacies, and lots of them. One point tokens, two point tokens, three pointers – he'd taken them all. He always targeted classes 1A, 1C or 1D, never 1B. Except Penelope, of course, whose pockets he picked daily. But he always gave her tokens back to her, rather than taking them to the Gardeners, just as she always gave his back to him.

A few weeks in, Gabriel had begun to realise that he could tell who in the older years was a Merit just by the way they walked and talked and stood. Small, hunched, curled into themselves, Merits were always quieter than their Legacy classmates. It was almost as if they were sorry they were still at Crookhaven, taking up a space that instead could have gone to a Legacy.

There was one Merit Robin, though, who had captured Gabriel's attention because he was just the opposite – the final year student walked tall and proud, his voice booming across the dining hall every lunch time. Leon Marquez. Every Robin had to take on a Crookling to mentor. A Criminal Confidante, they were called. Crooklings were allowed to request a specific Robin and Gabriel had put down Leon's name as his first choice, but so had every other Merit Gabriel knew. So when the tall, sandy-haired boy tapped Gabriel on the shoulder one Wednesday, he couldn't quite believe it was actually Leon.

'H-Hello,' Gabriel said. (Stupidly, Penelope would later tell him.)

'Are you the Crookling Merit who's been going around picking Legacy pockets?' Leon asked, grinning. He placed a large hand on Gabriel's shoulder. 'Heard you've already earned twenty points.'

'Twenty-two actually,' Gabriel said, and immediately regretted it.

Leon laughed and looked at Penelope. 'So he's pretty good then, eh?'

'He certainly *thinks* he is,' she said, looking unimpressed.

Leon raised an eyebrow. 'I know what you're like, Pen. You wouldn't be hanging around with him if he were useless.' He cleared his throat and launched into a spot-on impression of her. '*If I wanted to be average, Leon, I'd follow you everywhere.*'

Penelope crossed her arms. 'That sounds *nothing* like me.'

Leon turned Gabriel around and started to lead him towards the eastern side of the island. Gabriel looked over his shoulder and, to Penelope, mouthed 'Pen?'

She shrugged, as if a Crookling Legacy being on nickname terms with a Merit Robin was the most normal thing in the world.

'Do you think it's strange?' Leon said, catching Gabriel's glance. 'Pen and I being friends?'

'Guess so,' Gabriel said honestly. 'But she's grown up here, so I suppose it makes sense.'

Leon nodded. 'I first met her when I was a Crookling. Then the next year, when I was a Miscreant, I noticed that she would sneak into our classes and hide at the back. As a Lower Delinquent, I even had to stop her from raising her hand one time. But mostly she'd just be looking around at all of us with those big black eyes of hers. I think she liked the company.' Leon looked back at Penelope, but she'd already vanished. 'I was here when all that stuff happened with her mum, but she didn't really tell me about it until last year, when I was an Upper Delinquent. Closest thing to a little sister I'll ever have, that girl.'

Her mum? Gabriel thought, and tucked it away in the vault of his mind.

They walked along a winding path lined with foxgloves, eventually coming out by the lakeshore. It felt like winter now, and the bloated black clouds promised a downpour.

'Why didn't you pick Penelope as your Criminal Confidante?' Gabriel asked.

Leon picked up a pebble and skimmed it on the calm waters. 'Pen doesn't listen to me.'

'Because you're a Merit?'

Leon laughed. 'I don't know if you've noticed, but the three people she spends most of her days with are Merits. She's not that type of Legacy. She's not like her father.' He skimmed another pebble. 'The truth is, I didn't want to mentor her because she'd eat me alive.'

'Why did you pick me?'

Leon dropped his next pebble and walked over. 'Why? Because I can see that all your life you've been hungry. Like me. Hungry here,' he pointed at his stomach, 'but also here.' He raised his finger to his temple. 'I've seen you filling up your cans at lunch. I've been here for five years and I'm still always the first of my friends to finish their meal. That "just in case" feeling never goes away, you know. When you've been hungry – *truly* hungry – you never let yourself take that next bite for granted.' He sat down on the bank and gestured for Gabriel to sit too. 'Those of us who have lived like that have something different in us.'

Gabriel sat. 'Do we?'

'When things are at their worst, we make promises to ourselves. Don't we?'

Gabriel thought about that, then nodded.

'And they're the type of promises that keep us going just that little bit longer, even when everyone sane has long since quit.'

The way Leon talked – as if they were part of the same unspoken club, as if they were old friends – put Gabriel at ease. 'Do you think most Merits are like us? Hungry?'

'Nah. It's not that simple. Just because you earned your way into Crookhaven, doesn't mean you had a tough time of it. And just because you got in because of your family, doesn't mean you've had an easy time of it.' Leon jerked his head back towards the direction they'd come. 'Just look at Pen. That girl's probably never missed a meal in her whole life, but she's so hungry that she tells people she's going to become the greatest crook to ever live and they *believe her*.' He waved his hand in the air dismissively. 'The whole Merit vs Legacy thing is nonsense conjured up by the more traditional Crookhaven alumni and staff.' He gave Gabriel a smile. 'You'll forget that over the next few years, 'course you will. You'll want to beat them. I did.' He shrugged. 'I still do. But try to remember that there's no Merits vs Legacies in the real world. So when someone tells you that someone else is different to you, you don't have to believe them.'

Gabriel was a little in awe. Even as Leon sat there fiddling with a pebble, there was something so . . . confident about him.

'What's your promise?' Gabriel asked. 'The one that's kept you going after everyone else has given up.'

Leon nodded as if he'd expected the question. 'My mum wasn't in the picture and Dad was a gambler. He blew everything he earned on the horses. Most days we had breakfast and that was it. Then one day I got up for school and there was no breakfast. And no Dad. So my uncle took me in. Kindest man you're ever likely to meet. He's a taxi driver. Barely earned enough to feed himself. So when I fell into his lap . . .' Leon laughed wryly. 'With two of us to feed, things got rough. We moved around a lot because landlords wanted to, you know, get paid. That's when I started picking pockets. To try and help. My uncle never asked where I'd got the money. Probably because deep down he knew. And just when I started to get good, Crookhaven came calling. I didn't think twice. After I came here, Uncle found a smaller place he could afford. It's pretty grim, but he likes it.' Leon looked at Gabriel. 'So my promise to myself was that I'd do whatever it takes to give my uncle the life he deserves. I've already done a bit. Last year I got to leave the island to pull off a job I'd been planning for years. With my takings, I got my uncle a brand new taxi. But that's not enough.' He gave Gabriel a knowing smile. 'No matter how much I give him, it'll never be enough. You know?'

Gabriel did know. It would never, ever be enough. But that wouldn't stop him trying.

'And you?' Leon said. 'What's your promise?'

So Gabriel told him. About how his parents abandoned him and how Grandma had raised him on the move for all his life and how he wouldn't rest until his grandma never had to pick up another mop again in her life. When he was finished, Leon nodded, concentration etched on his face. A soft drizzle had begun, but neither of them moved.

'And your parents?' Leon asked eventually. 'You going to do anything about them?'

Gabriel still hadn't said it aloud, though he thought about it constantly. But there was something about Leon Marquez, something altogether familiar. As if Gabriel were looking at what he could be in five years if he made all the right choices. So he admitted aloud what he'd never admitted aloud before. 'Yeah. I think . . . I think it's time I learn the truth about them.'

CHAPTER
TWENTY-ONE

By the end of the sixth week, Gabriel had picked three subjects to dedicate most of his time to – Infiltration, Deception and, of course, Tricks of the Trade. He had gone back and forth about including Crimnastics too, but when he thought about the otherworldly speed and grace Amira had shown when she'd climbed, he'd given up the idea. He was naturally athletic so he wouldn't fail, but he could never be Amira-good.

He decided to leave Penelope to show off in History of Crookery and Forgery, and Ade and Ede to jointly dominate in Tech-nique, the one subject in which they lived up to the Brothers Crim name. Last was Cultivating a Crook class. Though he enjoyed this class a great deal, he wasn't really sure that dedicating more time to it would help him in his future life as a crook. They spent each lesson tending their own small patch of soil. Watering their seedlings, digging out weeds and listening to the delightfully dotty Mr Sisman spout endless quotes about discipline and patience. All of which, Penelope delighted in pointing out, were wrong. Still, being out in the woods and letting his thoughts drift while he tended his miniature garden was soon something Gabriel began to look forward to.

But there was something else he'd been looking forward to far more. He had finally, *finally* built up the courage to call Grandma.

It was Sunday night, which meant designated phone time. As he waited for Yasmin Anderson – the Crookling ahead of him in the alphabet – to finish her call, butterflies took flight in his stomach.

What if Grandma was so angry that she didn't answer? What if, without him, she hadn't been able to keep up with the cleaning and had been forced to move out of the summer house? Worst of all – what if something had happened to her?

When Yasmin finally came out, she was crying. Her whole body shuddered with each sob and she was muttering something that Gabriel couldn't hear. 'Are you all right?' he asked.

She looked up at him, bottom lip trembling. 'I . . . hate . . . lying . . . to . . . Mum . . .' she said, each word punctuated with a sob. Then she shook her head and trudged away.

The phone room was tiny and soundproof, and the phone itself was an ancient-looking thing with a long, curly cord and big, stiff buttons.

'They still use landlines here,' Ade had explained earlier,

when Gabriel had told them he was ready to call home. 'They're much harder to trace and nearly impossible to hack.' Gabriel had nodded along as if he knew exactly *why* that was the case, but he didn't.

Now, Gabriel sat at the table, staring at the phone and figuring out how exactly he was going to fib his way past the one person who'd never fallen for his lies.

Finally, he picked up the receiver and dialled. Even if he hadn't been cursed with perfect recall, he would have remembered Grandma's phone number, because the last three digits were 999.

It rang once. Twice. Three times. 'Hello?'

The sound of her voice set off fireworks inside him. 'Grandma.'

The line was quiet for a moment. 'Gabriel?'

'Yeah, it's me.'

There was a long exhale, as if all the breath she'd been holding for six weeks came out at once. 'You're safe.' There was no anger or accusation in her tone, only relief.

'I'm safe, Grandma. You don't need to worry about me.'

'Dear boy, telling a parent not to worry is hopeless. That's all our life is – a series of ever-worsening worries.' She exhaled again. 'Where are you? When are you coming to visit? Are you wearing enough clothes? Make sure you do. This past week has been bitter!'

Gabriel smiled at the flood of questions. 'I've got a uniform, Grandma. It's warm enough. And I'll be back at Christmas. Promise.'

'I just don't understand why you didn't tell me about this boarding school when you applied.'

So she had got the letter. 'Because it's quite far away and I knew you'd worry. But I love it here, Grandma. I really do. I have friends and everything.'

'Well, of course you have friends! You're a very clever boy.' Grandma cleared her throat as if she was fighting tears. 'Are you eating enough? You know how you get when you have low blood sugar.'

'We get three meals a day.' Gabriel lowered his voice. 'Plus I have a couple of cans of leftovers hidden at the bottom of the fridge.'

'Good boy,' she said, satisfied. Gabriel could tell she was gearing up for another flurry of questions, so he cut in. 'How's the mansion? I hope Mr Hartley has been helping like he promised.'

'Yes, yes. That great ogre's been around. His son too. Not a brain cell between them, of course, but they're hard workers all right.' His grandma chuckled. 'Oh, and I'm afraid you might not recognise me at Christmas, dear boy. Mr Hartley has been fattening me up with his sausage sandwiches. And you know the leak in your room? I can't quite believe it, but the great lump has managed to fix it!'

Warmth filled Gabriel's body. Grandma was safe and well fed and being looked after. At that moment, nothing in the world could have made him happier. 'That's great, Grandma. Maybe you can get him to sort the sink in the bathroom next?'

She chuckled again. 'Oh, I'm working on that, dear boy!'

There was a contented silence. Then, 'Grandma, can I ask you something?'

'Always.'

'Even if . . .' Gabriel trailed off.

'Yes, even if. Come on, out with it. Or I'll start wondering whether this really is my Gabriel on the other end of the line. He's never been one to hold his tongue.'

Gabriel steeled himself. 'Grandma, what do you know about my mother and father?' He'd always thought of them as that – Mother and Father. Not Mum or Dad. They didn't deserve those names. They'd abandoned him and, to Gabriel, that meant they didn't deserve *anything* from him, not even a second's worth of thought. But lately, thoughts of his parents *had* been bubbling to the surface of his mind.

Silence on the line. 'What's brought this on, dear boy?' she asked, her voice low and serious now. 'If one of those little blighters in your class are bullying you, I'm going to hop on the earliest train and give them a wallop they're not likely to forget!'

Gabriel couldn't help but smile. 'It's nothing like that, Grandma. I just . . . I've been thinking about it.'

'Well,' she said, growing calm again. 'That's only natural. But I really don't think that over the phone is the best way. Can't we talk about it at Christmas instead?'

''Course,' Gabriel said. 'But can you . . . do you at least know their names?'

Grandma sighed. 'I'm afraid even that is tricky, dear boy. The names they gave us were . . . well, I don't think they were *real*.'

'*Names they gave us?*' Gabriel repeated, stunned.

'As I said, it's all a bit tricky to explain. Especially over the phone. How about we—'

'They were complete strangers to you?' Gabriel interrupted. 'Then . . . how . . . *why* did you take me in?' They had never really spoken about it, but Gabriel had always assumed Grandma had known his parents somehow.

'You were only a baby. If I hadn't taken you, goodness knows what might have happened to you.' His grandma sniffed. 'Oh, dear boy. You've never asked about them. Not once. I tried to talk to you about them when you were little. Don't you remember? But you would always run away and hide. So today . . . out of the blue. And *over the phone*. There are some things you might not want to know . . .'

'What do you mean?' Gabriel asked, heart thumping. A knocking came at the door and the face of Trevor Bassett from 1C appeared. Gabriel gave him a thumbs up as if to say, *Nearly done*.

'The day your parents left you . . . well, there had been a robbery nearby. A heist at a casino. And it was when . . . it was when *the police* came to question them about it, that we realised they'd already gone. But it's like I said: the names they'd given us . . . well, they weren't real.' Her breath was coming faster, her words rushed. 'Nothing about them was, it seems. Because the police couldn't find anything. *Nothing.* It was as if they were ghosts. Here one minute, gone the next. Only, I know they weren't because I saw them with my own two eyes. So when I say it's tricky to explain—'

'It's OK, Grandma,' Gabriel said, trying to sound calm. 'Let's wait until I get home. Someone is at the door, so I've got to go.'

'Right then, dear boy,' she said, taking a deep breath. 'You stay warm. And if anyone makes fun of you . . . well, you just let me know and I'll sort them out!'

'I know you will, Grandma,' Gabriel said. 'Talk soon.'

He rung off and stood. He was trembling and his body ached. Trevor Bassett gave him a filthy look as he left, but Gabriel barely paid attention. He was thinking about Grandma and his parents and a nearby casino heist just before they went missing. But mostly he was thinking about one phrase Grandma had used. *It was as if they were ghosts.*

Of all the things Grandma had said about his parents, that stood out for one very unsettling reason – as far as Gabriel knew, only one place in the world taught people to move through the world like ghosts.

Crookhaven.

CHAPTER TWENTY-TWO

'**O**h, close your mouth,' Penelope said. 'Try not to make it *too* obvious that you've never been to a library before.'

Gabriel followed her as she strode into the library. 'I've been to libraries before, obviously. But this one's different.'

The Crookhaven library took up the entire top floor of the main villa. It was shaped like an enormous doughnut, with a hole in the middle. In the centre of the room, large windows wrapped around the Crooked Oak, with comfy reading nooks peering out at the enormous tree from every angle. In spring and summer, Gabriel imagined it would be a mesmerising sight, all bright yellows and greens. But winter had arrived, so the branches were bare and ugly, and the harsh winter light made everything appear a slightly different shade of grey.

The books themselves were kept away from the natural light, on polished wooden bookshelves. They were not set up in rows, like every other library Gabriel had known, but in circles around the room. The circle nearest the Crooked Oak was like a small o, while the one on the outer edge of the room was like a colossal O. The smell of old books and new furniture hung thick in the air.

Penelope walked with purpose, eventually finding a reading nook for two and slumping into a large maroon beanbag. 'This place has got the best view.' She gestured out of the window. 'Look.'

Gabriel sat on the beanbag beside her and followed her gaze. Under a large overhanging branch, a kestrel was feeding her babies. They watched in silence until the bird took flight.

'Why did you ask me to meet you here?' Penelope asked. 'It's Sunday. I should be doing HIIT and listening to my Cantonese lesson. So make it quick.'

'It won't take long,' Gabriel said. 'I just . . . didn't want to ask the librarians. This is something I want to keep private.'

Penelope sat up on the beanbag. 'Now I'm interested. What are you looking for?'

Gabriel peered over his shoulder. A slender, red-haired librarian strode past, her burnt-caramel eyes sweeping over the two of them and then moving swiftly on. She wore black jeans, a thick maroon fleece and thin black gloves, likely to protect the more precious books from fingerprints. When she was gone, he whispered, 'That's part of the problem. I don't really know.'

Penelope's eyes narrowed. 'Are you after a book? Records? Census information?'

'No idea.'

Penelope frowned. 'Gabriel Avery, I don't know if you've worked this out about me yet, but I'm not a very *patient* person.'

He'd only needed two Cultivating a Crook lessons to work that out. The way Penelope had tended her patch of earth with machine-like efficiency and then proceeded to glare at her seedlings for the remainder of the lesson had shown him that much. 'I want you to show me where they keep the information about Crookhaven alumni.'

Penelope stared at him. 'Why? Is this for History of Crookery or . . .' her eyes widened, 'or is this personal?'

'Personal,' he admitted.

'Are you going to tell me—'

'No,' Gabriel snapped. 'And if you ask, I'm going to leave, right now.'

Penelope raised an eyebrow. 'What kind of a threat is that? Why would I care if you left now?'

'Because,' Gabriel whispered, 'that would mean you'd lose your chance to have me owe you a favour.'

Penelope crossed her arms and leant back. 'Favours *are* the currency of the Underworld.' She tilted her head. 'But if you don't know what you're looking for . . .'

'All I want to know is where they keep alumni records.'

'But you don't know what you're looking for in those records?'

'No,' Gabriel admitted.

'Isn't that a waste of time?'

Gabriel shrugged. 'Maybe. But just like you're happy to waste your time doing HIIT—'

'It's *not* a waste of time. It's the best form of aerobic—'

'—I'm happy to waste my time looking through the alumni records. So, where are they?'

Penelope eyed him for a long moment. Then sprung to her feet. 'Come on then. I suppose a favour from you isn't *entirely* useless.'

Penelope led him through a doorway in the northeast side of the library, to a small, dimly lit room. Here, the bookshelves were arranged in a tight spiral. There was one way in and one way out, like a miniature maze. Thankfully, no one else was inside. And by the light smattering of dust settled on the shelves, it appeared as if very few students ever visited.

'Here you go,' Penelope said, and turned to leave.

'Wait,' Gabriel called after her. 'Where can I find the records in here?'

Penelope looked over her shoulder and laughed. 'This *is* the alumni records. The whole room. Every heist, every gambit and every wayward former student.'

'The whole room?' Gabriel said, eyes scanning every book and dog-eared scrap of paper sticking out of the shelves.

'Some of it will be redacted, of course. We wouldn't want the likes of Villette Harkness to stumble upon the real whereabouts of the Koh-i-Noor diamond.'

'Why is it not guarded?'

Penelope snapped her fingers. 'I knew I was forgetting something. Whatever you do, don't try and take anything out of this room.' She paused, thinking. 'Or, for that matter, bring anything destructive in. No water or shredding devices or, you know, matches to set the files on fire. There are sensors all over the place. The second someone tries to remove or destroy any of the files, the room goes into full lockdown, all the air is sucked straight out, and as for the person inside . . .' She moved her finger slowly across her throat, then smiled sweetly. 'Which would be a real shame now that you owe me a favour. Happy reading!' She strode off, waving delightedly.

Gabriel looked around and sighed. *This is going to take for ever.*

He didn't know what his parents' real names were, or what they looked like, or whether they'd ever even attended Crookhaven in the first place. He had no idea what exactly he was looking for. None. So the only sensible thing to do was to search alphabetically.

Gabriel found the As and, taking a deep breath, began his search.

*

'Time to wake up,' a soft voice said in his ear.

Gabriel blinked and looked up to see the red-haired

librarian smiling down at him. 'Good thing I checked in here after all, isn't it? We were about to lock up for the night. But here you are, dozing off.' She looked over her shoulder theatrically, then whispered. 'Not that I blame you. Dull as anything, this section.' She shrugged. 'But warm and cosy if you're looking for somewhere to nap.'

'I wasn't napping,' Gabriel protested groggily. 'I was reading and I must've . . .'

The librarian looked at the pile of papers in his lap and raised an eyebrow. 'Well, if you insist on reading about Geoff Acton, I can understand why. The man's as boring as they come.'

Gabriel looked down at the thin file in his lap with the name *Acton, Geoff* printed on it. 'It's not that. I just haven't been sleeping very well.'

The librarian reached out her gloved hand. 'Come on. Up you get.' Gabriel took the offered hand – her grip was firmer than he'd imagined – and stood. She wiped the dust off his blazer. 'No Crookling Merit sleeps well until at least after Christmas. Homesickness for some, nervousness for others. Can't tell you the amount of times I've found Merits snoozing in corners of the library these past few weeks. But Legacies?' She chuckled. 'Not one. They sleep like babies. They were basically bred to attend this school, so they're comfortable as anything.'

Gabriel slid the Geoff Acton file back on to the bookshelf and sighed. He'd barely made it halfway down the first bookshelf before he'd fallen asleep.

'Right, off you pop now,' the librarian said, opening the door. She wiped the handle clean with her handkerchief and mumbled, 'Crooks and their filthy little fingers . . .'

Gabriel walked out into the main library. The lights were off and the low rumble of chatter from earlier had faded away, leaving only an eerie silence. The librarian appeared behind him and they walked side by side through the stacks to the entrance.

'Right then,' she said, stopping. 'If you need help finding something next time, you come and find me.'

'Thanks. But I don't really know what I'm looking for.'

'Is that so?' she said with a chuckle. 'So I should expect to find you slumped over Felix Batley's file tomorrow night at closing time then?'

'I probably won't get that far by tomorrow night,' Gabriel said miserably. 'I've still got to get through all the As.'

The librarian tilted her head. 'There are thousands of alumni records in there. It could take you the whole year. Maybe longer if you don't know what you're looking for.'

Gabriel yawned. 'Maybe. But chances are the surnames of the people I'm looking for aren't something like Zim or Zorro.' He shrugged. 'Doesn't matter anyway. I'm just going to keep looking until I find something.'

'Is that right? Well, whoever you're after, I hope you find them.' She turned to leave.

'I don't think they want to be found.'

She faced him again. 'Ah, well that changes things . . .'

'Why?'

'If it's someone who went to this school, they probably know how to disappear. And crooks who want to disappear don't much appreciate being dragged back into the light. You want my advice? Don't go looking for people who don't want to be found.'

'Why not?'

'Because there's probably a very good reason that they want to remain in the shadows. And you might not like what you find when you turn on the light.'

CHAPTER TWENTY-THREE

'How did *you* find Crookhaven your first year?' Gabriel asked Leon as they sat in the Crookling common room, he on a large beanbag and Leon spreadeagled on the comfiest of the four sofas arranged haphazardly around the fire. The walls, like their uniform, were maroon, and hanging on them were paintings, some of which Gabriel was sure he had seen on those true crime shows that covered the world's greatest unsolved heists. In the corner by the door there were forty-eight white lockers, but only one, Decome's, had a lock on it. Everyone else had very sensibly come to the conclusion that placing a lock on a locker in a building full of thieves was a little like lighting a candle in a dark room filled with moths. Besides, Gabriel had no need for a lock – he had nothing at all to store inside his locker.

It was the last week of November and frost had begun to steadily creep across the windows.

'Well,' Leon began, but just then, two Crooklings from 1D wandered in and stopped dead when they saw Leon, eyes wide.

He grinned. 'How's it going, boys?' He asked about their classes and their teachers and, when they were beaming themselves, he sent them on their way with a 'Don't be strangers, boys. Matt, work on that scissors technique. If you can pick my pocket before the end of this term, I'll buy you a Snickers. And Ravi, let me know how it goes with Emily. Remember – confidence. Shoulders back, chin up and smile. Got it?'

When he turned back around, Gabriel was grinning. 'Do I get a Snickers if I can pick your pocket too?'

Leon laughed. 'Only a fool would make that bet with you, Gabriel Avery.'

A group of Crookling girls came in then, blushed furiously when they noticed Leon and quickly scuttled away. Gabriel jerked his head in their direction. 'Has it been like *that* since you were a Crookling?'

'Like what?' Leon asked, appearing genuinely oblivious.

'You're basically a Crookhaven celebrity.'

'Don't exaggerate,' Leon said, rolling his eyes. Just then, a third group of Crooklings entered and swarmed the charming Robin. After exchanging a few laughs, he politely excused himself and led Gabriel out of the room and up the stairs. 'Put on your coat. We're going to the roof. It's getting a bit crowded in there. Then again, I suppose it's not exactly normal to have a Robin hanging around in the Crookling common room . . .'

'It's not because it's a Robin. There are Robin Confidantes in the common room with their Crooklings every day. It's because it's *you*.'

'Come off it! You're telling me that if Marianna Sonorov was sitting in there, that place wouldn't be filled to the roof?'

Marianna Sonorov was the top ranked Merit Robin, one place above Leon. She had alarmingly pale skin, long fair hair and a crescent moon scar which clipped the edge of her lips. Wherever she went, whispers of awe and admiration followed. 'Well, OK. You *and* her then.'

Leon opened the door to the roof and pulled his coat tighter against the icy gust that spilled through. He smiled. 'Then maybe both of us should come along one afternoon. What do you reckon? We'd cause a *sensation*.' Leon walked to the edge of the roof and sat. 'You want to meet her? We're friends.'

Gabriel sat at his side. 'Wait. You and Marianna aren't . . .'

'Nah, we're not dating or anything. But we do have something in common.'

'What?'

'We both got an interesting offer recently. A job offer, you could say.'

'Since when are crooks offered jobs?'

Leon tutted and patted him on the shoulder. 'You're sharp, but there's still a lot you have to learn about this world. The top Robins are *always* courted by the most successful crews. Rookie Tier Two crews, established Tier Two crews that are aspiring to Tier One. Or if you're exceptional, one of the three existing Tier One crews. But none of those three have taken on anyone new in years.'

Gabriel was all ears now. 'Do you think it's a Tier One crew that's trying to recruit you and Marianna?'

Leon's breath spilled out of him like fog. 'Don't know. Some Tier Two crews have been in touch already, and I've been able to find out who they are and why they want me. But this crew . . .' He pulled his coat tighter. 'If they *are* Tier One, I suppose the secretiveness makes sense.'

'A crew,' Gabriel said, thinking about all he'd heard in History of Crookery. 'Is that really what you want?'

Leon shrugged. 'When I first got here, I thought I'd graduate and dive into the Underworld solo. You know, try and make it into Tier One without any help. But then I realised I actually liked working with the people around me. I was good alone, but when I was surrounded by people who outclassed me in Tech-nique or Crimnastics, I was so much better. Know why? Because the areas where I was weakest, they were strongest.' Leon took a breath and, without warning, howled into the night.

Gabriel blinked. 'What was that for?'

'When a wolf joins a new pack, they change their howl. Did you know that?'

Gabriel shook his head.

'It's true. They listen carefully to the howls of the rest of the pack and change their pitch and volume so theirs won't overlap with another wolf. Then when the whole pack howls, rather than it sounding tuneless or out of sync, it becomes a perfect harmony.' Leon gave Gabriel a smile. 'It's the same with a good crew. Alone you can become exceptional; together you can become unstoppable.'

'Why don't you form your own crew with your friends?'

'My classmates made me better. But the experienced crooks in the Tier One and Tier Two crews could help me become extraordinary. That's what I want. And that's what you want too, isn't it?'

Gabriel nodded.

'The reality is that very few crooks can survive in the Underworld solo, let alone succeed.'

'Penelope could.'

Leon laughed. 'I think you're right about that. Marianna too, maybe. But not me. I'm just a frontman. I need bandmates. And I may be wrong, but I think you will too. So keep practising that howl.' Leon leant back and howled again. He shot Gabriel a look of disapproval. 'Oh, come on. Are you just going to leave me to howl alone?'

Gabriel hesitated. Then he cupped his hands around his mouth, took a deep breath and he and Leon howled together. In the building below them, windows began to open. At first, the other Crooklings just listened, but slowly, one by one, they too began to howl. Maybe it was only his imagination, but Gabriel could have sworn each howl was ever so slightly different. As if each of the

Crooklings had subtly changed their own cry in order to create a haunting, tuneful song that echoed all around the island of Crookhaven.

When the last howl finally faded away, Gabriel and Leon were pink-cheeked and breathless. For a while they sat in silence and listened to the creak of windows closing below. Then Leon asked, 'Have you found anything on your parents yet? Last I heard you'd just finished the Bs and were about to start the Cs.'

Gabriel sighed. 'Nothing yet. But I'll find something eventually. I have to. And you? Are you going to join this Tier One crew?'

Leon leant back on his hands and gazed up at the moon. 'If they really are Tier One, then I'd be an idiot not to. If you get into a Tier One crew, you're made for life. I could help my uncle retire within six months. I could pay him back for everything.' Leon went somewhere then, his eyes glazing over dreamily. Gabriel wondered if he looked like that when he thought about Grandma and all he planned to do for her.

'Still,' Leon said, wincing ever so slightly. 'Joining a crew without knowing who they are or anything about them . . . It's a risk. I just have to decide if it's a risk worth taking.'

CHAPTER
TWENTY-FOUR

'You can't be serious,' Decome said, staring at the clump of nettles sitting on a stand in the centre of the Tricks of the Trade classroom. Hidden inside the nettles was a single white feather. 'If we stick our fingers in there, we'll get stung.'

'And?' Mr Velasquez said, tying his long hair into a topknot. 'Are you *afraid* of getting a little hurt, Mr Decome?'

Gabriel hid a smile as Decome shuffled awkwardly. 'It's not that. It's just . . . aren't there rules against this sort of thing?'

Mr Velasquez smoothed down his crisp black shirt. 'And what sort of governing body do you think regulates a school for crooks? Hmm?' He didn't wait for an answer. 'Anyway, the point of this exercise is to extract the feather *without* getting hurt. Not a single sting. So my advice to you, Mr Decome, is don't get hurt. Who wants to go first?'

'I will. This looks fun,' Villette said, stepping up. She

circled the stand, ice-blue eyes flitting from one nettle leaf to the next, looking for the best way in.

'Oi, did you hear?' Ade whispered to Gabriel. 'Me and Ed are starting a business.'

Gabriel chuckled. It wasn't the first time the twins had announced that, just the first time that day. Penelope, who was on his right, gave a huff. Gabriel and Ade looked over. She glared at them both and, slowly, menacingly, raised a finger to her lips.

Gabriel swallowed and turned back to Ade. 'Doing what this time?' he asked under his breath.

Ade gave him a knowing look. 'Feeding our fellow students mouth-watering meals, of course.'

Gabriel gave him a questioning look.

'Jollof rice,' Ade explained. 'We're going to sell it to other Crooklings.'

Two weeks before, Ade and Ede's mum had sent them a large package – or at least, she had sent it to an anonymous PO Box in Exeter, where all the Crookhaven mail was directed. From there, the Gardeners had collected it and brought it to the school. What was in their package was an ice box filled with a week's worth of jollof rice each. Gabriel, like many of the other Crooklings, had never tried the spicy chicken and rice dish before. But it had caused a sensation in the common room. People had tussled and shoved just for a single bite. So the brothers had split their servings in half and sold portions to anyone who would buy, even the odd Legacy, who they charged a higher rate.

When their supply had run out though, Gabriel figured that was the end of it.

'How are you going to get more?' Gabriel asked.

Ede pulled his brother aside so he could whisper, 'We told Mum that the teachers can't get enough of it. So this time she's sending *double* the amount.'

Ade jerked his brother back. 'Yeah, Mum will do anything if she thinks it'll help us get ahead in school. Bribing teachers is standard.'

They stopped to watch Villette, who had taken her time stretching her fingers, finally reach into the nettles. When her hand came out, it held the feather. 'Nothing to it.' She handed it to Mr Velasquez, smiling, then turned away. She started to walk off.

'Ah, ah, ah,' he said, stopping her in her tracks. 'Getting the feather wasn't the only point of this lesson. Miss Harkness, please raise your left hand.'

Villette's unwavering smile did waver then, just for a second. 'My hand? That's so silly. Why would you—'

'Let's see it,' Mr Velasquez said firmly, and, slowly, Villette raised her left hand. The teacher smiled. 'And there it is.'

Sure enough, a smattering of red blotches had blossomed all along the back of Villette's hand.

'You are quite remarkable, Miss Harkness. I have never seen someone endure the sting of the nettle without so much as a wince.' Mr Velasquez sighed. 'However, the task was to free the feather *without* receiving a single sting.

In this scenario, the nettles represent your mark – and every sting your contact with them.' He leant against the wall and swept an arm out in front of him. 'Anyone else up for the challenge? There's five points in it.'

Penelope went next. She took far fewer stings than Villette – only about four – but judging by the alarming shade of crimson her cheeks turned, that was four too many. Ji-a and Dmitri, Decome and Ede, Ade and Lulu, Dorian and Mona – everyone in the class took a turn and failed. Everyone but Amira and Gabriel. Then class was over and 1B piled out into the hallway.

'Mr Avery,' Mr Velasquez said, untying his hair and perching on his desk. 'Stay a moment, would you?'

Penelope gave Gabriel a disapproving look, as if she was certain that he'd done something dreadfully wrong, then took off down the corridor with Amira, chatting in fluent Italian. The Brothers Crim left too, animatedly discussing how they were going to split up their incoming jollof portions – thirds? Quarters?

'Sir?' Gabriel asked. 'Did I do something wrong again?'

'No,' the teacher said matter-of-factly. 'But you didn't do anything right either. Which wouldn't usually be an issue, except that I get the feeling you are holding back on purpose. Why? Do you not want the class to know how good you are?'

'It's not that, sir,' Gabriel said honestly. 'I . . . well I was going to go. But then Amira didn't volunteer, so . . .'

The teacher crossed his arms. 'So?'

200

Gabriel looked up. 'I didn't want her to be the only one who didn't volunteer.'

'Why not?'

'She doesn't speak much English and she's very shy so she's always left out in our class, sir. Everyone else has somebody. But not her. And . . .' Gabriel looked away. 'I was like her at all my other schools. Left out, I mean. It's not nice.'

Mr Velasquez sighed. 'It certainly isn't.' He gave Gabriel a weary smile and gestured towards the nettles. 'Go on, then. Give it a go now. Just for my sake.'

Gabriel wiped his sweaty hands on his blazer and walked over.

'Do you know what the others did wrong?' the teacher asked.

Gabriel nodded. He tilted his head, looking for the best angle. Then he reached in and plucked out the feather. He held it up between his first and second finger. 'They went in with their whole hand, which meant their thumb always got stung. Two fingers is all you need.'

The teacher chuckled. 'You know, you remind me of a boy I once knew. Best pickpocket I've ever seen. Warm-hearted, too. Like you.' His face grew sad. 'But he made all the wrong choices. Fell in with all the wrong people. And that warm heart turned cold.' He lifted his eyes to meet Gabriel's. 'You will not always make the right choices – indeed, you've already made a couple of dubious ones – but you must fight to keep your heart warm, Gabriel. A warm heart will always lead you back to where you need to be.' He tapped Gabriel's shoulder fondly. 'Oh, and you've just earned yourself five points. Good work.'

CHAPTER TWENTY-FIVE

'**T**oday we're going to be doing something different,' Friedrich said to 1B, who were sitting attentively on the padded floor at her feet. 'Up until now, you have been training. You've mastered using each piece of equipment safely. You have climbed, vaulted and learned to move efficiently, with no wasted movement. And I trust all of you have come to love the wall sits?'

1B groaned, and Friedrich's lips twitched upwards. It was the closest Gabriel had ever seen her come to a smile.

Ade and Ede were the only ones to reply.

'Love 'em.'

'Easy work, man.'

(Wall sits were, after all, the only part of Crimnastics they were any good at.)

'But with the Christmas holidays a week away,' Friedrich continued, 'it's time for a test.' She gestured behind her. 'I'm sure you've seen the assault course assembled behind me.'

They had. Vaults and monkey bars and springboards were assembled in an S-shape. In amongst the familiar equipment, everyday objects were scattered – a shopping trolley, park benches, even a red bicycle.

'Today you will each complete the course' – she paused significantly – 'if you can, that is. I will time you. The person who completes the course the fastest, wins ten points.'

1B looked at one another, anxious and excited.

'Did you see that?' Ade whispered to his brother. 'When she said "if you can" she was looking right at us.'

'Pfft,' Ede said. 'At you, maybe. Not at me. I'm gonna kill this course. Back home they call me "Black Thunder".'

Ade blinked. 'No, they *don't*. Who does? Give me one name.'

Ede shrugged. 'Jess from down the road.'

'Jess from down the road calls you "Black Thunder"?'

'Yeah, why not?'

'Rah, are you not giving this up? Jess is sixteen. She doesn't even know your name.' Ade tutted loudly. '*Lie. But never lie to yourself.* First principle of Crookhaven, little bro.'

'Whatever, man,' Ede said, in the way he often did when Ade mocked him. 'And you're only *three minutes* older. Don't try it with the "little bro" nonsense.'

'Why "Black Thunder"?' Gabriel asked, as he watched Friedrich demonstrate how to deftly navigate the equipment. 'Why not "Black Lightning" or "Black Hurricane"? What's so good about thunder anyway – it's just a loud rumble.'

Ede's face brightened. 'Nah, you're right actually. "Black Lightning" is better.'

Ade kissed his teeth. 'I once saw Nana pin you to the floor with a plastic fly swatter. No one's calling you "Black Lightning", Ed.'

'Gabe will. Won't you?'

''Course,' Gabriel said, knowing it would never catch on. Still, the smile that spread across Ede's face made it worth it.

It started to rain then. The heavy, relentless rain Gabriel had only ever seen on the moors. Wind whistled through the treetops and the branches above the roof creaked threateningly. The rain thrummed on the roof of the wooden Crimnastics building, echoing loudly inside.

1B looked up, listening in silence. It sounded almost as if they were in a stadium – the low rumble of cheers mixing perfectly with the high-pitched whistles. As though the weather itself knew that class 1B were about to face off against each other.

Again, they were asked to volunteer. Penelope called out her own name before the teacher had finished the question. She was wearing her usual all-black exercise outfit with the same ragged-looking violet ribbon holding her hair in a ponytail. Stepping forwards, she shook out her arms, lowered her shoulders and smiled determinedly at the first obstacle.

I doubt there's anyone in the world as competitive as

Penelope Crook, Gabriel thought.

Then she was off, springing over and under and through. Hanging and leaping and then sprinting her way to a time of 2.24.

When she returned to Gabriel's side, her skin was glistening and her palms were red from gripping the monkey bars, but she wasn't even breathless. 'Beat that, Avery.'

'Sure you don't want to use your favour now?' Gabriel asked. 'I can trip on the springboard or slip off the handlebars. Just say the word.'

Her eyes went wide with fury. 'I don't need you to . . . I would *never* ask you to—'

'Ji-a, you next,' the teacher said.

Ji-a had improved a lot since the first lesson, but she still looked a little like Bambi – slipping and sliding around the course, never really comfortable. Her time was 3.23.

Decome was third. He had improved drastically and, to Gabriel's surprise, had begun to work hard in class. The brashness and arrogance were still there, but when it had become clear he was in the bottom three in almost every class, he'd begun to try. Still, the best he could muster was almost half a minute slower than Penelope's score. 2.48. And when he was done, he had to be peeled from the floor by Dimitri, his blond hair matted to his forehead with sweat.

Ade and Ede were, as expected, disastrous. They insisted on doing the course together, and, to be fair, all went quite well until the monkey bars. Then Ede had clattered into

Ade mid-air and they'd ended up on the floor fighting. They finished the course hobbling and glaring at one another. 7.28.

Mona breezed to an impressive 2.39, Lulu swung to 2.51 and Dorian fell between them with a 2.45. It was Villette who came closest to setting a new record though. Her 2.30 brought a frown to Penelope's face.

'Almost got ya, didn't I?' Villette said, prodding Penelope in the shoulder. Then she winked and flopped to the ground to watch Dimitri.

Crimnastics was Dimitri's best subject, which was saying a lot as he was in the top five in most of 1B's classes. He was large, the largest in the class by some way. Only Decome was taller. Yet he moved incredibly fast. When Friedrich started the clock, he rocketed around the course. Had he not missed a grip at the monkey bars, he would have beaten Penelope's time. But his mistake cost him precious seconds, and first place. 2.28.

While Decome was high-fiving him, Gabriel leant over to Amira and whispered, 'You want to go next? Or shall I?'

'You,' she said, adjusting her maroon hijab. Each day she wore a different colour, but Gabriel was still fondest of the blue one he'd glimpsed flashing through treetops weeks before.

'OK,' he whispered, stepping past her. 'But try not to show me up too badly.' When he looked around, she was smiling.

Gabriel set his feet, took a breath and waited for his cue. The shout from Friedrich came and he took off at a sprint, springing over the bicycle, dodging the shopping cart and taking the monkey bars two at a time. At the last springboard, his foot caught awkwardly, sending him off balance. But he recovered, jumped over a balance beam and finished strong.

'2.26,' Penelope called out, and the look on her face was more of relief than triumph.

Gabriel sat beside Penelope. 'You're welcome, by the way.'

Penelope frowned. 'What for?'

'The trip,' Gabriel said, as if it was obvious. 'Are we even now?'

Penelope let out rasping laugh. When she realised she'd drawn everyone's attention, she cleared her throat and looked pointedly away. Once 1B's attention had gone back to Amira, Penelope turned on Gabriel. 'Gabriel Avery, if you're trying to imply that trip was *intentional*.' She stopped short, fuming. '*Even* if it was – and I don't believe for a second it was – then I would not consider that as a favour repaid. You know what I would do though? I'd drag you back to the starting line and make you go again.'

Gabriel raised an eyebrow. 'Don't you *want* to win?'

'Always,' she said. 'But I want to win fairly. If I wanted to cheat, do you think I would've helped you get the token back into Decome's pocket?'

Gabriel hid a smile. *This is fun.* 'It doesn't matter.

You're not going to win anyway. Look.'

Amira had flown off the starting mark and cleared the first vault before anyone had time to blink. She slalomed through the obstacles, bounded over the bicycle and, with perfect balance, leapt up on to the trolley and rode it as if she were surfing. When she finally leapt from the moving trolley, it wasn't on to the first monkey bar but the *sixth*, her hands moving at a dazzling speed.

There was something about the way she moved that was just . . . different from everyone else. She glided and twirled and danced while others simply moved. It was as if she had not been born to stand still, but to soar.

Out of the corner of his eye, Gabriel saw a figure pass him on the right, heading towards the finish line. Villette.

Amira ran towards the final springboard, on track not only to win but to break the two-minute mark. But as she leapt off the springboard, a pale hand reached out . . . and snatched off her hijab.

Amira's eyes went wide and she fell to the floor in a mess of arms and legs, just short of the finish line. She screamed and rolled into a ball, arms frantically trying to cover her head.

Friedrich moved fast, but Gabriel was faster. In a heartbeat, Gabriel had snatched the hijab up from the floor and forced it into the girl's clenched fist. Then he turned to face 1B and spread his arms. Penelope rushed to his side, then Ade and Ede and Ji-a, then Friedrich out in front. Together they made a wall around Amira, all looking away while she wrapped the hijab around her head.

Amira slowly rose to her feet, sobbing. All Gabriel felt as she ran from the Centre of Crimnastics was a rush of air. Friedrich went after her, calling back angrily, 'Villette, don't move a muscle. I'll see you after class.'

Shellshocked, 1B turned to look at Villette Harkness. She was wearing an expression that was somewhere between amusement and confusion.

'All a bit dramatic, wasn't it?' She addressed Decome, but even he was wide-eyed.

'Why did you do that?' Gabriel asked, unable to keep the fury from his voice.

'Why do anything?' Villette shot back. 'To see what would happen.'

'That was cruel,' Penelope said, her voice trembling with anger.

'No,' Villette said. 'It was just a bit of fun.'

'No one else here thought it was *fun*,' Gabriel said.

Villette rolled her eyes theatrically. 'That's because none of you have any *imagination*.' She sighed. 'Anyway. Congratulations, Crook. Looks like you're the winner.'

CHAPTER
TWENTY-SIX

That night, Gabriel couldn't sleep. He was furious with Villette for what she'd done and sad that he hadn't been able to find Amira afterwards, to check she was all right. But, underneath the anger, he felt a flicker of excitement too. Tomorrow he would take the 9.02 train from Moorheart to Torbridge. Then he would walk through the village he hated most in the world to the woman he loved the most.

Nestled inside the nook of the pine tree on the edge of the Headmasters' office clearing, that was all Gabriel could think about. The Gardeners wandered by occasionally, torches swaying from side to side. But he'd worked out their new night patrol pattern two days before and he knew that if he stayed where he was, he'd be just fine.

Gabriel imagined the look of surprise on Grandma's face when he opened the door tomorrow. He hadn't told her when he was coming home for the Christmas holidays. Partly because he didn't want her to wait at the train station, but mostly because Grandma loved surprises.

Gabriel pulled his legs closer to his chest. Even with two jumpers and his winter coat wrapped tightly around his legs, it wouldn't be long until he started to shiver. But until then he could enjoy the stillness of the frigid night and be warmed by thoughts of home.

Nothing new about the office's security system jumped out to him that night. He watched idly as an odd-looking crow swooped low, landed on the roof and then, seconds later, took flight again. In truth, though, he wasn't really concentrating.

After a while, Gabriel whispered, 'I know you're there. You can come down.'

For a moment, there was silence.

Then a soft rustling began in the branches above. Seconds later, a figure was sitting beside him. He hadn't even heard her land.

'I'm sorry about today,' Gabriel said, turning to look at Amira. Her maroon hijab was again perfectly in place, but the dark skin below her eyes glistened in the light of the moon with what he could only assume were very recent tears.

She said nothing, only stared at the army of trees ahead.

'Villette will be cleaning the sweat, dirt and blood off the matts in the Crimnastics Centre for the whole next term, Friedrich said. Plus, she's lost twenty points, so there's basically no chance she'll win the Crooked Cup now . . .' He trailed off. Then, 'We should have been faster.

212

To shield you, I mean.'

'Thank you,' she said softly. In the darkness, he saw the gleam of a small smile.

'You OK?'

Amira shook her head.

'Because of today?'

She shook her head again.

'Is it . . .' Gabriel paused, wondering if he should bring it up, '. . . because of your brother?'

Amira looked at him for a long while, as though considering, then nodded.

'Is your brother dead?' Gabriel asked softly. That was how it had sounded when Ms Lockett had spoken of him.

Amira sighed and looked at the ground. Crystals of frost had begun to form on the grass at their feet. 'To most people.'

'But not to you?'

'Not to me,' she echoed.

'Then . . .'

Amira opened her mouth but hesitated. Then, 'If I tell you, I will be dead to you.'

'You'll be dead to me?' Gabriel asked, shocked. 'Why?'

She started to shiver, from cold or nerves, Gabriel couldn't tell. He took off his coat and laid it carefully over her legs. 'You won't be dead to any of us. Not to me, Penelope, Ade or Ede. I promise.'

She looked up again and there were tears in her green eyes. 'Ishaan. I think . . . I think he join the Nameless.'

The 9.02 from Moorheart left exactly on time. Naturally, Crookhaven staggered their departures. The younger years left on the Saturday while the Lower Delinquents, Upper Delinquents and Robins left on the Sunday. Even then, they all took different trains, alone or in small clusters. They wore their home clothes or, if you were like Gabriel and had nothing suitable for minus three degrees and hail, then you borrowed some. Unfortunately, Penelope was the only one of his friends who had anything spare, so everything he was wearing – from the waterproof anorak to the too-small fleece to the too-tight jeans – was black. Still, he was grateful. When he'd said as much and wished her a happy Christmas, she'd flapped it away with, 'I don't have *time* for Christmas, Gabriel Avery.' Then she'd cleared her throat. 'But, you know, you too. If you go in for that kind of thing.'

Ade and Ede weren't much interested in Christmas either, but for a very different reason. 'Jollof rice,' Ade had said as they waited for their 8.43 train. 'That's all we're going to be doing, man. Helping mum cook it, sourcing containers for it and finding a better way of getting it to Crookhaven.'

Ede rubbed his hands together excitedly. 'There's money in this, I'm telling you. Forget being crooks. We're gonna be businessmen.'

Gabriel laughed. 'Remember me when the Brothers

Grub goes global.'

Ade nudged his brother. 'The Brothers Grub, I like it. Write that down.'

Ede frowned. 'Why do *I* have to write it down? You got a working hand, and I know you got a pen in your pocket so . . .' That was the last thing Gabriel heard as the brothers, still bickering, climbed aboard their train and rumbled away.

Gabriel boarded the 9.02 and sat by the window. Soon his thoughts drifted to the night before.

After Amira had revealed that her brother had joined the Nameless, she had told Gabriel all about why she was at Crookhaven and not the other crook school she'd originally planned on attending, in a remote region of Sicily. With four brothers, all of whom had gone to Crookhaven, Amira had decided early on that she didn't want to follow in their footsteps but blaze her own trail. That meant the other crook boarding school and, of course, learning Italian. She spoke other languages fluently, too, but pushed back when her father tried to get her to learn English. Because she associated English with Crookhaven and with her brothers' legacy at the school. If she learned English, Crookhaven could be her back-up plan, her safety net. And Amira had never wanted any kind of safety net.

She had gotten so good at climbing because she had never used any harnesses or nets to catch her. She had been willing to fall, to feel the pain of landing hard and learn from those mistakes. And so she quickly lost all fear and began to soar.

But when word spread that her favourite brother had joined the Nameless, she felt she had no choice but to enrol at Crookhaven. To learn *why*. So now she was at a school she had never wanted to attend, in a country where she couldn't speak the language fluently, surrounded by people who all thought her brother had betrayed them. Alone.

After that, Gabriel hadn't known what to say, so they had just sat in silence, shivering and staring at the moon shimmer on the lake. Then they had stood and, staying low to avoid the Gardeners, snuck back into their building.

Gabriel felt foolish now, for not telling her that she *wasn't* alone. He had wanted to tell her that he, Penelope, Ade and Ede would all be on her side. But the right words hadn't come. Though he had, as they'd gone their separate ways, given her a warm smile. One which he hoped said, *I'll see you soon.*

CHAPTER
TWENTY-SEVEN

Torbridge was as miserable as ever.

Gabriel trudged out of the train station and followed the familiar route home, sleet and icy wind sweeping through the empty streets. But as cold as he was, one joyful thought filled his mind, making him lower his head and quicken his step.

I'm home.

The Merciers had wised up and installed a sturdier lock, but he'd already picked far more challenging ones in Infiltration class, so it took him mere seconds. Once inside, he kept to the outside edge of the property, sneaking through the bank of trees that ringed the mansion. If he went near the house and someone saw him, he'd be forced into answering questions about where he'd been all these months, and he really didn't feel like it. Not today.

When the cabin finally came into view, the strangest thing happened – Gabriel smiled.

I never thought I'd be happy to see this place again.

He rapped on the door and waited. Seconds later, it swung open.

'Hello?' a stranger said. The woman was young and round and pink-cheeked. 'Who might you be, then?'

Gabriel blinked. 'I'm . . . My name is Gabriel. My grandma lives here.'

The woman smiled and crossed her arms. 'Are you one of Charles's friends? Is this some sort of game?'

'No. My grandma really does live here. Can I . . . is she in?'

The woman raised her brows. 'Here? Afraid not. I live here all alone. I'm the Merciers' housekeeper. Been here for, oh, about two months now.'

'But,' Gabriel began, peering past her and seeing that everything – the sofas, the cookers, even the fridge – had changed. 'I don't understand. Where is Grandma . . . Ms Avery?'

'Oh, the previous housekeeper?' the woman said, lengthening every word in the way people do when they think they're speaking to someone dim. 'Well, I don't like to gossip, but from what I hear the Merciers did a search of the cabin and found a stolen hat. A fedora, I think.'

Gabriel went cold. The fedora *he* had stolen. 'Do you . . . do you have any idea where she went?'

The woman stared blankly. 'Afraid not. All I've heard is that they found the hat and kicked her out the same day. I didn't get here until a week later. Is she—wait, where are you going?'

Gabriel had already swivelled and was striding back towards the gate. There was only one other place in the whole of Torbridge Grandma could be.

He knocked frantically on the door of Benson's Café. 'We're closed,' came a thunderous voice. Gabriel knocked again, harder.

Mr Hartley swung the door wide. 'We're bleedin' *closed*.' His eyes went wide. 'Lad, you're back. Hold on a minute, where you . . .'

Gabriel was past him, through the café and up the stairs before Mr Hartley could finish the sentence. And there, hunched over the kitchen sink in her yellow cleaning gloves and bleach-stained fleece was Grandma.

'Dear boy,' she cried, flying across the room and pulling him into a hug. 'Why in the *world* didn't you tell me you were coming?'

There was so much he wanted to say, to ask, but, after months without seeing her, without smelling that familiar blend of lavender and Werther's Originals, all he could do was relax into the hug.

Mr Hartley reached the top of the stairs, panting heavily. 'What kind of greeting was that then, lad?'

'Oh leave the boy alone, would you?' Grandma said. Then, to Gabriel, 'How about a bacon sandwich, hm? Does that sound nice?'

Gabriel nodded into her shoulder.

'Go on,' Grandma said to Mr Hartley without looking around. 'Sausage for me.'

The large man sighed and muttered, 'She's got me going up and down the bleedin' stairs all day long . . .'

When he was gone, Gabriel released Grandma and looked up at her. 'Why didn't you tell me?'

She sighed. 'You've been over there already, have you?'

Gabriel nodded. 'The new housekeeper told me that it's been two *months*.'

'Take off your shoes and socks first, please,' Grandma said. 'You'll catch your death if you keep those wet socks on.'

Gabriel did as she asked but refused to be distracted. 'Every time I called, you said—'

'I know what I said,' Grandma said, filling the kettle. 'I couldn't tell you the truth, now, could I? Not when you sounded so happy. I know what you're like, dear boy. You would've been on the first train home, and I couldn't have that.' She looked up from preparing the tea and laughed. 'Strange, isn't it? When you first left, I would've given anything to have you home. But now that you've found somewhere you love, I would've said anything to make you stay. Funny old world, this. Funny old world.'

Grandma placed a cup of tea on Mr Hartley's unstable table and sat down with a sigh.

Gabriel warmed his hands on the cup but didn't drink. 'I'm going to speak to the Merciers. Maybe if I—'

'You'll do no such thing,' Grandma said sharply.

'But your job.'

'Some job.' Grandma snorted. 'Paid a pittance to do the

work of three people. No thank you! Can you believe they kicked me out still wearing my cleaning gloves – before I'd even had a chance to get my mother's ring from the third-floor bathroom? The cheek! I'd taken it off to clean that disaster of a toilet but . . .' She trailed off. 'Anyway, truth is I'm too old and doddery to climb all those stairs these days. If anything, they've done me a favour.' But when she turned around, pretending to look for Mr Hartley, Gabriel thought he heard her swear.

'But our summer house . . .'

'Ha!' Grandma said, startling him. 'That's no summer house. It's a sieve made of wood. Rain just passes right through that place, wetting any poor sod that gets in its way. Let the new housekeeper have it. She's young and spritely and, I hear, an absolute dear. My old bones couldn't take another winter in that place anyway. Even the thought of it makes me shudder.'

Gabriel took a sip of his tea. 'We'll find somewhere else then, Grandma. We can move to another town. It's about that time anyway.'

'We?' Grandma said.

'Well, I'll have to leave the school.'

Grandma stood. 'You'll do no such thing! Not on my account. And who says we need to find somewhere else?'

Slowly, Gabriel began to realise that items from their cabin – the chipped floral egg cup, the red and green checked dishcloth and even a brand-new pair of Grandma's favourite fluffy blue slippers – were scattered about the room. 'Are . . . are you living *here*?'

Grandma smiled. 'That's right. Working here, too. Downstairs in the café. Washing dishes, making toasties, working that blasted coffee machine. Harry's nephew wasn't thrilled about me stealing his job, but he's in college now so he's got other things on his plate.'

'You're living *and* working here?' Gabriel asked stupidly. 'And Mr Hartley is all right with that?'

'All right with it?' Grandma chuckled. 'It was his idea.'

There was a clattering on the stairs and Mr Hartley appeared. 'That it was. I wasn't about to see her out on the street, was I?' He handed a sausage sandwich to Grandma and a bacon one to Gabriel.

'It's only been three months,' Gabriel said. 'But everything's changed.'

Grandma walked over to Mr Hartley and hooked her arm through his. 'Yes, a lot certainly *has* changed.'

Gabriel stared at their interlocking arms dumbly. 'But . . . but you two hate each other!'

Mr Hartley chuckled. 'We certainly bicker, don't we?'

'Something fierce,' Grandma answered.

'But the way I see it,' Mr Hartley said, 'what someone says doesn't matter so much as what someone does. Your grandma was there for me when my Maggie passed. Hardest time of my life, that was. But you saw me through, didn't you? Called me every night, no matter where you were living back then.' The large man rubbed Grandma's arm affectionately.

Grandma smiled. 'And he's been there for me through all this. Taking me in, keeping me fed and making me laugh. The bickering is nothing compared to all that.'

Still looking at them, Gabriel took a bite of his sandwich.

Grandma waited, but when Gabriel still hadn't said anything, she asked, 'Are you going to be OK with this, dear boy?'

The truth was that while he was certainly confused, he was also delighted. Grandma had never had anyone other than Gabriel to rely on. Now, it seemed, she did. And that thought made Gabriel smile. 'I reckon so.'

*

That night, while Grandma slept and Mr Hartley rumbled like thunder beside her, Gabriel, wearing all black, slipped silently into the cold night. He knew Torbridge like he knew picking pockets and, thanks to Crimnastics, he moved through the familiar streets with a new kind of grace – hopping fences, ducking low-hanging tree limbs and tiptoeing through an assault course of discarded children's toys in back gardens.

The Mercier mansion loomed large in the darkness. The lights were off and no smoke drifted from the chimney; clearly everyone inside had long since gone to bed. Picking the gate lock for the second time that day, Gabriel snuck in and stalked across the lawn. He pressed his back against the mansion wall and looked up.

Still too lazy to cut the vines, eh? Good.

Thick green tendrils grew up the walls to the third floor. But he only needed to climb to the second and in through the small window that had a faulty lock which had never been fixed.

He eased it open and slipped inside. Rather than use the stairs, which creaked in the way all old houses did, Gabriel leapt on to the sturdy banisters and, using his hands to help, monkey-climbed up to the third floor. And there, tucked away at the back of the bathroom cupboard, he found Grandma's ring, a large gold abomination that could have doubled as a knuckleduster.

Gabriel stuffed it into his pocket and was about to leave when he had an idea. A wonderful, awful idea.

He plugged the sink and switched the tap on low, so it made no sound as it filled. When the water began to drip over the edge, he moved the rug below the sink to cushion the sound.

Then he ducked out of the mansion and took off into the night.

This won't be known as my finest work, Gabriel thought, *but man, that was fun.*

That night, and for the first time in weeks, he fell into a blissful, dreamless sleep.

CHAPTER TWENTY-EIGHT

The Christmas holidays flew by in a wonderful blur of homemade food, belly laughs and bickering. More wonderful still, Gabriel managed to sleep most nights. And on the rare nights he couldn't, he would sneak out and practise his new skills on the sleepy cul-de-sacs of Torbridge. Breaking into all manner of houses – through windows, back doors, even a wine cellar. But he never stole anything. The people of Torbridge had been cruel to him and Grandma, but he had something to lose if he got caught now – the chance of changing his grandma's life.

For Christmas, Gabriel got a new pair of black trainers from Mr Hartley, who now insisted Gabriel call him Harry. After two days of mocking – 'your name can't really be Harry Hartley, can it? Sounds like a superhero name. Only, a really boring superhero that has the power to make bacon butties twice the speed of normal people' – Gabriel had agreed.

For Grandma's present, Gabriel gave her back her mother's ring. She was delighted at first, then immediately suspicious. 'Hold on. How did you get this, eh?'

'The Merciers said they felt bad about how everything ended, so they brought the ring back last week.'

'Is that right?' Grandma asked, but what she really meant was, 'What a load of old nonsense.'

'Mm,' Gabriel said, unconvincingly.

Grandma crossed her arms. 'You know, dear boy, you'll never guess what I heard in the post office the other day.'

'What?' said Gabriel, pretending to read a book of Grandma's about the world's most luxurious hotels.

'It was about the Merciers,' Grandma said. 'That awful bathroom on the third floor flooded. Can you believe that? They didn't know a thing about it until morning, when they came out of their rooms and their stairs had transformed into a cascade water feature. Water just pouring from the third floor all the way down to the ground floor. The tap's nozzle came loose, they think.' Grandma took a step closer. Gabriel kept very still. 'Know what's really odd though? It happened on the night you got back. Fancy that.'

Gabriel nodded absently. 'Yeah, that *is* strange.'

'Mm. Very strange *indeed*. If I were a suspicious person—'

'Which you're not,' Gabriel cut in pleasantly.

'Which I'm not, thank you. But if I *were*, I might think – what with the returned ring and the plumbing accident occurring on the same night as your arrival – that you, Gabriel Avery, were involved.'

'But you're not a suspicious person,' Gabriel reminded her.

'Me? Oh no, not at all.' Grandma sighed and turned away. 'But if I did happen to weed out the blighter responsible, do you know what I'd say?' She looked over her shoulder and smiled. 'Thank you.'

*

Gabriel got his Christmas present from Grandma on the day before he was meant to leave. She'd sent Harry away to run an errand, leaving just the two of them on the comfy blue sofa in the living room.

She began with a deep breath. 'Are you really sure you want to know all this? About your parents, I mean? This'll all be new to you because you've never once asked—'

Gabriel leant forward. 'I'm ready.'

Grandma nodded. 'Right then.' She settled back into the sofa. 'Where to start, eh? It's been a long time and my memory isn't what it once was.'

'Where did you meet them?' Gabriel prompted.

'They were staying at the hotel I worked at in London – I've told you about it before, the Palace. I was the maid for the VIP penthouses. All sorts of awful sods came in and out of that place. But your parents were different. Kind.' Grandma sighed. 'Though now that I know it was all an act, that doesn't mean a great deal any more.'

'And you said they gave you fake names—'

'Yes, yes, don't *rush* me.' Grandma sat a little straighter. 'A lot of the details have faded away, but I still remember welcoming them to the suite. They were both tall and elegant, with olive skin like yours. The man wore a smart grey suit – very handsome, he was – and the woman had these bright green eyes that sparkled. And there you were, clutched in her arms.' Grandma cupped Gabriel's cheek. 'Ugly little creature, you were.' Grandma let out a sharp laugh. 'Hairy as anything.'

'Grandma,' Gabriel said pleadingly.

Grandma waved a hand at him. 'I'm getting there. Anyway, that day they told me their names were Federico Guerrero and Isabella Cortes.'

Gabriel didn't need to write them down; now that he'd heard those names, he'd never be able to forget them as long as he lived. 'Did they say . . . what *my* name was?'

Grandma considered him carefully. 'What was I thinking getting into all of this without a cup of tea in my hand? Give me a minute.' When she returned, she had her favourite mug. 'No, dear boy, they didn't tell me your name.'

Gabriel nodded. 'Oh.'

'That first night, we know they went to dinner around the corner – they were spotted later on CCTV. The next morning when I went in to do housekeeping, their beds didn't look like they'd been slept in. But a man arrived at their room – he had the room key, so I assumed it had all been cleared by the front desk and they'd arranged for him to babysit. I could hear you crying and crying, poor thing. And we think he stayed all night – because your parents never came back.'

'Who was he?'

Grandma shrugged. 'We never found out. He left at the crack of dawn the next morning, looking exhausted. We assumed the parents had come back at some point in the night.' Grandma sipped her tea. 'But when I went to clean the room, there you were. All on your own. A little crying bundle of blankets.'

Gabriel sat back. *So it was true.* 'They just left me behind?'

Grandma worked an arm around his shoulders. 'Now we can't know that for sure, can we?'

'They never came back to get me, though, did they?'

Grandma fell silent for a moment. 'The police tried to track them down,' she said at last. 'There was a heist nearby that night and the police were going through all the CCTV footage in the area. They spotted your parents on CCTV at a posh restaurant just around the corner – but when they investigated, no luck. The names your parents had given the hotel were false, so no relations or friends could be found. The trail went dead. You were going to be kept in care until you found the right home. But the young police officer on the case, she was like me. Both of us had grown up in care, both of us knew what it was like wondering where you'd be living next. We wanted you to have a home as soon as possible. So she . . .' Grandma looked at the door as if, even now, someone would burst in and cuff her. 'She arranged for me to be your foster carer, with a view to adopting you. We left pretty soon after and, ironically, we've been bouncing around ever since. Haven't we?' Grandma chuckled and then sipped. 'I don't know what happened to that young woman. And I'm not sure how she sped up the adoption process like she did, but I'm truly grateful to her.'

'But why, Grandma,' Gabriel said. 'Why did you take me in?'

'Oh, well that's the easiest question of the lot,' Grandma said, with a hearty chuckle. 'Because you wanted me to.'

Gabriel stared blankly.

'You only ever stopped crying when you were in my arms. And you only ever slept if I was nearby. For some wonderfully odd reason, you adored me. And I adored you right back.'

As Grandma carefully sipped her tea, tears pricked Gabriel's eyes. 'You didn't have to do that. You could've stayed at the hotel. You could've let them take me away—'

'No, dear boy,' Grandma said. 'I couldn't. You'll understand one day. I was under your ugly little spell the moment I set eyes on you.'

Gabriel laughed through the tears. 'I wasn't *that* ugly.'

'You were a hideous, werewolf-looking thing,' Grandma said. 'And then you became *my* hideous werewolf-looking thing. And it's been truly miserable ever since!'

Still smiling, Gabriel wiped his cheeks. 'Things are going to get better from now on, Grandma. I promise.'

'Look around you, dear boy,' Grandma said. 'We've got a roof over our heads, food in our bellies and smiles on our faces. It can't get much better than that, now, can it?'

No, Gabriel thought. *I suppose it can't.*

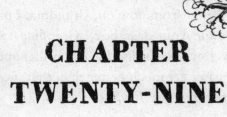

CHAPTER
TWENTY-NINE

Gabriel said goodbye to Grandma at the station early on a cripplingly cold Sunday morning.

'You just stay out of trouble, you hear?' Grandma said, her lips barely able to move.

'I'll try.' He couldn't exactly promise that he would, not when every lesson at Crookhaven was about getting him *into* trouble.

The journey back was uneventful. On his way through the woods surrounding the island, Gabriel stopped for a quick pit-stop at his miniature garden. The Gardeners had obviously been looking after the students' patches because they were all freshly weeded and dead-headed. They had even turned parts of the soil where it had started to freeze over. Gabriel's patch wasn't beautiful or anything, not like Ji-a's or Mona's or Penelope's, but he was happy with it.

At the top of the path, where it dipped, the terracotta tiles of Crookhaven came into view, and, for the first time,

Gabriel found himself truly excited to return to school.

Something small and hard hit him on the back of the head and fell to the forest floor. A pinecone.

'You've gotten slow,' a familiar voice called from somewhere high up.

Penelope sat on a branch in her black running kit, legs swinging.

'Charming,' Gabriel said, rubbing his head and taking off towards the lake without her.

He heard scraping and a thud and then she was by his side. 'Get anything nice for Christmas?'

'Mm,' Gabriel said. 'The truth.'

Penelope frowned. 'What's that meant to mean?'

'Not nice, is it?' Gabriel said. 'When someone half-answers your question.'

She nudged him with her elbow. 'Come on. What truth?'

Gabriel sighed. 'About my parents. I've got their names.'

'That's wonderful! Now you can—'

'No,' Gabriel cut in. 'Not wonderful. They're fake names. The police already checked them years ago. But at least I have something. I noticed that each file in the Alumni archive has a section called "known aliases". So I'm going to start there.' Gabriel stopped on the path. Turned. 'Hold on. Were you waiting for me? That's the second time now.'

'Don't be preposterous,' Penelope said. 'I'm a very busy woman. Why would I wait for the likes of *you*?'

'Then what were you doing?'

233

'It's Sunday,' she said, as if that explained it. Which it did, sort of. Every Sunday afternoon Penelope did her HIIT and listened to whatever language she was currently learning. She had recently moved on to Korean and was already able to hold short conversations with Ji-a.

'But it's *morning*,' Gabriel said, as they stepped on to the crooked pier.

Penelope shrugged. 'I heard that it was going to rain later.'

'It's not meant to.'

Penelope cleared her throat. 'Mickey's coming.'

The skinny man paddled the gondola over and tied it to the pier. In his winter gear, he looked like a piece of uncooked spaghetti wearing a coat. 'Hang about. Is this deja boo or what? You two, waiting here for me just like last time.'

Gabriel gave Mickey a high five. He got on well with the spindly boatman these days. After dinner, in the hour after the library had closed and before lights out, Gabriel liked to wander the island, and always seemed to find himself back at the crooked pier with Mickey. He was easy company. Better yet, he had stories of the Underworld, and he loved to tell them. So Gabriel listened.

'She was hanging around in the woods for me, Mickey.' Gabriel sighed theatrically and stepped on to the gondola. 'Just couldn't *wait* until I got back.'

'He's talking rubbish, boatman,' Penelope said, following. 'And it's déjà *vu*. Not *boo*.'

'Right you are, miss,' Mickey said, unfastening them from the pier. 'But there's no shame in it. Missing someone, I mean. There's someone I miss and I'm not afraid to say it.'

Gabriel looked at Penelope and, with his eyes, pleaded, *Don't ask. Don't ask!*

'Who?' Penelope asked, not understanding. Gabriel closed his eyes and sighed.

'Tommy, of course,' Mickey said, starting to paddle. 'My uncle only went and left me here for *months*. Can you believe that? I was meant to cover him for two weeks. *Two weeks*, mind you. Now look at me. My hands are practically leather and my back's all crooked. Ferrying this gondola back and forth all day'll be the death of me. You mark my words!'

'Did you get a break for Christmas at least?' Gabriel asked.

Mickey frowned. 'Not exactly. Mainly because a certain family I know,' he nodded unsubtly at Penelope, 'like to entertain every crook and their mother at Christmas time.'

'Is that true?' Gabriel asked Penelope.

'That's Father's doing,' she said grimly. 'I hate Christmas.'

'Why?'

'Because Mum loved it.' She looked away, and with that the gondola fell into an uneasy silence.

*

By that night, Crookhaven was alive again. The excited rumble of conversation filled the air, and the school kitchen filled their stomachs.

'We found a way around it,' was the first thing Ade said to Gabriel in the common room later that night. 'Remember the school was trying to stop me and Ed calling home more than once a week?'

The demand for their mum's jollof rice had been so high in their first couple of weeks of business, that they had needed to 'place orders' with her at least twice a week. 'I remember.'

Ede elbowed his brother. 'Nah, I get to tell him. We talked about this.'

Ade sighed and made a *go on* gesture with his hands.

'So Crookhaven scrambles signals for security, yeah?' Ede began. But when he saw the blank look on Gabriel's face, he explained. 'Means that phones and most communication devices don't work on the island – that's why the only phone we can use is that ancient one. But see they don't think about other old devices – like radios. Problem is the range of most radios is—'

'Rubbish,' Ade cut in helpfully. 'But we found a way to amplify it.' He leant closer. 'Like, *a lot*.'

'How are you going to smuggle in a radio?' Gabriel asked. 'The Gardeners check all of our luggage.'

'Nah, what you mean is how *did* we smuggle one in?' Ede said. The brothers shared a sly look, then their eyes slid down to the small fin-shaped bag at their feet.

'It's *inside* Sneaks?' Gabriel whispered.

'Nah, man,' Ade said. 'It *is* Sneaks.'

CHAPTER THIRTY

It snowed the whole first week back. In just a few days, the island of Crookhaven transformed from a paradise of evergreens and moorland wildflowers into a shimmering world of white. The snow settled on the immaculate lawn and on the branches of the Crooked Oak, on the balconies of the main villa and at the edges of the lake. The lake itself froze over, which delighted Mickey – until he learned that the gondola had retractable skates, so it was work as usual.

'For a place that's meant to be top secret,' he moaned to Gabriel one evening, 'there's a hell of a lot of visitors. Reckon they're handing out those ID cards at the train station like sweets.'

In the free periods between class, students were allowed to skate on the patches close to the shore, where the ice was thickest. The Gardeners stood guard on the thinner ice farther out, just in case someone was foolish enough to venture out there.

Having grown up at the school, Penelope was a natural on the ice, and she darted around, her face caught somewhere between intense concentration and pure joy. Surprisingly, Decome was good too. In fact, he was incredible. Almost all the Legacies were. Only Villette was dreadful. If anything, she moved as if she'd never put on a pair of skates before.

But if most of the Legacies were good, Amira was something different. Otherworldly. She zipped around with a dazzling combination of speed and balance, her red and gold hijab slightly loose and rippling behind her.

Gabriel and the Brothers Crim, meanwhile, watched on from the safety of the island. They were all bad swimmers, and the prospect of plunging into the heart-stopping water was enough to keep them a metre or two away from the ice at all times.

'Look at her,' Ade said nodding towards Penelope. 'Think she'll ever come back?'

'If I could move like that,' Gabriel said, leaning against a tree, 'I'd stay out there for ever.'

'Dimitri too,' Ede said, squinting. 'How is a guy that big so fast? Nah, it's unnatural.'

They all shook their heads, lost for words at the enormous bespectacled boy's grace on the ice.

'You heard the rumour about Penelope's mum?' Ede eventually whispered.

All Gabriel knew was that Penelope never wanted to talk about her mum. 'No?'

The brothers shared a look, then Ede piped up. 'We were testing out a bug we'd rebuilt for Whisper in one of the top floor classrooms and a couple of Upper Delinquents were talking about it. Apparently, her mum was taken . . . by the Nameless.'

'What?' Gabriel whisper-shouted back. He remembered what Leon had said about Penelope. *I was here when all that stuff happened with her mum . . .*

'It's true, man,' Ade said, hushing him with his hand. 'And those USBs that Whisper keeps giving Penelope – we're guessing that's new information she's found on the disappearance. Think about it. What *else* could be on there?'

'We could help, too,' Ede said. 'So why hasn't she said a word about it to us?'

Gabriel turned towards the frozen lake again. 'She will. But like everything else Penelope Crook does, she'll do it in her own time.'

After a while, Ade changed to subject. 'Any news on Leon?'

Gabriel worked his jaw. 'Nothing yet.'

Ever since Leon had failed to show up to their Wednesday afternoon catch-up, he'd been worried. The more Gabriel thought about the last conversation they'd had, the more worried he grew. Someone had been trying to recruit Leon. A mysterious crew Leon didn't entirely trust. What if he'd refused and they'd taken him by force? Or, worse still – what if his Criminal Confidante had taken the offer from the wrong kind of crew?

Ede patted him on the shoulder cheerfully. 'He'll show up, man. Don't worry. He probably just wanted to have an extra week with his family. Wish we had stayed longer, too. Might've got another backpack of jollof out of it.'

'You're probably right,' Gabriel said, trying to put his worries from his mind.

Penelope whizzed by, pink-cheeked and grinning. 'Have you told him about Whisper?' she asked the twins. Then she was gone again.

'What about Whisper?' Gabriel asked.

'She wants to be our tutor,' Ade said, shifting his foot. 'Can you believe that?'

'I thought we weren't meant to get tutors until next year?'

Ede shrugged. 'That's what we thought too. But she asked us and there was no *way* we were turning her down. I mean, it's Whisper – the greatest hacker alive!'

The brothers went to bump fists but mistimed it horribly. After several minutes of blaming one another, Ade turned back to Gabriel. 'It makes sense though. She knows we're rubbish at every other class. Might as well get focused now. Like you.'

'You're not bad at Deception, Ade,' Gabriel tried. 'And Ede's so much better at Infiltration now.'

'Hear that?' Ede asked his brother proudly.

'Don't get excited,' Ade said cruelly. 'He said *much better*. That's like getting the "most improved" award.

Means you were spectacularly crap and now you're slightly less crap.'

That was enough. Seconds later, they were on the floor scrapping. Gabriel left them to it. He no longer tried to break the twins apart when they fought – he'd quickly learned that, because they were so clumsy, there was never any danger of them hurting each other, only other people. Their punches and kicks were wild, but always wide of the mark.

It was Penelope who finally broke them apart. Not physically – she was far too clever for that. She slid to a halt and simply said, 'Last one to their feet gets dragged on to the ice.'

Both shot to standing, suddenly uncharacteristically obedient. Mumbling something rude about Legacies, the twins backed slowly away and skulked off towards the Crookling boarding house.

'How many tokens did you get?' Gabriel asked Penelope when they were alone.

Penelope raised an eyebrow. 'You saw me?'

He shrugged. 'A couple of times.'

She frowned and looked at her skates. 'That's a couple too many. Argh!' She looked up. 'Who?'

'Only Xavier Dobbs from 1C and Mercy Tetteh from 1A,' he lied. He'd seen her pick the pockets of Natalia Garcia from 1D and Radu Vanescu from 1A too, but he knew she'd fly into a rage if he told her the whole truth.

The frosty bank crackled as she sat to take off her

skates. Then she stood and leant against the tree, so they were shoulder to shoulder. The other Crooklings glided and slid and whooped on the frozen lake, the Gardeners behind them looking rigid and cold and bored.

'What did you see *exactly*?' Penelope said. 'Don't leave anything out.'

Gabriel held out his hand. Four tokens sat in his palm.

'Hey!' Penelope said, snatching them back. 'Picking the pocket of another pickpocket's picks is bad form.'

Gabriel laughed. 'Try and say *that* three times fast.'

Being Penelope, she did. And, being Penelope, she nailed it first try. Then, 'So? What did you see?'

'I didn't actually *see* the picks themselves,' Gabriel admitted. 'But I knew when you'd picked.'

She frowned. 'How? My hand position?'

Gabriel shook his head. 'Your face.'

Her frown deepened. 'My *face*?'

'You can't hide anything. When you're about to pick a pocket, you squint with concentration. And when you've picked the pocket, you grin.'

'I grin?' She snorted. 'As if . . . I would . . . Me! . . . Just *grin*.'

'It's the reason you're rubbish at Deception.' The moment the words passed his lips, Gabriel knew he'd made a terrible mistake. You couldn't joke with Penelope Crook about being bad at anything without getting pummelled with questions.

'What do you mean *rubbish*? In what *way*? And are

243

you saying my *face* is the problem?'

'Point is,' Gabriel said, when he could finally get a word in, 'picking someone's pocket isn't *only* about picking someone's pocket. It's about getting away with it. And if you're walking around grinning afterwards, you won't.' He sighed. 'If you get caught picking a pocket here, you lose some points. But out there, you could get in serious trouble.'

'I know that.'

'No, you don't *know it* until you've actually been out there. It's a different feeling. Everything can go perfect and your face can still give you away.'

Gabriel took a breath, ready for another barrage of questions. But instead, Penelope said, 'Control my face. Fine. I will.' She stared at the tokens in her palm for a moment, then slipped them into her pocket. 'You know, overall you're only ten points behind me.' She pursed her lips and gave him a sideways look. 'Mostly thanks to those fingers of yours.'

'That's your father's fault, you know,' Gabriel admitted. 'I beat his memory game once and he never let me play again. So I decided to pick every pocket in sight.' He smiled. 'He can't stop me doing that.'

'Stop you? Do you think . . . he's not asking you on purpose? So he can avoid giving you points? That would be cheating!' Penelope cried, outraged.

Gabriel raised an eyebrow. 'What do you think he's doing sneaking around with Villette? Helping her, obviously. There's a reason she's only fifteen points behind you right now, even with her twenty-point punishment. She's good, but she's not *that* good.'

'Why wouldn't Father come to me if he wanted to make sure a Legacy won?'

Gabriel laughed. 'You're a lot of things, Penelope Crook, but you're not a cheat. Your father knows that. But nothing is off limits to Villette. Remember that time in History of Crookery – she was talking about joining the Nameless? And just look what she did to Amira in Crimnastics. She'd do anything to win. And your father must be helping her. Why else would they be whispering together?'

Penelope furrowed her brow and looked towards the far bank. 'If Father and Villette really are cheating, I'll stop them.'

Gabriel nodded towards the tokens now sitting in Penelope's pocket. 'Even with the cheating, she's behind both of us.'

She clenched her jaw. 'Would it be cheating to break a finger or two on your right hand though? Because that's the kind of cheating I'd be just fine with.'

Gabriel laughed. 'It's not just me gaining on you. The twins are too. They've won every one of Whisper's challenges. And Palombo loves Ji-a—'

'*Anyway*,' Penelope cut in. Bringing up Ji-a – Penelope's biggest rival in Forgery class – was the fastest way to get interrupted these days. 'Come on. It's freezing.' She grabbed Gabriel by the wrist and dragged him back towards the Crookling houses.

'Leon told me there was no point in even looking at the overall points until after the Break-in,' Gabriel said, not ready to change the subject of points yet.

'He's right. It's worth fifty points, remember – that could change everything.' They ducked beneath a low branch and emerged on to the lawn. Footprints snaked through the thin dusting of snow, heading this way and that. 'Did you know that the Lower Delinquents and Upper Delinquents have their Break-ins in nearby cities? I can't *wait* for that. But everyone else has it here.'

'Even the Robins?'

Penelope smiled. 'They have the hardest Break-in of all – breaking into the grounds of Crookhaven itself. Only one person has ever succeeded.' Her smile widened. 'My mum.'

'She broke *into* Crookhaven? How?'

Penelope shrugged. 'Even Father doesn't know. She never told him.'

'I'm guessing you want to do it yourself one day?'

'I *will* do it myself. But first I need to win this year's Break-in.'

'Look at you,' Gabriel said. 'You'll be Marianna Sonorov in no time.'

'Better. Obviously. And, unlike Marianna, I would *never* leave Crookhaven before graduating.'

Gabriel stopped dead, Penelope's fingers sliding off his

wrist. 'She did what?'

Penelope turned. 'Didn't you hear? She left for Christmas and never came back.'

CHAPTER
THIRTY-ONE

Three Crooklings were caught trying to break into the co-Headmasters' office on the first night of the Break-in's heist phase – two Merits and one Legacy. Four more were caught on the second night. Gabriel liked to think that by the third night the Crooklings had wised up, and that was the reason no-one else was caught for the rest of the week. But the truth was far simpler – it snowed relentlessly every night. So even the Penelopes of the world, who were hell-bent on breaking in first, were forced to wait until conditions improved.

Gabriel didn't plan on breaking in any time soon. Instead, for those first two nights he merely sat high in a tree and watched as Crookling after Crookling was caught. He saw the first two get collared by the Gardeners before they'd even made it into the clearing. The third evaded them well enough but triggered a motion sensor five metres from the front door. The second night was an exact repeat of the first – two captured by the Gardeners, two triggered the motion sensor.

Every now and then Gabriel would hear a rustling above and glance up in hopes of seeing the tell-tale colourful flash of Amira. But it was never her.

The blizzard soon put a stop to his scouting missions. Instead he spent two hours after dinner every night in the warm, and often deserted, alumni section of the library. It was impossible for him to forget anything at the best of times, but the fake names of his parents were seared especially deep into his brain. *Federico Guerrero and Isabella Cortes.* He saw them when he closed his eyes to try and sleep, and when he zoned out in History of Crookery or Forgery. Sometimes he'd even find himself conjuring a face to go with each name. An olive-skinned face with amber eyes and wavy brown hair for his father. And the same, only with longer hair and green eyes, for his mother. These daydreams were often interrupted by the pale, red-haired librarian who popped by each night – sometimes with a drink (which of course he had to drink outside the alumni section), sometimes with a snack (ditto) and sometimes just with a smile.

'Are you this dedicated in your other subjects?' she had asked one night, to which he had to admit that he was not. 'And you're really not going to stop until you find these people?'

'No,' Gabriel had answered, fighting a yawn.

'Thought not,' she had said with a sigh. She'd

disappeared and returned a moment later with a smaller, comfier looking beanbag than the ones dotted around in the main library. 'Then you'd better have something decent to sit on, hadn't you? I pinched this from the teachers' section – yes, there *is* a teachers' section of the library and that's all I'm permitted to say on pain of excruciating death, so don't ask anything else – and I thought you might prefer this to the student beanbags.'

Gabriel had taken it from her gratefully and sat on it. He had looked up, mouth ajar. 'It's like sitting on a cloud. Thank you . . .' But he'd stopped, suddenly embarrassed that he didn't know her name.

The librarian had laughed. 'Marie-Elise. Most of the Robins don't even know my name. To them, I am Miss or "the librarian", so I am seriously impressed that a Crookling like you now does.'

Gabriel had smiled. 'Thanks, Marie-Elise.'

'Shall I hide this beanbag away somewhere that only you and I can find? That way you can go and get it whenever you're in here.'

They had decided to hide it inside one of the much larger three-person beanbags in the farthest corner of the main library. The three-person beanbag was old and stained and only half filled with pellets now. Besides, Gabriel had never seen any students using it, so it was the perfect place.

After that, every time Gabriel went to the library, he'd share a knowing look with Marie-Elise, slink over to their hiding spot, free his contraband beanbag and disappear into the alumni section.

Now that Gabriel was only looking in the 'known aliases' section of each alumni folder, his search had quickened, and he breezed past E and F. When he needed a break, he would go out into the main library, slum it on a student beanbag and watch the snowflakes twist and dance and settle on the branches of the Crooked Oak.

Ade and Ede never followed him to the library; they were too preoccupied with trying to tune Sneaks to the right frequency to call home. But with the terrible weather, and Crookhaven's non-existent signal, they were struggling.

Penelope visited him some nights, but only to say, 'Are you really just going to *let* me win the Break-in?' Then she'd sigh theatrically and say something along the lines of, 'I really thought you were going to be my toughest competition, Avery. Clearly not.'

At the end of each night, Marie-Elise would walk him to the door and ask him how his search had gone. Each night he'd have the same answer for her. 'Nothing yet. See you tomorrow.'

By the middle of the following week, Leon and Marianna still hadn't shown up. When Gabriel asked Caspian whether he knew what had happened, all he got was, 'Not yet, I'm afraid. But don't you go worrying about it, all right? I've got the entire alumni network on the case. Not even Tier One crooks can escape the beady eyes

251

of the Underworld.'

Even so, Gabriel couldn't help thinking that something was very, very wrong.

CHAPTER THIRTY-TWO

The second week into the heist phase of the Break-in, the snow melted and Crooklings again started to try and claim the points for themselves. Four more Crooklings – including Lulu and Dmitri – were eliminated that week. And Gabriel watched it all happen.

Them being eliminated meant the numbers were dwindling, which meant less competition. But Gabriel was far more interested in *how* they were eliminated.

Lulu, clever as she was, managed to bypass the Gardeners and the motion sensors, but set off pressure plates below the window on the east side – Gabriel knew something had been hidden under the uneven grass and this confirmed it.

Dmitri, on the other hand, tried something entirely new. Despite his size, he was quicker and stealthier than everyone in 1B – besides Amira and Penelope of course. He used that agility to climb a nearby tree and shimmy along a thick branch that stretched out into the clearing, its tip hanging over the office. Once at the end, he dropped and landed soundlessly on the edge of the roof. He looked from side to side and, seeing no one, tiptoed towards the chimney. Cautiously, he peered down it, and lowered a hand in. Then pulled it back sharply.

Fire's out, Gabriel thought, *but the bricks are still hot. What are you going to do now?*

Dmitri paused, clearly thinking. Then he moved cautiously to the edge of the roof. Just then, the crow Gabriel had seen lurking in the clearing landed on the chimney. Dmitri froze.

The crow stared at him, then tilted its head as if curious. It opened its mouth and suddenly released a deafening shriek. Within seconds, Gardeners spilled out of the trees and Dmitri was eliminated.

When Gabriel recounted the story to Ade and Ede in History of Crookery the next morning, the twins gawped at each other. 'Rah,' Ade said. 'Whisper is next level sick. She made a *crow-camera*?'

'I know,' Gabriel said, more troubled than impressed. 'Dmitri was barely up on the roof for one minute and the crow-camera caught him. So it's got to all be done quicker than that.'

'You think both crow eyes are cameras or just one?' Ede asked his brother.

'Both,' Ade answered. 'And I bet they can see 360.'

Gabriel thought for a minute. 'Does Sneaks have an

in-built Electromagnetic Pulse? It only needs to have a small range. A metre or so.' A plan was slowly taking form in his mind.

'Oooohhh,' they said in chorus now that he was talking their language. Ade said, 'Look at you, Gabe. Learning and stuff.'

''Course Sneaks has an EMP,' Ede chimed in. 'You think we're amateurs? And it's a *two-metre* pulse.'

'Mr Avery,' Miss Jericho called from the front of the class. 'If you are talking, I assume that means you will have no trouble telling me what infamous event occurred on September 16th 1987 in Korea, and what, if anything, crooks can learn from it.'

Gabriel winced. *On 16th September 1987, three crooks successfully robbed the K International bank in Seoul, Korea. They did it in broad daylight, with hundreds of people walking by, and no one noticed a thing because they struck at sunrise, when there was maximum glare on the glass separating the bank and the street. Nobody could see in, so nobody could see that a heist was underway.*

'Sorry, miss,' Gabriel said instead. 'I don't know.' He wasn't about to reveal his abnormal memory just to make himself look clever. He'd already made that mistake with Caspian. He'd earned some points in the moment, but he'd cost himself so many more in the long run, because Caspian had never picked Gabriel since.

Miss Jericho clenched her jaw. 'Then might I suggest you *pay attention.*'

At the end of class, Miss Jericho stopped Gabriel, Ade and Ede at the door. 'Would any of you care to tell me what was so pressing that you had to discuss it inside my classroom?'

'Sorry, miss,' Ade tried. 'We didn't mean—'

She crossed her arms in such a ferocious manner that Ade choked on his words. Gabriel could see an apology wasn't going to be enough. So he told her the truth.

'We were talking about the Break-in, miss,' Gabriel said, drawing startled stares from the brothers.

Miss Jericho's arms relaxed. 'Is that so.' It was a school-wide competition, so she couldn't exactly get mad. 'Merits sharing information. How very . . . cooperative.'

Miss Jericho was not shy about showing her favouritism towards the Legacies. Choosing to teach History of Crookery, a subject in which all ten of the top students in the year were Legacies, showed as much.

'Did you win a Break-in, miss?' Ede asked in that ever-curious way of his.

She let out an unpleasant laugh. 'Certainly not. In my five years here, I never once attempted it.'

Ede looked stunned. 'But . . . why not?'

'Hm, yes, I see the problem. You all reek of proactivity,' she said with a sigh. 'Well we, the reactive, salute you. But we also kindly ask you to do your proacting as far away from us as possible. History is to be made or to be studied, and *I'd* much rather study, thank you very much.'

And with that, she was gone.

'Is it me,' Ade said when they were back in the Crookling common room, 'or is Miss Jericho—'

'*Matilda*,' Ede cut in, imitating Penelope's accent.

'Right,' Ade said. 'Is it me or is Tilly one crisp short of a packet?'

Gabriel was sitting on the windowsill, looking up at the thickening clouds above. 'Any chance you have some jollof rice left?'

Ade and Ede looked at one another, then at Gabriel. 'We've got four. Why? You run out of leftovers in those cans?'

Gabriel sighed. 'Decome found them yesterday and threw them away. He did it because he thinks I'm the one who stole the mini-fridge his mum got him for Christmas.' Gabriel narrowed his eyes at the twins. 'It's a good thing for you two that he's not got anything between the ears, isn't it? Or he might have worked out that you need to store your jollof somewhere that isn't our common room fridge.'

The twins stood up, enraged. 'He stole *all* of your cans?' Ede said, bug-eyed.

'Nah, none of his crew are *ever* getting jollof off us again!' Ade added.

'Hold on,' Ede whispered to his brother. 'Those lot buy the most.'

Ade considered this carefully. 'None of his crew can get jollof off us for the next *week*! That's how much we care about you, Gabe.'

Ede gave his brother a nod of agreement and then turned to Gabriel, suddenly all business. 'We got chicken and we got extra spicy left. What you thinkin'?'

'Chicken,' Gabriel said, sitting down across from them.

Ede got up and went upstairs to the cleaning supply closet where they'd hidden the stolen mini-fridge. Ade, meanwhile, leaned forward and gave Gabriel a smile. 'We got you. That'll be three pounds, please.'

Gabriel frowned. 'It was two pounds two days ago.'

Ade nodded. 'Two days ago, we had eight servings left. Now we've got four. Price has gone up.'

'Even for me?'

Ede reappeared and put the container in the microwave. 'We don't do special treatment, Gabe. We're businessmen.'

'You're criminals.' Gabriel reached into his pocket for change. 'Good ones. I'll have to borrow some money from Penelope then.'

The microwave pinged and Ede brought over a steaming bowl. 'That's the nicest thing anyone's ever said to us, isn't it, Ad?' The brothers shared a look and fell about laughing.

Gabriel took a bite. The warmth and spice soon made him forget about the cold outside. 'When is the next batch coming in from your mum? Have you managed to contact her with Sneaks yet?'

The brothers fell silent. This time, the look they shared was something altogether different. Wary. 'Actually, Gabe, we wanted to talk to you about that,' Ade said.

Gabriel stopped eating. 'Huh?'

Ede bit his lip. 'When we were trying to tune Sneaks to our private frequency during the snowstorm, we . . . heard something.'

Gabriel put down his fork. 'Heard something? What?'

'We were recording in case our mum made us any promises over the phone and backed out later. She does that a lot. Ed'll tell you. Anyway, it means we recorded all of it,' Ade said, digging into his pocket and pulling out a voice recorder. Gabriel had seen the twins pull it out countless times over the last few months, usually when a new – and always terrible – business idea came up and they wanted to make sure they didn't forget it.

Ade placed it on the table between them and pressed play.

The audio crackled and warped, then two voices came through, low and urgent. A woman's voice and a man's, it sounded like.

Woman: How's it going in there?

Man: The routine is killing me. Every day is the same.

Woman: Not long now though. We'll be back together soon.

Man: That's all that's getting me through. How's it with you?

Woman: Don't worry about me. I'm back home. It's you I'm worried about, stuck in there with them.

Man: There's someone coming. I've got to go.

Woman: Remember, this is how we make them pay. We take *everything* from them.

Man: One piece at a time.

The recording ended and there was only silence. Eventually, Ade leant forward. 'What do you reckon, Gabe?'

'That man,' Gabriel said, stunned. 'It almost sounds like—'

The twins shared a look. 'Yeah, we know,' Ede said. 'Mr Velasquez.'

CHAPTER
THIRTY-THREE

For the rest of the week, Gabriel couldn't concentrate in Tricks of the Trade class. Instead he watched Mr Velasquez carefully. Was his favourite teacher really up to something?

Gabriel played the conversation over in his mind.

Woman: Remember, this is how we make them pay. We take everything from them.

Man: One piece at a time.

This is how we make them pay. Gabriel thought about the mysterious disappearances that term – Leon and Marianna. Were Mr Velasquez and this woman involved? Were they taking the most talented Robins from Crookhaven as part of some sort of revenge?

Gabriel thought about telling Caspian, but that would mean Ade and Ede would get in serious trouble. The only kind of communication allowed in and out of Crookhaven was the secure landline. So them trying to tune Sneaks to communicate with their mum about *rice . . .*

it could even get them expelled.

The worst part was that the three of them had realised they couldn't tell Penelope. Not because the Headmaster was her dad, but because Ade and Ede had broken a rule. And there was no one alive who hated rule-breaking more than Penelope Crook. A particularly strange trait for a girl who planned to be the greatest crook ever to live.

*

Late on Sunday, after spending the afternoon rifling through the alumni files G and H, Gabriel snuck out into the freezing night. Only two more Crooklings had been caught attempting to break into the office of the co-Headmasters that week – both from 1A, and both were nabbed by the Gardeners before they'd ever got close.

Gabriel zigzagged his way through the trees, past the patrolling Gardeners, and clambered up into his new look-out spot. The tree wasn't the tallest or easiest to climb, but the foliage halfway up was thick enough to cover him and it had a direct view of the clearing.

Two hours ticked by without any sign of a Crookling. So when a figure landed softly on a branch beside him, Gabriel started and jerked sideways. A hand reached out and grabbed his sleeve, saving him from tumbling to the forest floor.

'Sorry,' a familiar voice said. Amira stared back at him, green eyes glittering in the darkness.

Gabriel let out a breath. 'I didn't hear you up there.'

Amira smiled and shrugged as if to say, *well obviously*.

'Are you here to watch?' Gabriel nodded towards the clearing, the office still and dark and impenetrable at its centre.

'No,' she said, lowering herself to sitting, her dark purple hijab wrapped especially tight. 'The night-time . . . I like it. So quiet.'

'Aren't you going to try to break in?'

Amira looked off towards the clearing. 'No. No one will want me to win.'

Gabriel hesitated. *Should he ask?* 'Because of your brother?'

Amira nodded slowly. 'And other reasons.' She absentmindedly ran a hand along the bottom edge of her hijab.

'It doesn't matter what *they* want,' Gabriel said. 'Do *you* want to win?'

Amira shrugged.

Then a thought struck Gabriel. It was something Leon had said the last time they'd met.

Alone you can become exceptional; together you can become unstoppable.

'What if we work together?' Gabriel said.

Amira blinked. 'Me and . . . you?'

Gabriel smiled. 'Why not?'

'I'm Legacy . . . you Merit,' Amira said. 'Plus Break-in meant to be . . . alone.'

'I know,' Gabriel said, leaning forwards, suddenly excited. 'But I don't think there are any rules against it. Not really. What do you reckon? Think we can work together?'

Amira peered into the clearing. When she looked back, she was smiling too. 'Yes.'

'Perfect,' Gabriel said. 'Now we just need to get a few more people on board . . .'

*

Ade held up a hand. 'I'm going to stop you there, Gabe. Our answer is yes.'

The three of them were sitting at the back of Infiltration class, a particularly tricky window lock on the desk in front of them. Gabriel had barely been five seconds into his explanation as to why they should team up together for the heist, when the twins cut him off. He hadn't even launched into the bit about how wolves changed their howls.

'Really? That easy?'

Ede gave his brother a knowing look. 'Listen, man. At anything tech, we're like Mozart when it comes to composing—'

'—Tupac when it comes to rap—' Ade chimed in.

'—and Penelope when it comes to talking like a forty-year-old,' Ede finished. 'We're the best. But at everything else, we're pretty hopeless.'

'So teaming up with you and Amira,' Ade continued.

'Mr Pick-Your-Pocket and the Blur herself! Rah, we're *in*.'

Gabriel paused. 'Even if . . . I ask Penelope?'

The twins recoiled. 'Woah, one Legacy is enough, man,' Ede said.

'And you just *know* she'll try and take over,' Ade added, kissing his teeth.

'But she's the best crook in 1B,' Gabriel tried. 'Best in the whole *year*, actually, and you both know it. We could do with her help.'

'She's also the best at being *the worst*,' Ede added, unhelpfully.

'Doesn't matter anyway,' Ade said, absently fiddling with the lock on his desk. 'She'll never agree to join our crew. Wants to do it all alone, doesn't she?'

They were probably right. 'But *if* I can convince her . . .' Gabriel didn't need to finish the question.

Ade crossed his arms, and as he did it, Ede uncrossed his. 'Convince her first,' Ade said.

Ede nodded. 'Then we'll talk.'

*

Penelope held up a hand to cut Gabriel off. '*Non. Não. No. Nyet. Ani.* I can keep going if that's not already crystal clear.'

It was lunchtime and Penelope was prowling around outside her father's office, eyes flickering from roof to door to window. Gabriel almost had to run to keep up.

265

'There's no rules against it,' Gabriel tried. 'It's not cheating.'

'That's not the point,' Penelope fired back. 'I don't want or need anyone else's help.'

'I know. But *we* need your help.'

Penelope's steps slowed, faltered. Then she sped up. 'Well, you can't have it.'

'I've got Amira and the twins on board already,' Gabriel pushed on.

Penelope let out a sharp laugh. 'A crew? How preposterous.'

'Not if we manage to break in.'

'You won't get the chance. I'll be finished with this long before your little crew ever gets a sniff.'

'Penelope.' Gabriel stopped following her. 'If you do this alone, you'll get caught.'

Penelope froze mid-stride. Slowly, she turned. 'What did you say?'

'I've been watching Crooklings get caught for weeks and I was out here checking out the security features of the office for months before that. No one has even managed to get *inside* yet. Alone, this is impossible.'

'For you maybe,' Penelope snapped, her body coiled, her thick eyebrows low over her dark eyes. 'But there are things I know about my father and the way he thinks—'

'I know he has a perfect memory,' Gabriel admitted. 'So even if someone makes it in, he'll be able to tell what's been stolen.'

Penelope's eyes narrowed. 'How do you know that?'

'I worked it out.' Gabriel said nothing more.

Penelope shook her head. 'It doesn't matter. I'll think of a way around that.'

'We can come up with something together—'

'No!' Penelope shouted. 'I need to *show him*, Gabriel. I need to do this all on my own. Otherwise . . .' She clenched her fists. When she looked up, there were tears in her eyes. 'If I can't even do *this*, what hope do I have of finding her?'

'Penelope . . .'

But she had already turned and run from the clearing.

CHAPTER
THIRTY-FOUR

Penelope didn't speak to Gabriel for a full week. Gabriel had a feeling that it wasn't out of anger but out of embarrassment. Penelope Crook, the girl who no doubt would one day become the greatest living crook, had cried in front of him.

Gabriel tried to talk to her, to tell her that he was sorry. In Crimnastics and Deception and even Forgery. But she would change seats or immediately start a conversation with the person on the other side. And Gabriel would fall silent, defeated.

His new crew had begun to plan their Break-in, but they needed a fifth member for their plan to work. Ji-a was another option, but Gabriel couldn't bring himself to ask her just yet. She was talented and she would probably say yes, but Oh Ji-a was not Penelope Crook.

Three more Crooklings were caught attempting to break in that week, including Dorian MacArthur of 1B. The flame-haired boy had gotten closest too. Dorian, like Villette, was a bit of an oddity in that he was a Legacy who'd been recruited to Crookhaven for Infiltration. But where Villette could pick just about any lock, Dorian used tech.

In this case, he'd stolen a laser and a suction glove from Tech-nique and cut a boy-sized hole in the western window. He'd eased himself through and landed softly inside – the first Crookling to do so. But Dorian made one fatal mistake – he had forgotten that his suction glove still held the circular slab of glass. When he disengaged the suction, the glass pane fell and smashed, the pieces skittering across the office floor and triggering the motion sensors that had been pointed at the western window, eastern window and door. The Gardeners had descended on him in seconds.

Dorian had got close, and Gabriel felt sorry for him. Just not *that* sorry.

Gabriel had learned key pieces of information from all the recent Crookling Break-in failures, but he had learned one particularly important thing from Dmitri's.

There was no motion sensor watching the chimney.

*

It was ten minutes before the library closed and the words in the alumni files were blurring together. Gabriel closed Freddie Lonergan's file and yawned. He slipped it back on to the bookshelf and took out the next one.

Marie-Elise poked her head through the door from the main library. 'Thought I heard you in here. It's a Sunday night, Gabriel. Haven't you got anything better to do than sift through those dull old files?'

'No,' Gabriel said honestly. He hadn't used his voice in hours and it came out as a croak.

The librarian's eyes flickered towards the bookshelf beside him. 'Look at the mess you've made.' She sighed and closed the door behind her. 'You're usually pretty good at keeping things tidy. Is there something wrong?' She came across to the bookshelf and began straightening the files.

'Tired,' he admitted. The hours in the library and the all-nighters he'd been pulling to scout the office clearing were beginning to catch up with him. As he turned the pages, his usually nimble fingers felt clumsy and—

Gabriel sat bolt upright, a name leaping out at him. 'Federico Guerrero!'

The librarian dropped the file she'd been holding and whirled around. 'Look what you made me do now.' There was a strange wildness, even anger, in her eyes. But it melted away and left behind only kindness. 'I'm sorry, Gabriel. You startled me . . .'

'Sorry,' Gabriel said, suddenly wide awake. 'But I . . . I think I've found . . .' His heart thundered. Yes, there it was under Known Aliases: *Federico Guerrero*. No photo. Gabriel flipped the file over and read the name on the top left-hand corner.

'Luciano Lopes,' he said aloud.

Is that . . . my father's real name?

Gabriel read the file back to front, memorising every word. Then he stood and slid it back into the bookcase. 'Sorry, I've got to go.'

He needed to tell someone. No, not *someone*. Penelope. He needed to tell Penelope.

Gabriel swept out of the room, ran through the now-empty library and bounded down the stairs. He fizzed with energy. When he reached the bottom floor, he was breathless and panting.

What time is it? Where would she be right now? Who on earth would know?

Gabriel burst into the Crookling common room, a sweaty mess. Everyone looked up from their books or games or conversations. For a moment, there was no sound but the soft crackling of the fire in the fireplace. Then, 'Shouldn't you be up a tree somewhere, Avery? It's about that time.'

It was Decome, the flickering firelight causing his already sharp features to further sharpen.

Gabriel ignored him, eyes sweeping the rest of the common room.

Amira was nestled in a nook by the window, a book sitting in her lap. Gabriel rushed over and knelt down beside her. 'Amira, have you seen Penelope? It's urgent.'

Amira furrowed her brow. 'Thought she said—'

'It's about something different.'

Amira looked out of the door. 'She leave . . . ten minutes ago.'

'Wher—' He cut himself off mid-word. Of course. Where else would Penelope be at this hour?

Gabriel thanked Amira, then ducked out of the room and into the treeline. He supposed it was cold outside – the puffs of breath spilling out of him as he ran told him that – but he didn't feel it; only white-hot anger coursed through him.

Why now? Gabriel thought, as he ducked a low branch. *Why is she trying to break in now?*

Gabriel reached the edge of the clearing just as a figure clad in all black edged away from the safety of the treeline and into the clearing. By the way she moved – purposeful yet graceful – he knew it was Penelope Crook.

I'm too late.

Gabriel watched, powerless, as Penelope navigated her way past the pressure plates and motion sensors. Like Gabriel, she'd obviously watched the other Crooklings fail. So she knew the only route that would get her to the wooden building safely. Once there, she pressed her back to it. Gabriel could see her release a long breath. Then she turned to the eastern window lock, examining it.

Don't go in there, there's motion sensors just inside!

She peered through the window then jerked away, her back to the wall again.

Good; she's noticed them. Gabriel watched Penelope thinking, thinking, thinking. She looked up. *Yes, to the roof*. Gabriel blinked. Was he really rooting for her?

Her eyes swept along the lip of the roof, looking for a good handhold.

Something small and black and not altogether alive fluttered into the clearing. The crow-camera landed soundlessly on the roof. It pulled its wings in and glanced around.

Penelope seemed to have settled on a route up to the roof. She reached up for her first handhold.

If she pulls herself on to that roof, it's over. Gabriel took a step forward. Then he remembered what Caspian Crook had said on that first day.

Repeated failure humbles even the most brash. So let her fail.

Penelope had wanted this – to go it alone, prove herself to her father. Gabriel had warned her it wasn't possible alone. Not even for her. But she'd ignored him. Like always. He should let her fail, and he should win the Break-in with Ade, Ede and Amira.

That was what he *should* do.

Before Penelope could haul herself up the wall, Gabriel was there, hand across her mouth and finger up to his own lips. She froze in place, eyes wide. Gabriel jerked his head toward the roof and slowly eased them both closer to the wall. He removed his hand from Penelope's mouth then leant down and picked up a pebble.

Gabriel pointed back towards where they'd come, where hidden pressure plates and motion sensors lay waiting, and whispered, 'Can you get us back?'

Penelope nodded.

Gabriel looked up, waited for a moment, then tossed the pebble in the opposite direction. It struck a tree and the pop it made echoed around the clearing. A small black figure took off from the roof and swooped into the treeline.

Gabriel and Penelope shared a look, then ran. They leapt over pressure plates and swerved around motion sensors so fast that Gabriel lost track of his own feet. The treeline swallowed them, but they didn't stop running until they were back at the boarding houses.

Penelope turned around, seething. 'I didn't need to be *saved*.'

'I know,' Gabriel said, relaxing against the wall. 'That's not why I came.'

Penelope uncoiled slightly. 'Then . . . why did you come?'

'I wanted to tell you something.' Gabriel smiled. 'I think I've found my father.'

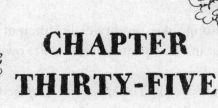

CHAPTER
THIRTY-FIVE

Spring arrived without warning. By the end of the week, wildflowers had bloomed in the woods surrounding Crookhaven and erupted at the base of the trees and along the banks of the lake, filling the air with an intoxicatingly sweet scent that brought some to life and others to their knees.

'Nah,' Ade said, stumbling through the woods, eyes red and swollen. 'Hayfever is no joke. Ed, you good?'

Ede was half a metre behind, eyes tightly shut and hands out in front. 'Can't see a thing, man.' He looked around. 'Gabe. Gabe!'

'I'm right here,' Gabriel said, grabbing his wrist and pointing him in the right direction.

'I think the plan's going to have to wait,' Ede said. 'At least until we can *see* again.'

'We're not ready yet anyway,' Gabriel admitted. 'We need—'

'It's been a week,' Ade said, fending off a tree that had

dared to block his path. 'She doesn't want to join us. Simple.'

'I still think—'

'She said no in, like, seventy-eight different languages, Gabe,' Ede cut in. 'She wants to win on her own. Let's just ask Ji-a instead.'

Ade shook his head. 'You saved her from getting caught and she *still* won't join us. So let's give up on her. Ji-a's perfect for this anyway.'

Gabriel sighed. They were probably right. It had been over a week since the night he'd saved Penelope and she'd barely said a word to him since. When she had, it was always about his father and what Gabriel was planning to do to next to find him. Never about the Break-in. Whenever the Break-in was brought up by people they were with, she would smile and nod along, but offer nothing. It was as if she'd wiped every trace of what had happened that night from her memory.

What a beautiful thing it must be to be able to forget, Gabriel thought, as they trudged the last few steps over to Mr Sisman and their miniature gardens.

The flamboyant teacher's lilac hair was tied into a loose ponytail today, his fingernails painted a uniform maroon to match his robe. 'Right, my dears! Today is a very important day. Spring is upon us, and, as the great writer Leo Tolstoy once said, *"In the spring, at the end of the day, you should smell like dirt"*. Gardening is the—'

'Actually, sir,' Penelope cut in, 'it was Margaret Atwood

who said that. Tolstoy said, *"Spring is the time of plans and projects"*.' Penelope pointedly avoided Gabriel's gaze.

Plans and projects. Hmm.

'Yes, well, smart fellow, Tolstoy. Are we sure he didn't say both?' Before Penelope could reply, Mr Sisman carried on. 'You have all done a wonderful job nurturing your gardens through what has been a very challenging winter. Some gardens have fared better; some worse.' Mr Sisman's eyes slid to Ade and Ede's patch, which was now little more than a graveyard of flowers. It could have been because the flowers they had planted weren't hardy enough and so were ravaged by frost and snow. Or, more likely, that they had been neglected to death.

'What you have before you now,' Mr Sisman continued, 'is a direct reflection of the care and effort you have put in. You should be very proud of yourselves.'

Villette twirled a trowel in her hand. 'So, who won, sir?'

Mr Sisman's eyebrows rose. 'Who won? My dear, there are no winners and losers in gardening.'

Penelope, too, looked pained by this. 'But . . . but whose garden is your favourite?'

Mr Sisman laughed his cartoonish laugh. 'My own, of course. Your garden, if you tend it well, is a reflection of your personality. So how could mine not be my favourite?'

'So *this*,' Villette said, gesturing with her trowel, 'was all for nothing?'

'For *nothing*?' Mr Sisman said, outraged. 'My dear,

you have created a self-portrait of yourself in flora form. It has taken incredible patience and discipline!'

It was true that each garden resembled its gardener. Gabriel hadn't noticed it before, but now it was perfectly clear. Villette's was wild and bright, with wildflowers and weeds growing beside bluebells and poppies. Penelope's was filled with flowers like roses and daisies, all perfectly pruned and organised into neat clusters by colour. Fittingly, most of the flowers that grew in her garden had thorns or spiky leaves.

Amira had chosen small, brightly coloured flowers, but had only planted in the middle of her patch, leaving thirty centimetres of soil between her and her neighbour. A few of her flowers were producing seeds, which were caught by the wind and thrown skyward.

Decome's was made up of the most showy but utterly impractical flora, all of which were not used to a moorland climate and so had been finished off by the bitter weather that winter. The few flowers that remained were organised in three neat, but pitiful, rows. It wasn't fair to judge the twins' gardens because, well, everything was dead.

'So we really have just been *gardening* this whole time,' Villette said. 'How exactly is this going to help us become better crooks?'

Mr Sisman blinked. 'Isn't it obvious?' He looked around and saw from the collective bafflement that it was not, in fact, obvious in the least. 'Well, *today* it is watering, feeding and pruning. But *tomorrow* it will be researching, planning and preparing. All good crooks value patience and discipline above all else. As the well-known saying goes, "Impatient crooks are often known by another name – inmates".'

Villette crossed her arms but fell silent.

'However, if I was to choose a favourite other than my own . . .' Mr Sisman began. Penelope immediately perked up. 'It would be the garden of someone who surprised me. For an old duffer like me, that is a rarity. Gabriel Avery, please come join me beside your garden.'

Gabriel blinked. 'Me, sir?'

'Yes, yes. There's no need to be nervous. Come on over.'

So Gabriel did. Penelope's face darkened like a thundercloud.

Mr Sisman placed a hand on Gabriel's shoulder. When he spoke, Gabriel caught a whiff of Skittles. 'Everyone else in your class chose to plant flowers. Yet you planted vegetables. Why is that?'

'Because that's what my grandma's always done,' Gabriel explained. When he looked up, Mr Sisman and 1B were quiet, wanting more. 'Wherever we went, Grandma would always plant vegetables. Sometimes in the garden, if we had one, sometimes in a pot on the windowsill.' *Just in case we ever went hungry*, was what Grandma would say. But Gabriel wasn't going to tell the class that part. 'Then we'd cook them.'

Mr Sisman smiled then, and, with great difficulty, bent

down and dug into Gabriel's patch. He pulled out a tiny carrot and held it up to the class. 'Look! Isn't it wonderful?' He stared at it, enraptured. 'Flowers are beautiful, certainly. But they don't hold a candle to vegetables. Why? Well because if you are going to put months or years into nourishing a garden, make sure it will nourish you in return.' He blinked, the spell broken. 'It is exactly the same in your criminal pursuits. Patience and discipline are for nought if you ultimately obtain nothing.' He took Gabriel's hand and placed the tiny carrot in it. 'It may not seem much, Mr Avery. I dare say you could eat it all in one bite.' Mr Sisman gestured to the rest of 1B. 'But that is still one bite more than anyone else will have tonight.'

*

'Go on,' Ade said, elbowing Gabriel in the ribs as they walked back through the woods to the gondola. 'Ji-a's right there! Ask her.'

Ji-a was just in front, walking alongside Lulu and Dorian but looking decidedly uncomfortable. Everyone knew Lulu and Dorian liked each other, but rather than admit that they preferred to walk beside one another in silence. Some of 1B thought it sweet, most thought it weird.

The majority, of course, were right. It *was* weird.

'You'll be doing her a favour,' Ede said, watching Lulu and Dorian with his face crinkled in pain. 'Getting her away from those two. Are we going to have five years of this? Of *them*?'

'Probably,' Gabriel said. 'Can't break up if they never actually talk to each other.'

The twins laughed. Then went wide-eyed. 'Oi, she's dropping back,' Ade said.

'She couldn't stand it any more,' Ede added. 'I don't blame her. Go on!'

They nudged him forwards. Gabriel swallowed and stepped closer. 'Ji-a?'

She turned and saw him. 'Mm?'

'Can I ask you something?'

She slowed to his pace. 'Is it about them? Because I didn't hear anything.' She paused. 'Actually, there's nothing *to* hear.' She shot him her semi-dimpled grin.

'No,' Gabriel said, with a chuckle. 'It's not about them.' He lowered his voice. 'It's about the Break-in.'

Ji-a furrowed her dark brows. 'The Break-in?'

Gabriel nodded. 'I wanted to ask—'

A person slid in between them. 'What are we talking about then?' Penelope said.

'Gabriel was just about to ask me a question—'

'Was he really?' Penelope cut in. 'Well if it's the question I think it is, then he already asked me and I said yes, so I don't think he'll be needing you. No offence.' But by the look in her eye, she actually meant, *Yes, offence, and a lot of it*.

'You said . . . yes?' Gabriel asked, as Ji-a looked on, confused.

'Only after a great deal of hounding on your part and thought on mine.' Penelope tilted her head and grinned. 'But yes, eventually I agreed.'

CHAPTER THIRTY-SIX

'**N**ah, not going to happen,' Ade said flatly.

It was after dinner and Gabriel, Ade, Ede, Penelope and Amira were standing in a tight circle beside the office clearing. 'You said no – in about twenty different languages!'

'I . . . I had a change of heart,' Penelope said.

Ede kissed his teeth. 'You heard we were going to ask Ji-a instead. That's what happened. Simple.'

'That's not true,' Penelope snapped.

It's a little true, Gabriel thought. But instead he turned to Penelope and asked, 'Then why?'

She looked at the office bathed in the fading sunlight. 'All I've done for the last week is watch this place. Watch Crookling after Crookling fail.' She glanced at Gabriel. 'You were right. It's impossible to break in alone. But together . . .'

Gabriel nodded. 'I think we can.'

Penelope inflated. 'So how are we going to do this?

If I was going to try again, I'd shimmy along that overhanging branch, drop on to the roof and go down through the chimney. It would have to be late enough at night that the bricks on the inside of the chimney would be cool, but it's the only entrance not covered by the motion detectors.'

So she had *noticed that.* Gabriel nodded. 'Exactly. But Amira will do that part. Not you.'

Penelope winced. 'Hold on. I'm exceptional at Crimnastics.'

'You are,' Gabriel admitted. 'But Amira's better.'

'He's not wrong,' Ade said.

Amira bit her lip. 'Me?'

Gabriel nodded. 'We only need one of us to break in and you're the best at Crimnastics. It's got to be you.'

Penelope balled her hands up so tight her knuckles whitened. 'Why are *you* the leader, hmm? I am far better suited to being the leader of this crew than you.'

The twins chuckled. Gabriel could see from their eyes that they were thinking *Told you.*

Gabriel had hidden the truth all year. He had slipped up once, with Caspian, and it had cost him countless points. But these were his friends. Not the rivals he'd thought they would become. So he took a deep breath and said the words he'd long held back.

'I . . . I remember things well,' he began. 'Too well, actually. I remember every detail of every conversation, of every class, of every room. I don't try to, it just sort

284

of . . . happens. So . . . yeah.' He cleared his throat. 'It means I can close my eyes and see every centimetre of that office in my head. Also means I can remember every detail of every failed Crookling Break-in. And every detail of the ones that nearly succeeded. So . . .'

When his classmates at his old schools had found out about his memory, before they inevitably drifted away, they all thought it was the coolest thing in the world. But something altogether different happened then. There was no surprise or delight or even disbelief on his friends' faces. Instead the four of them looked at one another, then closed in around Gabriel, patting him softly on the shoulder.

'Ah, that's rough, man,' Ade said.

'Dreadful,' Penelope added.

'So grim,' Ede said.

Amira nodded along, silently sympathetic.

Gabriel understood, then. He just *knew* that these four had known pain. Because for those who had led hard lives, a perfect memory was not a blessing. It was a curse.

After a moment, Penelope pulled away. She hesitated, and for a moment Gabriel thought she might tell them about her mum. But instead she said, 'So I assume the twins are handling the tech. If Amira is taking point on the Break-in and you're coming up with the plan . . . ' she added a small eye roll at this, 'what on earth am I doing?'

'Playing to your strength,' Gabriel said.

Penelope frowned. 'Don't be ridiculous. Everything

falls under "my strength".'

Now the twins rolled *their* eyes. Gabriel raised an eyebrow at her.

Penelope sighed. 'Fine. What exactly *is* my strength?'

Gabriel smiled. 'Now *that* is the right question.'

*

All of that week, the newly formed crew met after dinner in the trees surrounding the clearing and planned their Break-in. When darkness fell and they disbanded, Gabriel went straight to the library. He'd found his father's file. Now he needed his mother's. With both their real names, a whole new world opened up to him. A world the Brothers Crim could navigate better than almost anyone alive.

They hadn't had any luck with his father's name yet, but that wasn't surprising. All Crookhaven alumni were taught to disappear. But the twins had managed to enhance the audio of the conversation they'd intercepted. The bad news was that the clearer it grew, the more it sounded like Mr Velasquez. At least to Gabriel. The twins were far less convinced.

'This guy's got a Spanish accent,' Ade said. 'Just like Velasquez. But that's *it*. The voices are totally different. It's chalk and chips.'

'Cheese, man,' Ede chimed in. 'The saying is chalk and *cheese*.'

Ade frowned. 'Why would it be chalk and cheese?'

'Why would it be chalk and chips—'

And so began yet another Okoro brawl.

*

The crew called an emergency meeting that Sunday night, after Mona Moriarty's Break-in attempt. The night before, the Legacy girl had managed to bypass all the outer security, slip down through the chimney and get as far as picking up a marble on Whisper's desk before the alarm sounded. Though she hadn't succeeded, it was still way too close for comfort.

'If it had been me,' Penelope said, sitting on a low hanging branch at the edge of the office clearing. 'I would never have chosen Whisper's marble. She rolls them around in her hands all day to work her fingers. They're too precious to her. I knew she would have them rigged somehow.'

It was still just Penelope and Gabriel. The twins, as always, were late. But Amira was too, and that was unusual. 'What were you planning to steal then?'

'Something small from Whisper's desk. Not Father's.'

'Why?'

Penelope sighed. 'If anything is missing, he *will* notice.'

'Because he's like me?'

Penelope nodded grimly. 'Imagine having a father who never forgets anything you've ever done wrong. Who can bring it up and humiliate you with it whenever he wants.

But it's fine because *much is expected of a Crook*.' She sighed. 'Too much.'

'Means he remembers all the good things you've done too.'

Penelope laughed wryly. 'You would think that would be the case, wouldn't you? You'd be wrong, of course. When he wants to be, Father is just as good at forgetting as he is at remembering. Better, actually. Mum's been gone for three years, and he hasn't said her name once.' Penelope's hand unconsciously rose to the violet ribbon in her hair.

'Did your mum give you that? Is that why you wear it all the time?'

Penelope nodded. 'When she sees me again, even if she doesn't recognise my face, she'll recognise this.'

Tell me about her, Penelope. Trust me with the truth like I trusted you.

She seemed to come to herself again. 'Anyway. How did you work it out? About Father's memory.'

'It was something he said a while ago.'

Most would think it a gift, you know. Possessing a memory that never fades. But it's not, is it? When Caspian had said those words, Gabriel had known they shared a curse.

'And even knowing that, you still think stealing from him is possible?' Penelope asked.

'It is – but him believing it *isn't* is what is going to sell the final piece of our plan. That's your part.'

'What *is* her part of the plan?' Ade asked, late as usual. Ede was barely a step behind.

Gabriel looked left and right, then he told the twins Penelope's role.

'Rah,' Ede said, wide-eyed, looking at Penelope. 'So it all comes down to you then, Legacy. Think it'll work?'

Penelope stretched her fingers and grinned, all trace of doubt gone now that the twins had arrived. 'I've been working on it all week. It'll work. It's the rest of you I'm worried about.'

Ade smirked. 'No point worrying about us. Sneaks is all set up and ready to go. Once Amira has a few days to practise—'

'No,' a voice called from above. There was a rustling and Amira landed beside them soundlessly. 'I hear Villette talking now. She . . . break in tomorrow night.'

Ade kissed his teeth. Ede kicked a tree, hard. Penelope glowered. Then looked up. 'You don't think . . .'

'That your father has given Villette the perfect way in?' Gabriel cut in. 'That's exactly what I think.'

Penelope clenched her jaw and locked eyes with him. 'We can't let her get in first.'

'No, we can't,' Gabriel said. 'Which is why we're going in tonight.'

CHAPTER
THIRTY-SEVEN

Every Monday since phase two of the Break-in had been announced, the co-Headmasters had gathered the Crooklings outside their office and given them a round-up of all those who had been eliminated over the previous seven days. Judging by the looks of sheer delight they wore in the ten-minute-long meetings, this was the highlight of their week. For Gabriel and every other Crookling, it was truly miserable.

This Monday started out no different.

'Four more of you lot got caught this week,' Whisper said delightedly. She wore a royal purple loose-fitting suit and matching eyeshadow, her mother-of-pearl USB earrings glinting in the weak morning sunlight. 'Three of you by the Gardeners and one of you by Orwell.' The crow-camera, which she had named Orwell, sat on her shoulder, unmoving.

'Yes,' Caspian said, nodding to the Gardeners – one man and two women – who stood at watch behind the gathered Crooklings. 'Well done, all.'

'Now we're getting to the good bit,' Whisper said, holding up a card. 'Naming and shaming. Sophia Nordstrom. Yes, that's you. Up you come to the front. Oh, wipe that frown off your face, would you? We'll praise you to the heavens when you do something right, but we'll bring you right back down to earth when you fail. Fair's fair.'

The Crooklings parted and the fair-skinned Legacy from 1C trudged through to the front. She stood beside Whisper, head bowed in embarrassment.

Gabriel glanced at Villette, standing just ahead of him, watching with an especially sickly sweet grin, as though knowing full well that she would be getting into the Headmasters' office that night. Except . . .

You won't be grinning soon.

'Javier Serrano,' Whisper called out. 'Come on up. Takumo Kiyosaki and Rathi Khan, you lot too.' All three of them shuffled through the crowds, shoulders slumped. 'Pick your heads up, come on. You failed all right, but at least you went for it. You'll fail a whole lot more in your next four years. Nothing wrong with that. But we reserve the right to show you up when you do. Don't we, Crook?'

Caspian shifted uneasily. 'I wouldn't put it quite like *that*, Headmaster. But I do feel it's important to highlight successes and failures equally. Humility is a friend to the crook. If you learn now that failure is not only possible, but *probable*, you will be less careless in your future criminal pursuits.'

'Hear that, you lot?' Whisper asked the four disgraced Crooklings beside her. 'Remember how this feels and let it fuel you for next time. I've been in that same spot hundreds of times. Feels rubbish, doesn't it?'

All four looked up at her and Gabriel could tell what they were thinking. *The greatest hacker alive was once where I am now? Really?*

'But every time I was up here,' Whisper went on, 'I looked at what I'd done wrong and I never made the same mistake again.' She gave them a wink. 'Now, off you go. Consider yourselves named and shamed.'

Caspian straightened beside her. 'Now, there are only two weeks remaining of the—'

Gabriel raised a hand, cutting Caspian off mid-sentence. The silver-haired man pursed his lips. 'Yes, Gabriel? Do you have something to ask?'

The eyes of the gathered Crooklings fell on him. 'No, sir.' Gabriel's heart thundered. 'Not a question. Something else.'

Caspian nodded. 'Well? What is it?'

'Last night, just after three in the morning, we stole something from your office.'

Silence fell in the clearing.

The co-Headmasters shared a puzzled look. Then Caspian let out a laugh. 'Impossible. I checked thoroughly this morning and nothing was missing.'

Gabriel tried to steady his trembling hands. 'Something is, sir.'

Whisper chuckled. 'Crook doesn't get these things wrong, Gabriel. You got evidence?'

'We do.'

Caspian's smile vanished. He crossed his arms, a hand going to his chin. 'Who is *we*?'

Ade, Ede, Amira and Penelope stepped forwards to stand beside him.

For a moment, Caspian was speechless, his eyes on his daughter. Then they passed over Amira and the twins. 'Merits and Legacies . . . working *together*. What is this?'

'Ade, Ede,' Whisper called, equally as distressed, but for the exact opposite reason. 'Is he telling the truth?'

'Yeah,' Ade answered. 'He is, miss.'

'May I prove it?' Gabriel asked.

Caspian nodded, eyes again fixed on Penelope.

Ede handed him something small and square, wrapped in a white cloth. Gabriel took a breath and pulled it away, revealing a painting by Matisse.

Caspian Crook's painting.

The Crooklings gasped.

Caspian's face didn't even twitch. 'It's a fake. The original is hanging up inside. I saw it moments ago.'

'No, sir,' Gabriel said. 'This is the original.'

Caspian whirled around and disappeared inside. He reappeared with an identical painting clutched in his hands. He held it up to the Crooklings. 'As I said, this is the original. I would not—' He stopped, suddenly distracted by something on the back of the painting. He read it once. Twice. Three times. Then his eyes went wide.

He looked up at his daughter. 'You *forged* this?'

Penelope met his gaze. She stood tall, defiant. Proud. 'Yes, sir.'

Caspian stared for a long moment. 'It's absolutely . . . exquisite.'

That was all Caspian Crook said. But it was enough to force tears into Penelope's eyes.

'And you two?' Whisper said, pointing at the twins. 'What did you lot do?'

Strange, Gabriel thought, *it almost sounds like she's proud of them.*

Ade and Ede shared a grin and, collecting Amira en route, strode through the crowd, Sneaks in hand. 'We've got it all on camera,' Ade said.

Ede pointed at each Crookling as he sauntered past. 'Watch carefully, you lot. Might learn a thing or three.'

Gabriel followed at a distance, smiling. This was their moment.

Ade and Ede set Sneaks up facing the shaded side of the office. When they pressed a button, a beam of light spilled from it, projecting a square on the side of the building.

The Crooklings watched in silence as a video began to play. A small figure in black appeared in frame, crouching on a tree branch, something tucked under her arm. Amira. She tiptoed along the overhanging branch and eased herself down on to the roof. In a heartbeat she had ghosted all the way along the roof and pressed her back to the chimney. Peering inside, then laying a hand on the bricks and deeming it cool enough, she fed a rope around the base and, free hand working at unfathomable speed, eased herself down.

It all took less than thirty seconds.

While Amira was inside the office, another figure landed on the roof – small and stiff and crow-like. Orwell looked around in the same pattern as always – east, west, north, south Then it waddled towards the chimney to peer inside, but before it could jump on to it, a *third* figure appeared in frame. Sneaks landed behind the crow-camera. Seconds later, it activated its Electromagnetic Pulse (EMP) and Orwell flopped on to its side. Sneaks took flight and disappeared.

'So that's why Orwell malfunctioned for two minutes last night,' Whisper said, shooting the twins a look of admiration. 'Clever, boys. Any longer and I'd have known something was off.'

A minute later, Amira poked her head out of the chimney. Seeing Orwell on its side, she sprung out, the real painting under her arm, leapt up on to the branch and tiptoed out of frame.

Two rows in front, Villette cursed under her breath.

The square went blank, but Caspian stared at it for a full minute. Then he took a steadying breath and turned. 'Gabriel Avery, Amira Dhawan, Ade Okoro, Ede Okoro and Penelope Crook – you have succeeded in breaking into this year's chosen location, which was protected by the same security system as the DAM Museum in Holland, from which our infamous alumni Maravel stole the Geger Tapestry.' He worked his jaw as if the words hurt. 'Each of you will be awarded fifty points.'

Ade and Ede attempted a wild high-five, while Penelope and Amira whooped and hugged.

'Moreover,' Caspian continued, 'each of you wins the right to ask me a single question. One which I must answer truthfully, so long as answering it would not put Crookhaven or its alumni in danger.' He glanced at them in turn, and, for the first time since Gabriel had arrived at Crookhaven, he saw true rage in the Headmaster's eyes. 'I urge you to use it wisely.'

CHAPTER THIRTY-EIGHT

When Gabriel entered the office of the Headmaster later that night, Caspian was sitting at his desk, gazing at the corner where the real Matisse hung once more. He waved Gabriel in without a word.

'Sir,' Gabriel said, sitting down in the plush leather chair opposite the Headmaster. 'I want to ask my question.'

Caspian nodded absently. 'Hmm. I have several of my own I wish to ask you, starting with – how did you manage to convince four other students to join you?'

'I told them the truth. About everything. About how it would be impossible to break into this place alone. About me and my memory.'

Caspian turned slowly. 'The truth about you? Are you sure *you* know the truth about yourself, Gabriel Avery?'

That was exactly why Gabriel had come. 'I don't think I do. That's why I—'

Caspian held up a hand. 'I have more questions first.

How exactly did you convince my daughter to play second fiddle to Miss Dhawan?'

'She wasn't second anything, sir,' Gabriel said. 'Amira is the best at Crimnastics in our year. Probably the whole school. Penelope knows that.' Gabriel shrugged. 'And Penelope is the best in the year at Forgery. It just made sense.'

'Swapping the paintings was very clever.' The words came out more like an accusation than praise. 'Where did that idea come from?'

'You,' Gabriel answered honestly. Then he repeated Caspian's words back at him. '*Only the most skilled crook can steal without their mark ever learning something is missing.*'

Caspian nodded. 'People are perfectly happy to listen to advice, but they seldom hear it. I suppose I should be glad that for once someone did.'

'Didn't Villette listen well enough, sir?' Gabriel asked.

Caspian's eyes narrowed. 'What are you implying?'

'Nothing, sir. I just noticed that you've had a lot to say to each other this year. I wondered if maybe you were her tutor for next year?'

Caspian chuckled. 'Certainly not. I'm afraid the reason Villette and I have been catching up regularly is confidential. I can assure you, though, that it's not related to cheating. Beyond these walls, Gabriel Avery, the Underworld is in upheaval. Villette understands that better than most. That is all I will say on the matter.' The Headmaster smoothed his silver hair. 'Now tell me –

what is it that you've come to ask?'

Gabriel took a steadying breath. 'I know you didn't recruit me to Crookhaven just because I'm a good pickpocket. Penelope told me that you've never personally recruited anyone. Not in twenty years. I'm the only one. And I think I know why.' Gabriel leant forwards. 'You recruited me because of my parents, didn't you?'

Caspian's face was blank, unreadable. But where his skin met collar, a muscle twitched. 'I didn't recruit you personally because you are a good pickpocket. I recruited you because you are an *exceptional* pickpocket. Maybe the best of your age I've ever—'

'Luciano Lopes,' Gabriel cut in.

Caspian flinched. 'I'd rather you didn't say that name in this office.'

'That's my father's name,' Gabriel said, anger swelling within him. 'But you already know that. How. *How* could you know that, when even I didn't?'

'For the safety of Crookhaven and all its alumni, I cannot answer your—'

Gabriel stood and slammed his coin down on Caspian's desk. 'It was this, wasn't it? It's the only thing I have from them. Whoever was scouting me from the alumni network saw it and told you. Then you came to see it for yourself.' Gabriel picked the coin up and held it out, showing Caspian the charred side. 'What is this really?' There was desperation in his voice now.

Caspian's hands trembled. 'Gabriel, you do not want

to open this—'

'I *need* to know!'

Caspian glared at him for a long moment. Then he sighed, the tension leaving his body. When he met Gabriel's eyes now, he too looked desperate. 'That is a Mark. It is the only known symbol of the Nameless.'

Gabriel felt like he'd been punched in the stomach. 'What . . . no. My parents . . . they weren't in the *Nameless*.'

'I'm afraid they were. They still are, Gabriel.' Caspian leant over and plucked the Mark from Gabriel's limp hand. 'I'd seen pictures of these, but yours was the first I'd ever seen in person. Fitting really. An ugly symbol for an ugly organisation.' He set the Mark down. 'As soon as I heard about the coin from my alumni contact, we started investigating you. With Whisper at my side, it wasn't hard. She had your entire life mapped out in minutes. And when I saw that you had been abandoned in the same hotel that Federico Guerrero and Isabella Cortes, their aliases, had stayed in before they disappeared . . . Well, I grew suspicious. And when I saw you at Torbridge station, there was no doubt left in my mind.' Caspian surveyed Gabriel carefully. 'It's the eyes.'

Gabriel slumped into the seat again. 'But why . . . why did you want me here?'

Caspian slid open his drawer and pulled out a silver-edged picture frame. Slowly, he turned it around to reveal a woman, beautiful, with long wavy hair and brown skin like Penelope. She was alone and smiling, her hand reaching out as if to block the camera. Gabriel had seen her face once before, projected on the wall in his first History of Crookery lesson – one of the nine who had made it into Tier One. Caspian ran a thumb over the photo lovingly. 'Penelope's mother. She was kidnapped by the Nameless three years ago.'

Gabriel looked at the photo, his mind swimming. 'Why? What did they want?'

Caspian shook his head. 'Nothing. They've never asked for anything. They simply took her. To prove they could best me.'

Then Gabriel understood. 'So I'm . . . bait?'

Caspian met his gaze, unflinching. 'I wasn't lying when I said you are the best pickpocket of your age I've ever seen. But yes, you are also bait. I put the word about you out into the Underworld months ago. You, Gabriel Avery, are infamous. I'm certain your parents will have heard by now. And they will come for you.'

The voices of the woman and the man on the recording came back to Gabriel then. *Mr Velasquez.* Suddenly he was on his feet. 'Unless they haven't heard because they were *already* here. Undercover.'

Gabriel swung around and pushed open the door – and then he ran.

CHAPTER
THIRTY-NINE

G abriel threw the door to Mr Velasquez's classroom open and stepped in.

The Tricks of the Trade teacher looked up from his desk, stunned. 'Gabriel. It's late. You should be in bed.'

Gabriel just stood, staring at his teacher.

Mr Velasquez swivelled in his chair. 'I heard you broke into the Headmasters' office. Is that why you're here? Because you could've waited until morning to show off—'

'Luciano Lopes,' Gabriel said.

The teacher went rigid. 'How do you know that name?'

'I know a lot more than that now,' Gabriel said, stalking across the room.

Mr Velasquez closed the book he'd been reading. 'Why do you want to know about him?'

'*Him?*' Gabriel let out a bark of a laugh. 'We recorded the whole conversation.' Gabriel had kept the voice recorder hidden in his pocket since he'd heard the recording, but now he pulled it out and pressed play. Mr Velasquez stared at it blankly as the voices spoke again.

The recording stopped. 'That's your voice.' Gabriel pocketed the voice recorder. 'And after everything Headmaster Crook just told me, I'm sure that man is Luciano Lopes.'

Mr Velasquez blinked, as though shaken from his daze. 'You're right. That is Luciano's voice.'

It was Gabriel's turn to stiffen, his breath catching.

Mr Velasquez added quietly, 'But I am not Luciano Lopes.'

'That voice is—'

'It's not me, Gabriel.' The teacher reached for his phone, unlocked it and pressed record. Then he repeated every line the man had said on the recording. When he was done, he replayed the file. And his voice sounded . . . nothing like the one in the first recording.

Gabriel slumped against wall, the energy sapped from his limbs.

Mr Velasquez sighed. 'I think I know the answer to this question. But who is Luciano Lopes to you?'

Gabriel thought he'd worked it all out. He thought he'd finally, finally found something in his life that was *true*. He had wanted Mr Velasquez to be Luciano Lopes because then he could have pulled on that one strand of truth until he unravelled who Gabriel Avery really was. But now . . .

'He's my father.'

Mr Velasquez nodded slowly. 'I see.' He let out a long

breath. 'What year were you born, Gabriel?'

It was a long while before Gabriel answered. '2009. Don't know my real birthday. Sometime in October or November, Grandma thinks.' He shrugged. 'I picked October 31st.'

'I was back in my hometown for all of 2008 and 2009,' Mr Velasquez said. 'Laying low after a job went wrong. I have proof if you don't believe me.'

Gabriel shook his head. 'I don't need proof. It's not your voice. I hear that now.' Gabriel pulled his knees to his chest. 'No one else at Crookhaven fits. So even if he was here, he's gone now.'

'Was that the only reason you suspected me? My voice?'

'No,' Gabriel admitted. 'People said we also . . . look quite similar.'

Mr Velasquez's serious demeanour broke, and he laughed. 'Well I'm flattered. But you are at a school where we teach students to become anyone they wish. Give me five minutes in Mr Khan's classroom and I could pass for Caspian.'

Gabriel nodded. 'You helped me, though. Even outside of class. If you were him, that would make sense. But you're not. So . . . why?'

Mr Velasquez stared at him for a long moment, then stood, rounded the desk and slid down the wall beside Gabriel. 'Because you're talented, Gabriel.' He smiled kindly. 'And because you're hungry to learn.' He stretched out his legs. 'Besides, us Merits need to stick together.' The teacher's eyes widened. 'Oh, but you're not a Merit, are you? Not if you're Luciano's son.'

That thought hadn't crossed Gabriel's mind. Even now, he was too exhausted to react.

'Do you remember that boy I told you about, the best pickpocket I'd ever seen?'

Gabriel nodded. *He made all the wrong choices. Fell in with the wrong people. And that warm heart turned cold.*

'That was Luciano. I didn't know him well. He was three years below me.' Mr Velasquez stopped. 'Do you want to know this? I will stop if—'

'No,' Gabriel cut in, sitting straighter. 'I want to know.'

The teacher nodded. 'Well, he was a Merit. Very shy as a Crookling. Then he was put in a new class as a Miscreant. That's how he met Adria Vivas. They were inseparable after that. By the time I left, they were best duo the school had ever seen. He was an Infiltration savant and she was known as the Chamelienne.'

Gabriel sat bolt upright, energy flooding his body again. *Adria Vivas*. He hadn't heard that name before. But he knew where he could look for it . . .

'Sorry, sir,' Gabriel said, shooting to his feet. 'I need to check something.'

CHAPTER FORTY

Gabriel burst into the library. It was deserted but for a small group of Robins in the far corner.

Gabriel looked up at the clock. *Ten minutes before closing time.* He looked around, trying to spot Marie-Elise. Seeing no sign of her, he sprinted through the main area and slid open the door to the alumni section. The familiar scent of new dust and old glue washed over him as he closed the door and rushed past the files.

S, T, U . . . V.

Adria Vivas, he repeated in his head as he began rifling through the folders. *Adria Vivas.*

When he found himself at *Fedor Voronin*, he stopped. Then started again, this time slower. And again, more carefully still.

'It's not here,' Gabriel said aloud. 'Why isn't it here?'

'I might know why,' a voice said from behind.

Gabriel turned to see the librarian leaning against the

door, the file marked *Adria Vivas* clasped in her hand. He swallowed. 'Why . . . why do you have that?'

The librarian laughed. 'Am I not allowed? After all, it is my file.'

Gabriel froze. 'But Marie-Elise, you're . . .'

The woman cupped her ear. 'A librarian? Mm. But people don't really *see* librarians. They are simply there – the kind, unthreatening guardians of stories.'

Then it hit him. The conversation Ade and Ede recorded. The woman's words: *Don't worry about me. I'm back home.*

For alumni, Crookhaven *was* home.

It was never the man who had been undercover; it was the woman.

Gabriel searched Adria Vivas's face. Like with Mr Khan in Deception that first day, something about her eyes was different now. In the dim light of the alumni section, her real eyes glittered. Green rather than amber. Cold rather than warm. Her trademark smile was gone too. She stood tall and calm. And dangerous.

'Those gloves you wear,' Gabriel said, eyeing the thin black gloves on her hands, dirt speckling the fingertips of the usually pristine material. 'They're not for the books at all, are they? They're to stop you getting your fingerprints everywhere.'

'Well, Crook has a rather nasty habit of having the Gardeners do random fingerprint sweeps of Crookhaven. To prevent outsiders from posing as staff. I couldn't have the fingerprints of the infamous Adria Vivas appearing in the library, now, could I?' She chuckled. 'Of course, the sweeps only work if the "outsider" doesn't know about them.' She slid down one glove. 'Plus, they helped cover this.' Unlike the startlingly pale skin of her face and neck, her hand was olive-skinned. Just like Gabriel's.

Gabriel took a step back. 'Why . . . why are you here?'

'I didn't come here for you, if that's what you're worried about,' she said. Even her voice was different now. Lower and rougher. 'I came for Robins, like your friend Leon. Nice boy. Perhaps a little too trusting.' She smirked. 'We were short on numbers and, as you can imagine, it's not exactly easy to recruit new talent when the entire Underworld think your crew are kidnappers and murderers. We felt the personal approach would be far more . . . persuasive.' She gestured towards Gabriel. 'You were just a happy accident. In more ways than one.' She placed a hand over her mouth theatrically. 'Couldn't resist.'

'We overheard you speaking to a man. He sounded trapped so I thought he was the one undercover at Crookhaven.'

She tilted her head. 'Heard that, did you? I bet it was those twins you're always hanging around with. Clever and nosy, they are. Traits that, together, can get you in serious trouble.' She smiled. 'I wouldn't worry – Luce isn't trapped anywhere. He's been pulling a long con. You'll hear about it on the news one day soon. Or maybe not, if it goes well.'

Gabriel's hands trembled. 'Every night I was here, you sat with me, brought me food, drink, you even walked me to the door at closing time . . . and you never said anything.'

She shrugged and took a step towards him. 'I didn't know who you were. My crew probably tried to get me a message about you, but I've only managed to make contact with them three times in a year.'

She took another step. 'All I knew was that this sweet, naive little boy was looking for someone that they had no hope in hell of finding.' Her face darkened. 'Then you found Luciano's file. The shock of hearing his name – it startled me.' Gabriel recalled the librarian dropping her file, the uncharacteristic wildness in her eyes. 'Then I thought about it. About *you*.' Adria studied Gabriel. 'You really are just like Luce before I made him fun. Strange, isn't it? No contact for fourteen years and yet I can see us both in you. I suppose that's why I've always believed in nature rather than nurture. The truth is that who we are is decided the moment we are born. That's why you've ended up here, a crook, like both of your rotten parents.'

Gabriel's head throbbed. 'I don't *hurt* people. I only steal because I need to. I'm not like you and the Nameless.'

His mother took a step closer. 'You know, I deeply regret not giving our organisation a name. Having Crook and all his little alumni calling us the *Nameless* is far worse than any name we could've dreamt up. Giving us a name means that, by definition, we are not nameless. Doesn't it? Or am I mad?' She flapped away the question. 'Anyway.

What I'm saying is that you belong right by our side. It's what you wanted, wasn't it? To find us. That's what every long night in this library has been about, hasn't it?'

'I wanted to find you. But not to join you. To ask *why*.' Gabriel's quivered. 'Why did you . . . leave me?'

His mother tutted. 'Are you really still bitter about that? It happened so long ago. Can't we chalk it up as a mistake and move on?'

Gabriel couldn't speak. *Still bitter about that*. As if it had been nothing.

'Look,' Adria said, taking another step closer, her tone softening. 'I've done what I came here to do. I'm leaving tonight. This is your only chance. Don't you want to know the truth about us, me and Luce? About you? You don't even know your real name.' She took another slow step. 'We can tell you *everything*. We're the only ones who can.'

Gabriel felt himself take a half-step towards his mother, pulled by the power of her words. She was right – he wanted the truth more than almost anything else. Adria Vivas and Luciano Lopes had the answers to every question he'd ever had. It would be as easy as 'OK'.

But now she was standing in front of him with those cruel green eyes, those questions had vanished, leaving only two.

Can I really leave Grandma behind after all she's done for me?

And what about my friends?

Gabriel took a step back. 'I can't.'

Her jaw flexed. 'Don't you *want* to know the truth about that night? Don't you *want* to know the real reason you were left in that hotel?'

I do. I do!

'Take my hand and we'll tell you everything.' Adria reached out with her olive-skinned hand. Gabriel stared at it. All the answers he'd ever wanted were right there, cupped in a hand that looked just like his own. All he needed to do was take it . . .

Gabriel looked up. 'I'm not going with you.'

'That,' his mother said, taking another step forward, 'is the wrong choice.' She grabbed his wrist tight.

'Oi, Gabe,' a familiar voice called from the main library. 'Where are you?'

'Ade!' Gabriel shouted. His mother clapped a hand over his mouth. But he bit it and sprang away. 'I'm in here!'

'I should've known you'd be—' Penelope froze when she opened the door and saw the scene in front of her. 'What—'

'Stay where you are,' his mother said. In one hand she held her folder. In the other she held a lighter. 'If you take another step, I'm going to light this.'

Penelope backed away. 'Don't! All the air will be sucked out in seconds. You'll suffocate.'

'And so will he,' his mother said, jerking her head towards Gabriel. 'So here's what's going to happen. I'm going to leave. If anyone tries to stop me, if anyone so much as sneezes, I'm going to start a little bonfire. Is that clear?'

Penelope pushed Ade and Ede back. Amira too. 'Yes, fine! Just . . . don't.'

As his mother edged towards the door, Gabriel pressed himself against the bookshelf. If she set that folder alight, his only option would be to climb towards the vent in the ceiling.

Adria Vivas reached the doorway, lighter now lit and raised to the paper. Penelope and the others had backed away so far he could no longer see them. Then his mother turned. 'Until our next family reunion.' She winked. 'Now, take a deep breath.'

The folder burst into flames.

An alarm squealed above, and the inner door clunked and started to close. A deafening roar followed as air was sucked into the vent, paper and folders with it. Amid the whirlwind of pages and noise, Gabriel started to climb. But flailing limbs by the door caught his eye.

All four of his friends were blocking the door, arms and legs straining against the crushing power of it. But that was impossible. How could they . . .

Then he saw it, clamped at the base of the door. Sneaks.

Gabriel took off running. They were shouting, screaming at him to run faster. But his chest was heavy. The air had gone from the room, causing stars to blossom at the edge of his vision.

Then hands caught him, pulled him, dragged him through the tiny gap.

They collapsed on the floor of the library in a heap. There was a sickening screech of metal crumpling, the twins' pained cries of 'Sneaks!', and the door slammed closed.

Gabriel wobbled to standing, muttered a croaky thank you in his friends' direction and looked towards the library entrance. Gardeners were rushing in but . . .

Where is she?

He took off again, legs heavy, vision still swimming. He ran past the Gardeners and down the stairs, stumbling every few steps. Then he was outside and he could *breathe* again. With each breath his legs grew steadier and his pace quickened.

A trail of discarded clothes led into the trees, so he followed it.

He broke the treeline and ground to a stop at the lake's edge. Twenty metres out, a figure cut through the flat-calm lake with smooth, powerful strokes. His mother. A second figure waited on a jet ski. He was tall and wore a black wetsuit, his face covered but for his eyes.

They were Gabriel's eyes.

Amira arrived at his side first. Then Penelope.

His mother climbed on to the back of the jet ski and turned towards the island. The pale make-up had washed off, revealing her true face, olive-skinned and with a distinctive mole over her lip. Seeing him, she smiled a strange smile. Almost as if she was proud he'd made it out alive. The amber eyes of the man lingered on him, too, just for a moment. As if he was memorising Gabriel's face. Trying to somehow discern the kind of life the child he'd abandoned had lived.

Then they turned away and sped off across the lake, vanishing into the darkness.

'*Who* were those two?' Penelope asked breathlessly.

Gabriel looked down at the scorched but still intact file in his hand. 'My parents.'

CHAPTER FORTY-ONE

At the request of Ade and Ede, they held a funeral for Sneaks. Penelope was especially annoyed about this. 'You're going to rebuild it—'

'*Her*,' Ade cut in. 'Have some respect for the crushed, would you.'

'You're going to rebuild *her* using the same parts anyway. Why are we having to miss lunch for this nonsense?'

'Sneaks gave her life for Gabe,' Ede said, outraged. 'How can you be so cruel about this, eh? It was her that was made of metal, but it's you that's a robot, Penelope Crook!'

'Call me whatever you want,' Penelope snapped. 'But if I don't get my bolognese, I'm going to melt Sneaks down and give her to Ms Lockett to make into a lock. How would *she* feel about that?'

That more or less ended the funeral.

*

The news that Adria Vivas had infiltrated Crookhaven made it to the teachers but no further. Nobody other than Gabriel's crew and the Gardeners had seen anything, and that was for the best. Yuri Malenko, one of the best trackers Crookhaven had ever produced, was a Gardener that year, so Caspian sent him after Gabriel's parents. For the last two weeks of term, twice as many Gardeners roamed the grounds at night.

Caspian grilled Gabriel, and Gabriel told him everything he knew. None of it was helpful. His mother had infiltrated the school to recruit the most talented Robins. She'd learnt about Gabriel purely by accident. There wasn't much more Gabriel could say. He didn't know *how* she'd sneaked in, though she had successfully imitated a librarian who had been at Crookhaven for nearly ten years. She was, after all, known as the Chamelienne for a reason. Or maybe his mother had been right when she'd said that no one really noticed librarians.

Gabriel had filled in the other four, as they sat cross-legged in the clearing they'd conquered. No one spoke for several minutes.

Then Ade, tactful as always, said, 'So your parents are in the *Nameless*?'

Gabriel nodded. He and Amira shared a look. She was the only one who understood what he was feeling.

'Rah,' Ede said. 'That's kind of scary but . . . also kind

of sick.' Penelope shot him a glare. 'Mostly scary, though, yeah,' he clarified.

'But this isn't over, is it?' Penelope asked the group. 'Gabriel's parents are in the Nameless. Amira's brother is too. You two recorded their voices so they'll be after you—'

'Hold on,' Ade cut in. 'That was an accident. They couldn't get mad about that. Could they?' The brothers shared a worried look.

'And my . . .' Penelope looked to Gabriel. He nodded encouragingly. 'My mum was kidnapped by the Nameless three years ago.' She didn't wait for reactions. 'So we need to learn everything about them.'

'Ah, she finally said it!' Ade said with a theatrical sigh.

'I thought we'd be all grey and wrinkled by the time she fessed up,' Ede chimed in.

Ade nudged his brother playfully. 'Reckon that means she likes us now. Or at the very least she doesn't *abhor* us or *loathe* us or, you know, something else that a forty-year-old might say.'

'You all knew?' Penelope asked, sounding more surprised than angry.

Ade, Ede and even Amira nodded. 'Me and Ed heard about it at the start of this term. When you've got bugs set up all around the school, you hear things. Didn't want to say anything because, you know . . .' Ade shrugged.

Penelope turned to Amira, who blushed. 'I overheard the Gardeners talking about it while I sat in a tree.'

Gabriel had started to notice that Amira's English had

improved in the crew's presence, and it got him wondering about whether she had underplayed how fluent she was so that others underestimated her. Or, at the very least, so they didn't bother her. It wasn't something he would ever mention to the Crimnastics prodigy, but the thought that Amira was relaxing into her true self around them made him happy.

Penelope prodded Gabriel in the shoulder, hard. 'And you?'

'Ade and Ede told me,' Gabriel admitted. 'But now we all know, and we can help you.'

Something happened to Penelope then. It was the subtlest of changes. Probably only Gabriel, whose cursed memory made him recall every detail that usually made up Penelope Crook, even noticed. Her shoulders slackened, and her dark eyes warmed, and she let out the smallest sigh. As if the unburdening of her secret had made her lighter. And then, voice trembling, she asked a question Gabriel had never dreamed she'd ask. 'You'll really help me?'

'I mean,' Ade began, 'we all want to learn more about the Nameless, so we wouldn't only be helping *you*—ow!'

Gabriel withdrew his elbow from Ade's ribs and smiled at Penelope. ''Course we will.'

'We might have to break some rules,' Ede said.

'Sneak around,' Ade added, rubbing his ribs and glaring at Gabriel.

'Go into areas of Crookhaven we shouldn't,' Gabriel

finished. 'Will you be OK with that?'

Penelope nodded firmly. 'For mum, anything.'

Gabriel nodded. 'Good.' He stood. 'But right now, Miss Crook, you need to go and claim your Crooked Cup.' Penelope had beaten Gabriel by two points in the end, which hadn't hurt as much as he thought it would. He had won the Break-in and asked Caspian his question, which had led to the truth about his parents. That was enough. Besides, winning the Crooked Cup meant everything to Penelope. He tapped the twins on their shoulders, then. 'It'll be ours next year.'

Ade and Ede sprang up. 'I've already written my acceptance speech,' Ede said. 'How's this: Firstly, I'd like to thank my mum. If it wasn't for her jollof selling out, we wouldn't have been able to upgrade Sneaks and—'

Ade kicked him in the shin. 'You don't get a speech. Sorry, Ed. And as your big brother, I'm going to have to win it first. You know, set an example.'

It was the girls' turn to spring up. 'Excuse us, boys,' Penelope said. 'I have a very Crooked Cup to claim and my right-hand woman is coming with me.'

'That's some real big talk for someone who would've lost by nearly *fifty points* had we not graciously taken her into our crew,' Ede said. 'How about a "thank you", eh?'

'You can't teach class, Ed,' Ade said, arms crossed. 'You either have it or you don't.'

Amira gave the boys a playful shrug. 'Good luck . . . for next year.'

The twins looked at one another. 'Did we just get roasted?' Ade asked.

'Think so, Ad,' Ede said. 'I reckon we put a jollof ban on the both of them for that.'

With that, the girls turned and walked away, cackling.

*

After that day in the library, Gabriel began to sleep like a baby. He didn't know why, exactly, but he guessed it was because now he knew where he'd come from, and he didn't want any part of it. Adria Vivas and Luciano Lopes were not his family. He already had the only family he needed waiting for him in a tiny flat above a tiny café in a tiny village just a short train ride away.

The five of them left Crookhaven at sunrise on a Saturday. As always, the Crooklings were on staggered journeys. The twins and Amira took the 7.36. The train sputtered away as they were still calling out promises to rebuild Sneaks and return with twice as many backpacks of jollof next term. Amira only smiled and waved.

Penelope waited for the 9.02 with Gabriel. She relayed all her summer plans, which mostly consisted of mastering a new (but very old) method of sculpting, practising free diving in the lake and learning Korean fluently enough to insult Ji-a without getting in trouble.

Gabriel only listened. He had no summer plans at all, which was just perfect.

The train pulled in and Gabriel boarded. He sat in a window seat and eased the window open. 'If you want to visit, you can come to Torbridge whenever you want.'

Penelope raised her eyebrows. 'Really?'

'Don't expect a villa on a private island or anything. But yeah. 'Course you can.'

Penelope smiled. 'OK, I will.'

The train pulled away from Moorheart and Penelope.

The journey was excruciatingly slow, but when the train finally stopped at Torbridge, Gabriel jumped off and bounded over to Benson's. The bell tinkled its welcome as he stepped in. The café smelled of bacon and coffee and home.

Grandma was at the counter, red-faced and smiling at a customer. Then she saw him. 'Dear boy! Oh, come in. Come in and sit down.' She gave him a hug and ushered him upstairs before Harry could get a word in. 'Tea? Water?'

'Water, please,' Gabriel said, slumping into the comfiest sofa. Everything in the flat was wonderfully, perfectly the same.

Grandma shuffled over with his water and sat beside him, beaming. 'Well, go on then. Tell me everything. Did anything exciting happen this term?'

Gabriel shook his head. 'Exciting? Oh, not really. I'm just glad to be home.'

Grandma clapped. 'That's reminded me.' She leant down, opened the drawer on the coffee table and pulled out a postcard. 'This came for you.'

Gabriel took the card and turned it over. His mouth fell open. On the front was a photograph of a wolf pack perched on a stone overhang that reached out over a thick forest, their faces upturned and howling at the moon.

Gabriel flipped the card and read the one line written on the back.

ALONE YOU CAN BECOME EXCEPTIONAL;
TOGETHER YOU CAN BECOME UNSTOPPABLE.

Relief swept through Gabriel, then. *Leon's alive.* It had to be Leon. He'd said exactly that to Gabriel the night they'd howled at the moon together. But did that mean . . . could he really mean he *knew* he was joining the Nameless? That he wasn't kidnapped or tricked into joining them at all? That he had *chosen* to?

'Friend of yours, is it?' Grandma asked, leaning closer.

'A friend?' Gabriel blinked. 'I . . . I don't know.'

'You don't know if it's from a friend or not?'

No, that's not it, Gabriel thought. *If Leon really chose to join the Nameless, then he's not my friend. He's my enemy.*

But instead he said, 'I don't recognise the writing, that's all.'

'Well, it's an odd thing to write anyway, isn't it?' Grandma stood and took the squealing kettle off the stove. '*Alone you can become exceptional; together you can become unstoppable*.' She clicked her fingers. 'Ah! Maybe it's an advertising ploy. They're getting craftier, those lot, dear boy. Only the other day . . .'

Grandma's words faded into the background as Gabriel's gaze fell on the postcard again. There was another message there, he realised. This message, though, wasn't written out and it didn't need to be – the postcard itself said it clearly enough.

The Nameless knew where Gabriel lived.

ACKNOWLEDGEMENTS

First and foremost, I want to say a heartfelt thank you to every single person who appears on the credit page in this book. Having worked in this industry for four years, I know that publishing a book is a true team effort. You are all hugely appreciated.

I want to say a special thank you, though, to my former agent Josephine Hayes, who took a chance on me and my little crew of crooks, and my current agent, Jordan Lees, who seamlessly took the baton from Jo and has been a guiding light and my number one advocate ever since.

I am also wholeheartedly grateful to Lena McCauley and Nazima Abdillahi, my endlessly patient and ever-enthusiastic editors, for helping me turn this story into the best possible version of itself. Knowing that I will get to work with you both on more *Crookhaven* books is enormously exciting.

The beautiful artwork for this book comes from the wildly talented Euan Cook, who has created a truly captivating and magical cover. You have brought my story to life, and I cannot thank you enough for that.

To Cheyenne Kotch, without whom I would not have come up with the idea for this crooked school. To Emmanuel Antwi Bawuah and Lateef Jinadu, whose personalities I may have (slightly) nicked for Ade and Ede. To Peter O'Boyle, Sebastian Streeting, Alex Satterfield, Niall Smith, Michael Weeks and Theo Mefsut, whose support throughout this process I have truly treasured. And to the Circle of Chaos – Lilidh Kendrick, Jasmine Horsey and Allegra Le Fanu. Your own meteoric rise continues to inspire me. To all my friends – I am grateful for you. And to the delightful Annie and Alec, who read and loved the book long before anyone else – I will treasure the letters you sent me, always.

Finally, my family, who have each given me so much. My grandma, Mary Williams, gave me a love of story and always encouraged my imagination. My mum, Jenny Arcanjo, gave me self-belief and a love of words. My brother, Marcus Arcanjo, gave me an unquenchable thirst for learning (and several scars). My mum's partner, Mark Paine, gave me his infectious enthusiasm and a belief in the series that never wavered – I promise I will see what I can do about getting you a cameo on the TV adaptation. And my grandpa, Bryn Williams, when I most needed it, gave me his undivided attention and unwavering support. Without them, I would not be writing my acknowledgements in the back of a published book. But since I am, I am fortunate enough to get the chance to say: thank you for everything.

CREDITS

J.J. ARCANJO is a half-Portuguese, half-English writer who grew up between the Algarve and Devon. He has a degree in Criminology and Psychology from Aberystwyth University, a Masters in Creative Writing and Publishing from City University, London, and currently works in editorial at Bloomsbury Publishing. He's published two crime novels for adults. *Crookhaven* is his middle-grade debut.

JOIN GABRIEL AND THE REST OF THE
CREW FOR THEIR SECOND YEAR
AT CROOKHAVEN IN ...

CROOK HAVEN

THE FORGOTTEN MAZE

COMING
AUGUST 2023